NOSTRAND
AVENUE

NOSTRAND AVENUE

KENJI JASPER

Kensington Publishing Corp.
www.kensingtonbooks.com

DAFINA BOOKS are published by

Kensington Publishing Corp.
119 West 40th Street
New York, NY 10018

All Kensington Titles, Imprints, and Distributed Lines are available at special quantity discounts for bulk purchases for sales promotions, premiums, fund-raising, and educational or institutional use. Special book excerpts or customized printings can also be created to fit specific needs. For details, write or phone the office of the Kensington special sales manager: Kensington Publishing Corp., 119 West 40th Street, New York, NY 10018, attn: Special Sales Department, Phone: 1-800-221-2647.

Dafina and the Dafina logo Reg. U.S. Pat. & TM Off.

ISBN-13: 978-1-4967-1570-8
ISBN-10: 1-4967-1570-5
First Kensington Trade Edition: September 2018
First Kensington Mass Market Edition: August 2019

ISBN-13: 978-1-4967-1571-5 (e-book)
ISBN-10: 1-4967-1571-3 (e-book)

10 9 8 7 6 5 4 3 2 1

Printed in the United States of America

For Carla McCullough Jasper
for reminding me how the game is played

CHAPTER ONE

A TEASER BEFORE THE FIRST ACT

The Spark

You are falling, maybe not for the last time. But you'll never fall like this again. You can't afford it. It won't be allowed, because you have seen where this kind of thing leads to.

Sometimes you wish that you'd never met Jenna Ann Campbell. You wonder if it would've been better for both of you if you hadn't asked your boy Mike to hook you up with the same girl that did his cornrows. He had the spiral joints like Allen Iverson, and you wanted some braids like that for the barbecue you were throwing Fourth of July weekend 2000. If you hadn't gone over to that basement apartment she was working out of on Lewis Ave., where you could hear the roomful of pit bulls barking into the floor overhead, then you wouldn't have seen that she was the same girl from the night of your first J'Ouvert during West Indian Parade weekend the year before, when you were just visiting NYC from DC. J'Ouvert was the pre-party that went all night, rain or shine, hot or cold, the soundtrack to the lining up of the countless parade floats that would spend Labor Day crawling past crowds of island folk waving every flag the Caribbean had to offer in the name of their heritage.

The first time you met Jenna, you might as well not have met her at all. She had on her Virgo "Nigga I'm Not Impressed" face, the one most Black women learn around age two (and sometimes before). She had on a sling-back denim catsuit with block wedges and a gold herringbone choker thick enough to be a collar. You were about a foot away from her taking in that first night of music, liquor, and humid heat in the hours before the best day to be Caribbean in all of the New York year.

Jenna was still with the dude she'd been with since she was 18, a Rohan Marley wannabe who pushed a 4.6 Range and had four kids by three baby mamas by the time she met him. You would later suspect that it was a Biggie/Lil' Kim kind of thing they outgrew. But according to her, when they were together it was like lightning striking, with the whole rest of the world blinded by the flash. This was back when you couldn't understand Jamaican patois at all. To you it sounded like a Shabba Ranks duet. But you knew they were arguing, and that they were already drunk and yelling about some kind of thing involving some other woman, and she slapped him twice, harder than most dudes punch.

Then he backhanded her into a car. Then two Trini members of the Flatbush NYPD beat half of dude's face in before they put him in the squad car. Jenna just stood on the corner, Dunhill lit, and stared down that police cruiser until it disappeared. Then she kept staring at the void it left behind. The rest of the world had gone back to the party, except the two of you, her looking at him go and you being worried that she wasn't all right. Because back then you used to worry about people, even people you didn't really know.

There was this hardened quality to Jenna's features. She had these really sharp cheekbones with these narrow-slit eyes. And there was this fire behind them, a fire that you, as water child, wanted to tame somehow, because that was what you were into. You always had a thing for the wild ones.

You stepped up, knowing that it wasn't the smartest move to make considering the Negro theater between them that you had just witnessed. But you were freshly twenty-one and prone to not giving a fuck. You were even too young to know that most fucks were actually worth giving.

"How long you been with him?" you asked.

She turned to you, unsure of what to make of the question, until she answered.

"Too long," she said.

Then, like something out of the movies, a gypsy cab pulled up. She got in and left you without another word in a cloud of dark filter and tobacco. You didn't see her again until you came knocking on her door to get your hair done, having no idea that it was the same woman. You were just there to get fresh. But that changed as soon as y'all kissed outside of Larry's Liquid Love. Your nonchalance went out of the window under that cheap-ass comforter you bought from the furniture place on Flatbush the same day you got your first Brooklyn futon. After that, Jenna was all that mattered. She became the blueprint, the schematic for structures that never held their weight long enough to go the distance.

Still, you were ready to stab the one dude because he started talking out of the side of his neck about how she looked like a whore because "tight and revealing" was usually the first way she chose to go. But she held you back from poppin' dude in the mouth that time, because she said that "real rude boys kill before they see the consequences coming." She didn't think you were for real until she saw what you did for a living. That humbled her a little bit. But still, most times she was ready for a fight. And when it came to any war on her battlefield, you were the first and only soldier who was always ready to go.

You either had to roll with Jenna or not roll

at all. Apache's "Gangsta Bitch" comes to mind. Looking back, the two of you probably smoked so much weed to keep tempers down and stayed inside for as many hours as you could to keep all your flaws from getting out into the world. Jenna was not a character from a movie. She didn't do dishes. She didn't cook, and sex with her was always on her terms, which meant that you had to wait to get it and deal with however long it took for her to be in that mood.

When it all went south between you, bursting into flames like a piñata soaked in gasoline, its ashes scorching everything in the path you'd laid together one stone at a time, you convinced yourself that it probably would have ended better if the two of you had never met at all.

These were the thoughts going through your head somewhere between Saturday morning and that fateful Thursday in 2005, when this story both begins and ends. It would take you close to 20 years to realize, as the cursed cement had fully settled in a newly gentrified Bed-Stuy, that the right people always end up where they're supposed to be. Coming back to Nostrand Avenue had very little to do with Jenna or Khujo, the Asanas, the Arsonists, or Gilda.

This was all about you.

You are not "back" in the *John Wick* or "new album out now" senses, as these might give the reader expectations of a story about gratuitous sex and violence, family feuds free of Richard Dawson (without the flask), and the most expensive misunderstanding you ever came across. You are back like Newman in the final frames of *The Color of Money*, energized like Scotty from *Star Trek* behind the boards, doing what he did best and giving it all he had for every season he earned a paycheck.

After 15 years, you finally know where you and your karma stand, with them, with her, and with the dude in the mirror who picked up some good sense along the way. Things have changed, but you can't do a thing about what's already done: a Pandora's box you teased open like a fleshy pair of thighs, and a mistake similar to the previous metaphor that you wish you could take back in exchange for a sober night and keeping to yourself at the bar. But life just doesn't work that way.

These paragraphs are the thought process you use to distract your mind from the debilitating fact that the first house you ever owned is burning out its insides while you fall toward the street from three stories up. And you are burning, but not in Milton's *Paradise Lost* sense. Your actual skin feels like it's on the verge of blackening like rotisserie chicken over an open flame with too much barbecue sauce on it. Shrapnel and shattered glass are hanging in the air above you.

There is nothing for you to do in this state other than pray. So you just breathe, one white-hot breath after the other, until it all goes dark. This is how you lost your house. Everything else you lost 15 years before, when you worked magic in the presence of Muggles wearing a Darth Maul tee and that pair of vintage Jam Master Jay Adidas you scuffed while fighting for your life on Winthrop Street. This is where the intro ends. Now you can get to the real beginning.

CHAPTER TWO

A Prelude to the Kiss of Death,
July 8, 2005, 10:16 a.m.

If there's one thing you learned from all of this, it is that the rules are there for a reason. Hierarchy exists for a purpose, particularly when dealing with high-value content that must be handled with care. In youth, the right person, the maverick, the rogue personality, believes à la some Neo in *The Matrix* sense of being the exception, that they are the Chosen One, one who can bend reality without breaking it, which is complete and utter bullshit. You truly believed this about yourself and, in turn, shared the idea with others, and thus found yourself taken back to school like Rodney Dangerfield looking to avoid the death of a marriage.

This is a cautionary tale about what happens

when you go swimming with sharks in the East River and convince yourself that you can dog-paddle your way to safety. Enter the yoga class.

The class isn't packed. There are only five people, spaced two arm's lengths from one another, standing on thin mats made of perfectly biodegradable and perspiration-absorbing material. The whole neighborhood knows this place as a dance club on the weekends, a second-floor calypso and soca hole for folks that speak English with accents you often struggle to understand. You are from the South, after all, a distant land known as Chocolate City. And before you try to argue about cultural geography, DC is most definitely below the Mason-Dixon Line.

There is more fluid motion between the movements than in the yoga classes you've taken down in the Village or on the West Side. You are all in cobra, your flat palms pressing your upper bodies, heads and faces toward the sky, midway through the sun salutation process.

Jelly trained under some yoga Jedi Master from India, and she has organized this little free gathering to share what she has learned with a few African American bohemian types whom she hopes will jump others into the gang. Only a little money changes hands, ten bucks at a time, enough for the owners to make it worth keeping the lights on for 90 minutes.

You are not here seeking enlightenment, merely to strengthen your aura. A person's aura can have different properties at different times. Step into one person's aura and your wounds heal more quickly. Someone else's might be solid enough to break bones or boards when something collides with it. Others, with full concentration, can permeate matter to walk through walls, or literally step into a shadow and come out on the other side somewhere else. But to maximize the potential of your aura, you must practice, and yoga, one of the many tools used to hone body, mind, and spirit, is perhaps the most readily available gym for this purpose.

But right now, you're not thinking that deeply about your aura or the process of tuning and toning it. Right now you're going through the motions because you don't want to think about Jenna Ann Campbell, your kryptonite, your weakness, the bane of your twentysomething existence, because right now, approaching the end of summer, she is a problem that you cannot fix. Plus there is work to do. And the job takes priority over all else.

Jelly is telling a story about her yoga experiences in DC. Unlike the other strangers here, you have known her a long time, since before the husband and child, before the three cities where you intersected repeatedly after growing up in the same town. After some research, you even learned that ancestors of yours and hers were buried right next to each other in some graveyard on Bolling Air Force Base back in the homelands, the town where the feds caught that mayor on tape smoking crack while he patiently waited to get some tail from a so-so sidepiece.

But now you and Jelly are both in Brooklyn, and she is telling a story about her and her yoga teacher, who has a name that you are never going to be able to pronounce.

"Sometimes we'd drink Guinness, get drunk and do shoulder stands . . ."

You move through the remaining positions in the series, from the warriors to the tree pose to downward facing dog and the dolphin. It ain't like doing push-ups or lifting weights. The burn in your deltoids and quads is subtle, almost exercise without exercise. You don't fully feel it until it's all over.

There're a lot of ways to deal with what the Stuy doles out. Some drink. Some get high. The most despicable beat the shit out of the spouse or child, whoever is within closest reach. You prefer to vent your frustrations through the act of intercourse. This is not to say that you do not engage in the act of making love, but the woman you love has put you on an indefinite time-out, which is why you are here in striped Adidas sweats, finding solace in pain and endurance. You are not emotionally unavailable by a long shot, but you do have an ego problem. And there is no larger ego boost than bringing a fine-ass woman to legitimate orgasm with her legs folded forward as far as they will go, your iron rod pointing toward the uterus. You love it when her head almost indents the drywall from the force of a poorly timed thrust, when your sweat lines the valley that runs from between her shoulder blades to the crack of her ass. While these are not all acts of *intimacy*, you too often consider them "therapy."

An erection is the last thing you want as the only guy in a class full of women. And you're far from that frame of thought. There truly is freedom in the movements and the vibration of hatha, vinyasa, and/or kundalini. But yoga alone will not calm the nagging butterflies at the bottom of your gut. You smell money in your sinus cavities, a sign that cash might soon appear for you in the land of the living.

The class ends with the most casual Black people "Namaste" on record, and you find yourself standing on Nostrand Avenue, mat in case slung over your shoulder like a soldier's rifle as you make your way to the Kyoto bodega at the corner at Fulton and Nostrand. Designed with delicate paper windows encased by iron bars and Plexiglas, this corner store is an ode to modern-day Tokyo. There are video screens all over the place, some announcing winning lottery numbers and others filled with animated characters from Pokémon to the '80s classic flick *Akira*. There's a rack of katana swords on the wall, recently added after the success of Quentin Tarantino's *Kill Bill*.

Actual sushi might be a stretch for a bodega's capacity to stay up to health code. But there is a miso soup and rice breakfast option to go along with your standard New York coffee in the signature blue and white cup with those Roman columns on it. The brothers who once owned the place have since sold it to a group of Turkish gentlemen who are all, at one point or another, smoking Dervish brand cigarettes, a foreign offering they suck down exclusively but don't offer for sale. You glide in for a bottle of water and a two-pack of Reese's Peanut Butter Cups, the only sugar you allow in your life that isn't distilled or fermented.

The water goes down cool as you head south down Nostrand toward Hancock Street and hang a left. You climb the stairs to the first-floor entrance of the brownstone you own and rent out to two tenants, and take a good look at the day's copy of the *New York Daily News*, which for some reason or the other has a Photoshopped President George W. Bush in drag. All you have to do is take a good look at that newspaper and you know where you have to head next. It looks like money is indeed on the way.

"How come white people get to have everything?" Shango Oluwande asks between bites of French toast at the Doctor's Cave, the little hole on Marcy Avenue where you take a meal every once in a while. Shango's there every day, though, mainly to eye Jean, the dreadlocked and beautiful better half of Tim, who prepares all the meals she loves so much when she's not working shifts as a nurse at Brooklyn Hospital. Everybody in this town has a side hustle.

Shango is not your direct handler, but he gets stuff handled. Imagine if you could put Al Sharpton and Stringer Bell from *The Wire* into the same body and make him around 55 with a whitish-gray temple taper cut and a matching beard cut close with a surgical shape-up.

"I put in the best bid on that pair of brownstones down on Greene. Had the shit locked for like three days, and then eight hours before the cutoff, some white boy coalition comes in and chops my head off."

"Hey, real estate's a cutthroat business," you say. The frown on his face softens into a smile. He knows something you do not.

"You're right. That's actually why I called you down here."

You and Shango never use landlines, cells, or even email. If he needs to see you, the right corner of the front page of your *Daily News* will be missing. If it's a little piece, you'll find him at the gym over on Kingston. If it's a lot, he's over at Jean's. This is a system you developed the year before, when you negotiated a truce between his crew and the Crown Heights chapter of the Bloods a little farther north up the Avenue. And before that he helped you out with a certain situation, involving certain people that you don't need to mention just yet.

"So, what's the deal?" you ask him.

"Reuven's got a problem," he says, dabbing his lips with one of the packets of moist towelettes he carries everywhere he goes.

Reuven Horowitz owns a nice piece of Fulton Street, mostly storefronts that have been in the family for almost two generations. Needless to say, any problem he has is likely to be an expensive one.

"What kind of problem?"

"Yardies want that corner building he's got on Fulton and Nostrand, you know the one with the optician and the furniture store up top?"

"I see it every time I go to the train," you say. "So, what? They're putting the squeeze on him?"

"You could say that," he replies. You are trying not to notice that he's chewing with his mouth wide open. "More importantly, they've got us under contract."

"Under contract to do what?"

"A little FYI."

"FYI?"

"We need to let him know they're not fuckin' around."

"And let me guess, he wants me to come up with a plan."

"Plan and execution."

"For how much?"

"Five."

"That's a little low, isn't it?" you say, knowing that it's more than you need. But you know the kind of cake that this dude pulls down, and you tell yourself that you value your time enough to make it your business. Greed is the deadliest of all sins.

"You can use it to get your girl something nice," he says, signaling Jean for coffee just so she can show him her behind before she grabs the pot off the maker and pours.

"Always ahead of my game, huh?"

"I gotta be to take fifteen percent." Your brain calculates options at the speed of light. Then your compass points you north. "I already took my fee out of the number, by the way."

The cost of doing business is that everybody takes their tax. There are rules. And they are there for a reason.

"Figured as much." You nod, still pensive. Then it comes to you.

"I'm gonna need to see Sam."

Shango smiles again. "I told him you'd be there in thirty minutes."

"You know anybody that needs four .45s with no firing pins?" Sam asks, twenty-three minutes later.

He's a barber by trade. But he picked up a few other skills during the early nineties, when that nappy 'fro trend kept a lot of his usual cake out-of-pocket. On the table before him is a half rack of short ribs. He bites and chews in twenty-second intervals, using the nostril that isn't outlined with crusted blood.

"I might," you say, never revealing any more than you have to.

The rear of Sam's is the local arsenal. You come to him for both offense and defense, for gaining ground and covering your ass. For pistols, rifles, hollow tips, and even explosives, he's the undisputed muthafuckin' man, and the key element to your equation on this particular Thursday.

"But what I need," you continue, "is something that makes a bang. Compact with high impact."

"What for?"

"It's on a need-to-know basis, my friend," you say with the wave of a finger. "Besides, curious cats end up in the carry-out."

"You make any money from that writing shit?" he asks, his gray T-shirt now smeared with barbecue sauce and pork grease.

"Sometimes," you say.

"What about the rest of the time?"

"I do this. But look, Sam, I'm kinda on a schedule. Can you get me what I need?"

"Already got it. It's right there under the blanket."

You remove the fabric to see a half-liter nitroglycerin charge with a twelve-second trigger. He makes them for a third of what seasoned pros invoice for. A half-liter is a little much, but it'll have to do.

"Did I hit the nail on the head?" he asks.

"More like a fly with a hammer. But I'll take what I can get."

You and Sam don't deal in cash. Favors are your particular form of currency. So while such equipment would easily go for five figures on the Stuy market, you'll take it off his hands for no money down, if you get him what he wants.

"You know, there's only one cruiser on each precinct with a shotgun right now?" he asks, as if making small talk. But you know what's coming.

"Nabors," you begin.

"He's the day-shift patrolman for the Marcy projects. Pump-action Mossberg with a wood-grain slide. Takes a large curry chicken for lunch around 2:55 every shift at the Golden Krust by the train station."

"Yeah, I know that dude," you say. "The one that looks like a tall Danny DeVito?"

Sam nods.

"What a coincidence." You grin. "That's what you want?"

He doesn't want the gun to sell but for something more inventive. You just set things up. What happens after all of that isn't your problem.

"Yup, that's it."

"I'll send my man by for the hardware," you say on your way out. "And pencil me in for a shape-up tomorrow at 4." Arsenal or not, Sam gives the best cuts in the Stuy.

"I miss jail," Brownie tells you from the bean-bag recliner by the window. He did six months in Otisville for intent to distribute before they gave him time served for rolling over on some white boy suppliers, one of whom had something to do with Brownie ending up in there in the first place. Very few folks around the way know this. But you do.

Brownie is six feet and 295 pounds, is down for whatever, and happens to deal the best weed close to your house. Thus you allow him into your home from time to time, for as long as the high lasts. More importantly he trusts you im-plicitly, because he knows that for some reason you're not afraid of him. You're not afraid of him because he's a man that doesn't want to be feared, who needs people to embrace his softer parts so that he can feel better about himself.

"What do you mean, you miss jail?" you ask, pulling on what remains of the once-ample

Phillies blunt stuffed with Chocolate Thai. He is called Brownie because of his fudge-colored face. His real name can only be found on the lips of his elderly mother or on a rap sheet longer than the spread on your bed, that $300 thing Jenna bought you for your birthday.

"A nigga like me needs some discipline," he says. "I realize that now. In there they told me what to be and where to go. Kept me in a cage and made me follow the rules. Out here I just get into shit. Out here I'm a fuse ready to blow."

Sam used to be married to Brownie's older sister, Davina, but that was before she divorced him and moved back to Panama. Sam had apparently been tapping some girl barely out of high school. But Brownie and Sam are still like brothers, the kind that keep each other out of trouble when they need it.

"Are you sayin' that you wanna go back?" you ask, swigging bottled water to wash away the taste of charred leaves. "What you gonna do? Go out and fuck up on purpose?"

Instead of answering, he climbs to his feet and goes over to one of the windows to look down at Hancock Street.

"That's the only thing I hate about the inside." He grins. "You never get windows this big."

"You don't get to leave either. You don't get to see your kids. You don't—"

"Fuck my kids!" he explodes, turning to me. "Neither of them bitches won't even let me see 'em nohow, unless I got some paper. Besides, it ain't like I'm even close to bein' a good daddy.

I'm a street-nigga, man. That's the only shit I know."

Looking back, it's clear to see that he should have been recording interludes for gangsta rap records. He missed his calling.

On any other day, there might be a speech for you to offer, something about him not needing to go back to jail to find the happiness he seeks. It would be a perfectly crafted existential rant about how what he does isn't wrong, that he only does what God wants him to do. You would say it with all the conviction that you could scrape out of the depths of you, just so he'd have that thirty-dollar bag for you every Tuesday free of charge. You are trying to cut down. You really are. You also need him to play a part in your plan.

"Can I ask you a question?"

"Shoot," he says.

"What do you do all of this for?"

He turns to you with a confused look, like a five-year-old trying to solve a Sajak puzzle. And he never answers.

"Where you goin' with all that food?" Miel Rodriguez asks you, her bedroom eyes electric with interest outside of the Splash and Suds at Nostrand and Halsey. You are carrying two large bags of food from Yummy's carry-out: a half gallon of shrimp fried rice, three small wonton soups, four egg rolls, and a six-pack of grape soda.

Miel would dig you if she weren't all about

the Benjamins or if you drove an Escalade with gleaming twenty-two-inch rims like the one she's seated in, compliments of her man of the moment. But you're a writer, and she doesn't read. So you only flirt in passing moments like these, though you wouldn't mind getting your lips on those D-cups of hers. But intuition tells you that Jenna could outfuck her any day of the week.

Miel is beautiful, though, with those dark brown eyes and golden delicious skin tone, long Native American–like hair as shiny as a Barbie doll's. The man of the minute is a lucky one, if he can hold on to what he's got.

"I got some people in town," you tell her.

"From where?" she asks.

"Atlanta," you say. "I went to school there."

"Oh," she replies, interested in nothing beyond the five boroughs. Twenty-three years old and she suffers from the worst ailment of them all, Hoodvision, the inability to see past the blocks where she was born.

Behind the front seats are two different shopping bags, each topped off with a folded knit sweater. Beneath one is her current man's stash of product; the other, his take for the week, to be dropped off at an undisclosed location at the end of the day. Heroin has been in short supply since the DEA raid on Jefferson a few days ago. Her boy was suspiciously the only one who had a feeling it might not be a good day to check in at base camp right before the siege.

It's not that you don't know her man's

name. You just choose not to use it. He's an X factor in the day's proceedings, perhaps a catalyst, perhaps a not-so-innocent bystander. You'll know soon enough.

"How come you never try and talk to me?" she asks, offering a sexy smile, her slight overbite gleaming in the sunrays from above.

"I'm talking to you right now," you say.

"That's not what I mean," she says.

"What about your man?" you ask.

"His days are numbered," she says.

"What's he doing in the laundromat anyway?"

"Droppin' off his clothes. We gotta come back and pick 'em up at 5."

You glance at the bags in the rear again and know that Miel is carrying. Something small, but bullets of any caliber can kill you. There's no other way this guy would leave her alone in the ride for this long. You see him starting out of the building and take that as your cue.

"Well, lemme get this food, girl. I'll holla at ya."

You start away, knowing she'll do anything to have the last word.

"You didn't answer my question," she says, just as her boy hits the sidewalk.

"I know," you yell back, picking up the pace. It's almost 1:00 p.m. You have to move quickly.

The Starving Artist Café has barely been built, but there are already rats living in the basement. Not the disease-carrying rodents that infest the city, but four motherfuckers with whom you have a score to settle. They are two sets of brothers, Trevor and Neville of Gates Avenue by way of St. Kitts, and Dave and Francis of Harlem by way of grandparents that moved there from the Carolinas in the 1940s.

Weeks ago, they took a stab at looting your crib while you were away at a speaking gig. Half the hood knows you own the place but can never tell when you're in or out. They made off with some DVDs and your 100-disc changer, ignoring the art and the gear and generally keeping the place mostly looking like you'd left it.

Lisa Forsythe saw them from across the street and told you about it. Now the time has come to make things right. They live in the basement beneath this café. Blankets and space heaters have kept them alive since the autumn chill began. Various hustles keep them fed and functioning, all to keep their habits up. The lap of luxury isn't something they aim for anymore.

"Good lookin' out," Dave yells, draped in the same Pittsburgh jersey he's been wearing since Monday. They're all short on costumes since most of the dough vanishes into the good veins they have left.

Food won't make their jonesing any easier, but it will give them more energy, which they'll be needing shortly. They immediately tear into what you've offered.

"Anything I can do for my peoples," you say. The "peoples" part is not fully untrue since you used to play ball together a few summers back, before they started sniffing and shooting, be-

fore the internet crash that killed their entre-
preneurial dreams. But that's another story.
Everybody in the Stuy has a story.

"Besides, I know y'all sufferin' right now."

"What you talkin' about!" Trevor demands,
pulling a sleeve down over the arm he punc-
tures most often.

"It ain't like he don't know," Neville argues
between mouthfuls of shrimp fried rice. "The
man looks like he got somethin' to say."

"Only if you want to hear me," you reply,
watching them tear into the food.

"We want to hear you," Frank assures you as
he slurps his soup. The warm liquid returns the
color to his fair skin.

"All you need to know is that he drives an
'04 Escalade. Twenty-two-inch rims. Two shopping bags in the back seat. He's picking up his
laundry at 5. Just him and his girl."

They all look at each other. They don't
think it all the way through, just the potential
payoff and the nagging for the chemical of
choice coursing through their brains. They just
react, moths drawn to the proverbial flame.

"But we ain't got no heat," Dave laments. "I
mean, we can't just run up on the car with
nothin'. You know he's gonna be holdin'."

"His girl is too," you say, clearing your
throat. "But I got that part covered."

It is a quarter to two when you get the urge
for something to drink. It happens every once
in a while, during *Texas Justice* on the 30-inch
screen in the bedroom of the unit you've taken
as your own. And today is no different. But

you're also in the mood for another yoga class, even though you just took one. So you grab the carrying case for your mat on the way out the door but leave the mat itself behind. You also take an old white bath towel.

Both sides of Nostrand are packed with beings headed in every direction. You're never sure of what the unemployment rate actually is in this hood because there are always people on the street in the middle of the day. They move from the Nostrand Avenue A train to their homes, or from those homes to the produce markets, fish stores, and greasy spoons that make up every block of Fulton from Kingston to Clinton Avenue.

You see Officer Nabors enter the Golden Krust carry-out at the corner. You see Miel Rodriguez and her man pull up to the laundromat between Halsey and Macon. You see a gypsy cab slow to a halt in front of Reuven Horowitz's precious storefront. Then it all unfolds.

Brownie emerges from the cab's rear with a half-liter nitroglycerin charge. He kicks a hole in one of the storefront windows and tosses it in. The boom all but deafens everyone in a four-block radius and coats the entire street in shards of glass. The blast knocks Brownie to the ground. He hops up quickly and begins to run down Fulton Street and right into Nabors's field of vision, knocking over a grandma and a pack of teenage moms and their strollers. The babies cry like a chorus, unhurt but more than aggravated.

Pandemonium is a virus infecting the four

blocks in each direction. Sirens rev up and make their way toward the vicinity. Fire and rescue and the cops are going to converge on this place like 9/11 in less than three minutes.

Nabors IDs Brownie as the perpetrator and calls for backup, dropping his large curry chicken to the ground as he begins to chase the man on foot. Fulton Street, or at least the people on it who are not still climbing up from the explosion, cheer both men on as the chase moves westward.

You then spin around to see four armed men surrounding the Escalade that's just pulled up in front of the laundromat, their .45 pistols trained on the driver and passenger. The junkie thieves are shocked to find that the pistols they'd gotten on loan from a man called Sam don't have firing pins. Moments later they are chased off by the working and loaded weapons of those inside the vehicle. Impossibly, none of the four end up with wounds from the clips Miel and her current boo fire in their direction.

Backup units arrive to aid Nabors, and some splinter off to chase the armed men fleeing from the laundromat. But none of the blue boys notice that the driver's-side window on Nabors's squad car is down. Nor do they see the young writer reach through the opening to commandeer the Mossberg shotgun in the holster next to the shifter. The writer wraps the weapon in a towel and then slides it into the cotton sleeve normally used for his yoga mat. He slings said sleeve over his shoulder and fights his way through the crowd looking on at the burning disaster and enters the local Bravo supermarket for a bottle of Snapple Peach Iced Tea and a king-size pack of Reese's Peanut Butter Cups.

Brownie is tackled, clubbed, stomped, kicked, and then arrested by several white officers who don't have the brains to make it in any other profession. Trevor and Steve take one for the team as they too are apprehended by men with few other career options two blocks from the shootout in front of the laundromat.

Twenty minutes later the fire department has tamed the blaze. Three men are on their way to central booking, and the young writer is on his way back down Nostrand to his residence, having never earned so much as a glance from the authorities during the entire mêlée.

Sam has his Mossberg by 4:35 p.m., beating his 5:00 p.m. deadline. Shango has your money fifteen minutes later. Reuven has a concussion and a cake of shit in his pants. It's time for you and Jenna to get out of town for a second, take a trip, do something special and forget about all the bullshit you put her through a few months before, events there is no need to mention now that you've executed another successful operation.

You are smiling on the inside as you turn onto Madison, anticipating the surprise you'll find on Jenna's dark and lovely face. It's the last house on the left at the end of the block, a sublet she grabbed after your "altercation" because she said she just couldn't live with you anymore.

But then you notice the taxicab in front of her rented residence. She's out front in denim and a top made of spandex, her hair in micro-braids blowing Beyoncé-like in every direction. There is a man with her, and they have rolling suitcases. Are they going on a trip?

The dude doesn't look like much to you. Maybe they're headed into the city to buy him some testicles, or maybe a rug for that hairline that starts at the crown of his head. He carries her and his bags to the car like a perfect gentleman. And she's right behind him, holding what appears to be a pair of plane tickets. Or least they could be from a few hundred feet away.

You will later learn that they're headed on a trip to Brazil that begins today. Though the details will not fully be clear until after she returns, you will eventually understand that no matter how good you are at what you do, there is no salvaging what you had before. But there is the chance that something new can begin in its place, or at least you tell yourself that. You are Sisyphus rolling another rock up a long steep hill, only to have it roll over you before you have to start back at the beginning.

The two of you are the only loop you have never managed to escape, a checkmate you still can't recover from. She is like the sound Coltrane chased in his dreams, never to be had, never to be held, never to be won, in a season of games that lasts forever. But you keep trying. And the summer isn't over . . . yet.

CHAPTER THREE

START, August 20, 2005, 5:15 a.m.

When it happens, it's a random occurrence. One week it's twice in a row. The next it's every other day. It's your penance, the way she sees it. You fucked up what should have been one of those love affairs that turns into a great marriage, and the whole neighborhood knew it. The blocks and corners have a mental highlight reel of the Kango and Jenna golden era: back when you walked the streets arm in arm, lighting up the intersections and train platforms like an infestation of fireflies, kissing like you were auditioning for one of those Big Red commercials back in the day. There was a soundtrack to it, a rhythm with a rubbery bassline that vibrated with the sway of her narrow but ample ass, her skin so dark that it was almost a mirror.

But that's the old school now, a month after that Thursday that gave birth to this Friday. *This* is something else.

Your phone scurries across the nightstand, ringing and vibrating all at once, the combination barely enough to pull you out of last night's blunt-fueled haze. The crusty seal of eyelid on eyelid breaks and you flip the phone over to view the screen. It simply reads "downstairs."

At twenty-five, you pop up with the contoured core strength of a gymnast and the standard erection you hope to shake off by the time you get down to the front door.

Too many young women walk the Brooklyn streets with little sense of decorum when it comes to their hair. The hood trend of the moment seems to be walking out in the open with their wigs still wrapped and all of the pins still showing, blasphemy to the sistas of prior generations. It's the equivalent of a pimp with a perm hitting the streets with his bandanna still in place.

Jenna Ann Campbell is the third generation of the Jamaican class who has servants, who only sets foot on common folk soil in Kingston when she's driven and walked to a front door with an escort. Then, of all things, she came to Brooklyn to go to cosmetology school. Underneath it all the girl has issues. But as you've mentioned before, so do you.

"I have a thing 'bout heads," she would say when anyone asked, though you never believed this as the real reason she decided to do hair. You think she wanted to come down off the mountaintop and meet the people her pedigree told her were trash to be stepped over. Then she got to the States and saw that there were a lot of layers in the middle. Putting her fingers in other people's hair was how she learned how the world worked beyond her homeland. People, especially women, pass the time by talking in the chair, whether they're getting Senegalese twists or a press and curl.

Jenna worked Harlem. Jenna worked Washington Heights. She was the kind of chick who could talk her way into any chair, work for like a day and have a shop begging her to stay there forever. Then she would stay a month or two and move onto the next thing. Then her mom flew over for six months, made some moves, and bought her a salon. A $115K investment out of thin air. She never told you what her mama did or how she was so well connected. Her pops was an even bigger mystery.

But back to the current morning moment after her "downstairs" text. You gallop down two flights of stairs and open the front door.

The sun ain't even up and she is wearing shades two times the size of her face and some kind of cloak thing that looks directly out of a *Lord of the Rings* flick. It probably costs five hundred dollars. You open the door just as her manicured green fingernail is hovering in front of the buzzer. She has no compunction about disturbing your other tenants.

"Are you ready for me?" she asks. This is her best impression of all those clients that made her feel like shit, all the toxic heads she got tangled up in, a storm she keeps down deep inside her to be unleashed in the place she once called home, a set of rooms she only visits now when she has the urge to look backward.

The cloak thing has a belt around her narrow waist, accentuating the hips. Chocolate block wedges make hard clacks on the stairs as she climbs them. You follow behind, entranced by her infamous sway. Today she's wearing thick cornrows that crawl down her back, a fetish thing she knows that you like. She has spent at least 45 minutes preparing herself for this and takes a certain joy in you being fresh out of bed, almost exactly the way she left you all those months before.

"So how you?" you ask, breaking the silence as she disrobes. After this she'll head to the gym in the sports bra and yoga pants hiding under her *Vogue*-ready cloak.

"I didn't come here to talk," she says, masking her accent in something that sounds like Angela Bassett talking with her glutes clenched. She leans back onto the platform bed, on what she knows is *your* side, slides out of the wedges, and raises a bare set of toes. Her arch says that there was some dance training in her past somewhere.

You know the drill as you put fingers and thumbs to work at the meridian points of her feet. She exhales, leaning back on the bed she always got out of before you did, the only human being who lives comfortably on four to five hours of sleep and then moves around like she's had nine. You enjoy this act of service, as you used to do it for her when she came home after long days, full of energy but sick and tired of standing on her soles. Your fingers move to her palms next, releasing the tensions from days (and now years) of her work.

She's completely casual about the way the other foot travels toward that erection you've never lost. Being the nosiest girl on the planet, she found her way to the private bookmarks for your online fetish collections, taking in even the most graphic videos of men of a lesser caliber than yourself getting off to the slightest touch of a woman's toes. This is all meant to remind you of how much she knows about you, of the miles you've traveled both together and apart. This is as close to tantric sex as you're going to get at 25.

Her eyes narrow, glancing up at you with a focused kind of indifference, one that you know as a bold-faced lie. But forgiveness was an express train racing by while you were seated at a local station. You feel this heat rising through your core, climbing from one chakra to the next, stacking itself on top of guilt heavier than a ton of bricks. She broke you down to the point of having tears welling in the gutters beneath your eyeballs. But she wasn't having it. This is all that you get. Then there is a shift in gears.

You peel the pants off of her thighs, listening to the spandex slide off with just the slightest bit of perspiration. And then you smell her; it is something that you would never call an odor, which will linger in the air until long after she's gone, reminding you of your failure . . . one more time. You bury your face into her, feeling it moisten your mustache and the hairs at the end of your chin. You flick her clit back and forth, sucking on it, probing the southern end of the slit with your fingers. Her hips jerk. Her pulse quickens. And you feel a pulse of power, just a little vibration of the earthquakes the two of you used to make; dessert before dinner, so to speak.

She unhitches your mouth from the faucet and brings it to her own. Tongues knot. Body parts get intertwined. Her tiny breasts heave. Her legs rest on your shoulders. You enter her and that's all she wrote. Fifteen minutes later she's puffing on the half L sitting in the cluttered ashtray. And she doesn't offer you any, not a single puff.

"You're like the Tin Man now," you say, lying next to her, watching her smoke your weed.

"What's that supposed to mean?" she asks.

You never understand how she goes to the gym high and then makes it to the salon at the starting bell without missing a beat.

"You don't have a heart anymore," you say, pulling the slightly dingy white sheet over you.

"It's still there," she says. "You just don't have it anymore. And whose fault is that?"

Her words impale you, just as they were designed to.

"That would make you the Cowardly Lion," she says, twisting the blade Frida Kahlo'd through your heart. You deserve this for your crime against humanity.

You wonder when and how this will finally end. And this is when she tells you, as she climbs out of bed, her silhouette outlined by the daylight filtered through closed blinds. She stands and stretches all 5' 8" of her, fingers interlocked, palms reaching for the ceiling as her back bows into an arch. Then she starts dressing.

"I think I'm ready for something else. I can't just keep coming here to remember. You prop yourself up on one arm, lookin' like some *Playgirl* centerfold from the '80s."

"We don't have to live in the past," you say.

"No," she replies. "But we don't have a future."

"How many more ways can I say I'm sorry?"

"It's past that, J. It's been six months and you're still here, still doing the same shit and thinking it won't catch up to you. Yeah, you make moves. And you're good at what you do. But you don't go anywhere. You don't do anything. We never went anywhere. You never even took me out of the city. Even when you had the money. All you want is Nostrand Avenue. You act like there aren't a million other worlds out there for you. Sometimes I think you smoke out to keep your eyes all chinky so you don't see what's going on, that any minute something can come along and take it all away from you."

By now she has the cloak back on and the shades in hand, and she's starting for the doorway.

"So this ain't about love, is it?" you ask, the only words you can squeeze out of a face half-swollen by all the verbal hooks she's tagged you with.

"No, J. This shit is about you. Get it together and get it moving again. Don't make the same mistake twice."

It's 6:48 when the door downstairs closes behind her, sending the echo back up to your ears. This wasn't the battle. This was the war. You'll never see her on this side of your front door again.

All kinds of feelings start to crawl across you like phantom insects. To add insult to injury, she took what was left of the blunt with her. Now you have to start all over. But you really don't know how.

The only reason you broke down in the apology was because you'd never actually been caught before. You always got away clean. You covered your face or masked your phone number. You kicked open the fire exit and ran like hell before the security guard ever got wise. You talk out of the side of your neck and those words never reached the right set of ears to call in the DA to make a case. You were slicker than K-Y on a bathroom floor, and you had the ego to show for it all.

But Jenna had you dead to rights in that bedroom the two of you used to share, and you thought that showing the heart you hadn't used on the night in question was enough to get you off with parole or probation. But that wasn't *this* time. This time you actually heard what she'd been saying for six months. These visits weren't for you. They were for her to get over what she was giving up in the name of a new start.

The twenties are all about new starts until

you get it right. As time moves on, each change, each transformation costs you. But the time you're in the railroad-style kitchen, firing up the coffeemaker and the vegetarian breakfast patties, you're doing the math and it's like trying to fill a crater with a bag of potting soil.

At the same time, you can't let the streets see you in crisis. You can't walk into the bodega on the corner for the paper and show the Yemenis behind the counter, with their photo collage of the three of them standing in front of a Jeep with a 50mm cannon on the back, that you are vulnerable, that you can hurt, because then those men in the shadows who pay your bills won't come to you for the work anymore. They'll think you're soft. They'll know that if anyone boxes you in—cops, rivals, karma, etc.—that you'll melt like wet tissue.

So you'll have to stand in the kitchen and look out the window down at the yard your basement tenants enjoy, and slowly put your face back together. You've got your text message alert set as theme from *Jaws* for one person. And that's Khujo. Addicted to Black & Mild cigars and Beanie Sigel, she doesn't text this early unless there's money on the line. So, you go back into the bedroom and check your phone. She wants you to meet her at the Franklin Avenue Shuttle in 30, which gives you time to shower, shave, and plot a route across the four blocks that allows you to look as few people in the face as possible. After one look at you they'll know that your dick couldn't win her back. They'll know you fucked up the best thing you had, and the rest of your young life is going to be irredeemable.

The thoughts pile in your head like multiple cars in a highway collision. How could you have been so stupid that night? Why did you bring garden-variety tourists back to the place where you lived with someone else?

These women who ruined your life were basement girls, orisha princesses who smoked cigars and channeled spirits and danced the dances of their ancestors to bring light and healing into the world. You knew because of the eleke beads around their necks and wrists. You knew because you had blipped on that community's radar once or twice. But their affiliation wasn't what drew you to them when you came offstage at the open mic. It was their thirst.

You had gone up there and freestyled something hot and juicy, rhyming "eyes" and "thighs" with a "Black queen" and "Yemoja fantasy" thrown in there for good measure, and they'd thought it was all for them, that the spotlight you stood in onstage somehow had a mirror where they were sitting. They went in for the kill when you came to the bar, which created the exact opening that they needed.

Larry's Liquid Love was trying its hand at open mic poetry, a sign of changing times for a place once known as home to pimps, playas, ostrich shoes, and all kinds of bowler hats, the perfect set piece for a documentary like that *Pimps Up, Ho's Down* thing that had run on HBO not that long before. The one from Queens was chocolate-colored with the spaghetti-thin locks dyed blond and rocking a Moshood two-piece that fit her form like paint on skin. The other was a geeky girl built like a brick house with peanut butter–colored skin and a line of cleavage that stood nearly a foot out in front of her.

"You should be on *Def Poetry*," she said. "Russell Simmons would sign you in a minute."

You knew some of the folks in that Russell crew. You'd even scored tickets to one of the shows when they were on Broadway. But what you couldn't tell them, two whiskies in, was that when it came to actually writing it down, getting past the spotlight, where you were an ace at surfing the brain waves coming from the crowns of the crowd, tapping your foot to whichever hiphop instrumental the DJ had on underneath you, you sucked at the actual writing process.

You didn't carry some little notebook slaving over every little line and stanza. You were just a rhymer who didn't rhyme, the Wu-Tang Masta Killa of the cipher who managed to get away with whatever came from between your lips. Doing a book tour was second nature, but finishing the book was another story.

A major publisher had thrown you five figures once upon a time, mainly because you used to write record reviews for *The Source*. And you had actually tried to be the real deal for about a year and a half. But in reality, you were perpetrating a fraud and they found you out when the pages you handed in ended up in a barrel fire for the homeless. That was actually how you found your way into your current profession. But your crime in the United States of Jenna was cleaning up those groupies on the shores of Larry's fantasy island, a perfect slice of cake before the guillotine.

You finish your wallowing flashback in the shower, scrubbing yourself down with that Buf Puf of Jenna's she left hanging on the soap rack along with the assortment of bank-breaking soaps and body washes that you dip into whenever the red-bearded Muslim you buy from on the corner of Fulton and Kingston goes missing. You shave without a mirror, shaping up your own sideburns with the edge of the disposable blade. Then the water goes off.

You jump into a Star Wars Darth Maul tee and jeans with green and white Adidas Torsions, and you're on your way up Hancock, past the ball courts and the library and then up the iron staircase into Franklin Avenue station, the fastest gateway to Flatbush at any time of the day. You get there ten minutes late, and Khujo is pissed about it.

"Be punctual, nigga," she says, filing her nails with a small emery board. She checks the time on her old-ass Nokia cell that requires twenty minutes of key shifting for her to type out a simple text. She doesn't like when you're late.

Believe it or not Khujo got her name from getting bit by a rabid dog back when she was seven. Some German shepherd that got slashed by a raccoon got loose on the ball courts off Halsey and damn near tore her leg off before some hero cop beat the thing to death with his Mace and nightstick. Khujo is pretty with big doe eyes and Hershey-colored skin. But you can't focus on the femme underneath because of all the window dressing: the coarse fabric head wrap, the two scarification marks on the right side of her forehead, the hand-carved stars on her knuckles she got while she was in juvie for slashing another chick's face with a "buck fifty" box-cutter. And there is what's left of a Black & Mild cigar clutched between her teeth.

"Head Wrap bitches," she says, not looking directly at you, twirling some thought in her mind like some girly girl might play with a wisp of her hair.

"You know you're wearing a head wrap, right?" you say. She's not amused. But you've made your point.

Khujo, like you, had done some time with the people in white. She had been marked a child of Ogun, a child of the train track, a child of war. But then she lost some people and got out the game. She, like you, had to find her own way.

"When I say Head Wrap I don't mean me," she replies. "Got a text from this broad that wants to beef about why I'm calling her man. Why? 'Cause he got a box of Rolexes I can move faster than it takes for you to get knocked up again, bitch."

Khujo is a middle for whichever ends need to come together, which makes her kind of like your manager. She takes 20 percent for putting you at a place and time with any particular client. The official rules are that they get two meets with you: one to set it up and a second for the plan. That's it.

All cash. No checks. No credit cards. No wire transfers. All you're in it for is the money in the bag.

"Sorry about your Head Wrap problem, but what's up with the gig? I need to get my mind right. Me and Jenna just—"

"Ain't no just," she barks. "That shit is deader than them shows on Nick at Nite."

She puts her hands to her temples like some fake-ass psychic. "I see . . . I see . . . some new pussy in your future. Get paid and go find it."

She pulls an envelope out of her purse and hands it over.

"That's 2 gs right there. Another two after you deliver. There's only one problem. You gonna have to go see dude up in Harlem. The white boy just don't come down this far."

"White boy?"

"You always said the only color you see is green when it comes to this, right?"

You think about shaking it off and handing the money back. It has nothing to do with his race. Suddenly you just don't feel like working. You want to wallow some more. Take a couple yards out the bank, buy a quarter ounce and a bottle of Jameson, and take Khujo up on the idea of going hunting for tail on some foreign blocks where they don't know your name. But the very idea of that triggers another Jenna flashback, that whole bottle of Jameson shattering on your and Jenna's living room floor along with a flurry of loose 9 mm Luger rounds you were loading.

You had the first clip loaded and were working on your second. The pistol was chromed, like the one Richard Grieco had on that show *Booker*. Marquis and some of the dudes you ran with over on Madison and Lewis had Jedi mind-tricked you into going on a "hit and run" with them to get at some Serbians from Bay Ridge who had beat Marquis down at some off-brand pool hall. Even Jenna knew that if there were Serbs rubbing shoulders in Flatbush, then they were probably connected to somebodies, the kind of somebodies from places where lynching whole families was on the cheap side for keeping a reputation solid.

That was back in the first six months of whatever you and Jenna had started doing. She was working as the shampoo girl for Lil Magic on Grand, not far from the Botanic Garden. She comes in from work and sees you at the kitchen table with a nine and a yet-to-be-loaded 12-gauge sitting in Marquis's lap. And that was when she went the fuck off, the kind of "off" you never want taking place when your homeboy is there to witness it.

She snatched the piece out of your hand by the trigger guard and grip and started going on in a gutter patois you barely understood. But the words you could make out said that she wasn't happy.

You told her to shut the fuck up, that she didn't know shit about you (even though she knew everything), and that if you were gonna handle some niggas she needed to understand. That was when she slapped the fuck out of you with an open hand that felt like an iron fist. You staggered three steps back and Marquis put his eyes as far away from the two of you as he could, which happened to be on the photo of Jenna you took of her lying topless on the bedroom mattress.

"You like what you look at, Marquis?" she yelled, displacing her anger at the innocent bystander, which gave you just enough time to come with a comeback, even if it wasn't the right one.

"I don't need a woman all in my business!" you yelled, standing tall, playing off how much your face still stung. She came charging toward you, and you were ready but hoping to God the only things to go back and forth between you were words. She was fighting the tears, but they came anyway.

"And I don't need you to die on me!"

She'd hit the bottle with her hip on the way over to you, and the splintering glass was the soundtrack for her words. And just like that you forgot about the whole thing. Why were you about to let off on some dude over a pool hall beef you didn't know a damn thing about? You had made it out of the '90s alive and without a record. What possible reason did you have to take chances you didn't need to?

And that was the last time you picked up a pistol while you were with her, and the last time Marquis came over to your house. He loaded that shotty on your kitchen table and took it to back his boy up, and the two of them ended up hanging from the Verrazano on dog leashes. Somebody even put it in a rap line that turned up on a mixtape you used to have. Liquor was poured out for the homies and life went on.

Then the flashback ends and you're back in the corridor of the Franklin Shuttle with a 2g envelope tucked into your back pocket the way some dudes might carry a grocery list.

"You can't keep holding on," Khujo adds. "It's only gonna hurt you in the end. Dude wants to see you tonight. His name is Josh. The address is in the envelope." Without another word she starts down the hallway toward the shuttle train. The soles of her construction Tims make a loud squeak against the linoleum as she starts moving.

You let out a sigh about having to head uptown. Then you make moves for the closest ATM. Weed and whiskey might not be such a bad idea.

CHAPTER FOUR

The Bends

There is no shortage of liquor stores on Fulton Street. They tend to appear every four blocks. Some cater to the least common denominator, stacked to the brim with pints and freezers full of more malt liquor than Dr. Dre's "Nuthin' But a 'G' Thang" clip. There are others that have selections of fine wines and keep the pricey shit in clear view, aiming for the weekend champagne set, the middle-aged enthusiasts and perhaps most importantly, the corner boys turned day walkers looking to celebrate one more week of being alive and free from their former J.J. Evans from *Good Times* existences. You prefer Min's, right next to the Tak King take-out joint (which has a competing liquor license).

Min herself is a soft-spoken Korean woman

in her 50s. Widowed by a chain-smoking husband who fell to lung cancer, she only deals with the customers when she has to. Most of the daily operation falls to her son, Daniel, who is maybe 30 and as dark as his father in the framed photo on the wall but otherwise looks just like Min herself, except he always has some kind of cover (be it a hoodie, ball cap, or even sun visor in summer) around his features. It's like he's the face of the place but is somehow ashamed to be recognized.

Jigga and Jeezy's "Go Crazy" bumps on stereo behind the Plexiglas counter. He smiles, happy to see you.

"What you need, dog?" he asks.

"Gimme a fifth of Jamie and a Reesy Cup," you say, sliding a twenty through the steel semicircle. He puts the bottle in a bag and spins it through the service turnstile. Then you're right back on the street, the sun resting just above the tops of three- and four-story buildings as the day walkers make their return home from Manhattan and deeper Brooklyn. You, however, are headed to the corner, where the Warriors live.

Raheem, Wes, and Michele (he's Haitian) sit perched on milk crates cushioned with throw pillows they probably got out of a dumpster five years earlier. They are the neighborhood watchdogs. Raheem is the slickster, the panhandler/scammer. Wes is an army vet who used to teach at a college at some point but now lives on disability. And nobody knows Michele's real deal, but his thoughts are always ahead of everyone else's.

"You know how I know they about to run us out of here?" Raheem remarks. "They put a Applebee's in Restoration Plaza."

"And they started making the streetlights real bright," Wes adds.

"The more you can see, the less happens," Michele finishes. "What do we have when they take our darkness away?"

You crack the seal on the bottle, pour a little into the intersection, and then fill the plastic cups they have waiting.

"You know what would go good with this?" Raheem proposes. "Tastykake Koffee Kake. Like four of them bitches." The words go without answer, as you are not springing for dessert to go with their sips.

"What you seeing out here today?" you ask. This is not a casual bullshit question but a thermometer they have come to understand.

Your visits have a purpose. If you're about to run a job, you'd like to know the warrior state of mind. They are your first line of defense against any foolishness out here, though it's the Twins who have the deeper insight for you personally. You fold three twenties into tiny squares and slide them into their palms with a sliding slap of hands. Paying the toll is part of the process.

"Fulton is always a no-go," Wes explains. "But it's still quiet on the side streets. We still own those."

"I heard your old girl came to see you this morning," Michele says. He always gets there before anybody else. "Where the fuck did she get that coat?"

All three of them laugh like they were at this exact spot at five in the morning when she walked past. When you think about it, they probably were.

"Yeah, she came through," you say, taking a hard sip from the bottle to the head before refilling their cups again.

"That girl is dangerous," Wes says. "Can't nobody hold on to somethin' like that forever. That's Helen of Troy right there."

"Or any bad bitch on any block in Black America," Raheem adds. "Same thing."

This is the preamble to your planned drinking binge. But first there must be food. You leave what's left of the bottle with the boys on the corner and hoof down Fulton, skipping the train, feeling pulled toward what they now call Clinton Hill, where the Notorious B.I.G. was born and bred.

The blocks between Franklin Avenue and Putnam are sparse and underdeveloped, a snapshot of what the hood was like before its sister, Fort Greene, became all the rage, a center of bohemian buzz after Erykah Badu landed there for a while in the late '90s. You weren't born in Brooklyn, but you know its history. Even when you were growing up back at home, folks always thought you belonged in the Big Apple.

You put a curve in the brim of your caps, kept your jeans hip-hop baggy, and only played records and tapes that came out of the five boroughs. You weren't a street kid, but you knew the corners and the folks who lived and worked there. You grew up around crews and sets, but you were the smart kid. The right folks (and of course God Almighty) steered you away from the things that should have killed you.

That, of course, didn't save you from stray shots smashing the windows of your mama's house in Capital Crossing territory, or all the shot-up parties where dudes you knew went out on stretchers or in black bags when one hood took on the other, or when it was the MPD versus killers, thieves, and hustlers. All of it seems to come with more casualties than the body count in a Stallone or Schwarzenegger flick.

You pass the Mount Moriah Baptist Church, a beat-up storefront with paint peeling like dried skin. There's Mr. Felix's tax and accounting office, a barber shop that still has the spinning striped pole painted on the plate glass front window and enough baggies and splintered bottles to let any passerby know that pain still lives in these parts.

Sometimes after dinner you and Jenna would come back outside and walk down this way, playing in the shadows between the streetlights that actually worked. Her aura was special. It glowed yellow when she danced and purple when she was angry, and when the two of you shared space it turned into a pulsing kind of orange. You liked the way she would stroke the back of your neck whenever you got a fresh fade.

The sun has tumbled out of the sky completely now. A crescent moon ignites the rich blue left behind.

Some Head Wraps have taken over the intersection at Putnam and Fulton by the laundromat. Two police cruisers are posted at either side as a buxom sista in a blue dress spins in circles while carrying a full bucket of water. She travels in a razor-straight trajectory as singers and drummers play on.

A DJ wearing a white turban cuts and scratches on top of the rhythm, adding a new-school element to songs older than the country you live in. This is a cleaning. The bucket is meant to take on all the negativity of challenges of those who surround the bucket holder in question, to clear the space of all that should not leave with the worshippers and witnesses once the drumming is over. This is not a job taken lightly in their faith, as the crowd of maybe 50 or so have come to see and hear from the many faces and names the Creator goes by.

You watch from a distance, enjoying the final moments of the show. Soon the crowd will disperse and go back to their other lives in their other clothes. But for you the workday is just beginning. You're on your way up to the hell that is Harlem.

The Stardust bodega is a sight for sore eyes when you get topside from the A train at 125th Street. Just a few blocks from the infamous Elbee's Heart and Soul, it's the last sign of light before the avenue takes that sharp curve leading toward Riverside and the Fairway under the bridge. But you're headed east.

The Stardust was the retirement plan for an Atlantic City casino dealer who wanted to come home to the Lenox Ave. of the '70s. Even though that era was long gone, he put all of this money into vintage (and broken) slot machines, signed and framed 8x10s of Wayne Newton, the Rat Pack, and Elvis, and posters for shows featuring Liberace, the Rolling Stones, a Motown revue, and a host of others. He used it all to line the inside of a relatively basic bodega. The outside sign became a mini-rip-off of the neon monstrosity from the famous Vegas hotel where so many of the performers on its walls had played. The idea was "Vegas Come to Harlem," one man's personal paradise while he sold milk, eggs, and loose cigarettes until the day he died.

The place changed hands a number of times over a number of decades, but instead of giving it a makeover and dumping all the old junk, each successive owner added to it, bringing images of everyone from Siegfried & Roy (pre-mauling) to David Copperfield, and Redd Foxx, Lola Falana, and Britney Spears. The Palms, Caesar's, Treasure Island, and Paris are represented with figurines, mirrors, and even, strangest of all, tourist photos from random people who contributed their vacation photos to the place. Its owners are now Afghani in origin. But they rent the place to a Serb family whose English isn't the greatest.

"You seem like smart guy . . . different," Dragan remarks. Thirty years ago, any hockey scout in the country would've given a kidney for this dude: He's 6' 4" and built like Paul Bunyan in a Karl Kani ensemble that was in in style around 1996.

"Why Newports, like the rest of your brothers?"

No one has ever questioned your taste in cigarettes before. This is mainly because you only smoke when you drink. And since you're planning on doing a lot of drinking, you might as well be prepared.

"I never thought about it," you say.

"I think you need a better brand," he replies, leaning on the Plexiglas counter with images of McCarran Airport underneath his scarred elbow. Sinatra plays through speakers that sound like they should be hooked up to a cheap laptop. "I'm Gonna Live till I Die."

You don't know if this is casual conversation or something more. The only reason you remember the guy's name is because there's a Serb with the same name in a flick you dug called *Layer Cake* that came out two years before.

"It's bad for you anyway," he says. "Like Mr. Spock, live long and prosper."

"I'll do my best," you say, tucking the smokes and green lighter into your messenger bag. Then you walk out without another word, wondering if somehow he or the Stardust know something about the future that you most certainly don't. You take a cab to 145th and Edgecombe to the address Khujo masking-taped to the cash in the envelope.

"I hear real estate is on fire around your way," Josh explains as he lines a split Dutch Master with what smells like exceptional herb, the hood equivalent of a bottle of Buffalo Trace shared between billionaires. He seals it up, sparks it, and takes a long pull before he passes. What good are you in this game at twenty-five if you can't do business high?

"You ever want to take over something, be a thug and just snatch it from someone?" There's a flicker of light in his emerald eyes as he says this.

Josh is tall and slender like a shooting guard. His voice is affected but not necessarily effeminate. He could be gay but he could have just gone to really good schools. It doesn't matter to you either way. You're just here for the business.

"About a year ago I was studying for a doctorate in biochemistry. Had a nice job lined up at NIH when I finished. Then I'm driving my brand new Z3 and I run into an MTA bus headon. I break both legs but I fucking live. I walk straight. I talk straight. Eighteen months later it's like it never happened. But it, like, changes me, you know? I almost feel like it happened so that I could see my real potential, my place in the world. I wasn't happy, you know?"

You're tempted to suggest that he's mistaken you for some kind of a therapist, the same way Brownie used to, but that is *not* what you do. Still, you decide to keep your mouth shut. You try to stay present before the drug and the mood and the distance from your base in Brooklyn have you shift through shadows on the walls, as your aura tends to allow you to do. You hold tight and ground yourself as he meanders toward the point you're looking for. Intuition tells you that he's almost there.

"Now I want to step up my game. I want to do something real. And there's this strain of weed that only comes out of your hood, some crossbred hydroponic madness that only one dude has. And I want it. All of it."

"You want to heist out somebody's weed stash? That's what this is all about?"

"No, I want to turn it into a business unto itself. Jack the supplier. Make it scarce. Make it like it never existed and then bring it back to the marketplace as a nationwide franchise. Not a stash. I want the whole supply, the entire strain from seed to stem, and it's all right there, right on Nostrand between Halsey and Macon."

"But it's just weed," you argue. "You got a million different strains. Nobody cares enough about one to turn it into anything special."

"You're not a man of vision, Kango?" He grins. "Just the facts, right? You want to draw me a blueprint, get paid, and be on your merry way. You don't invest in anything, do you, not even yourself? I think that might be your weakness."

"I don't like paper trails, systems, hierarchies," you say.

"Lemme guess, you get comfy on somebody else's playground until they kick you off."

"That's the thing," you say, feeling the slightest bit insulted. "I don't get kicked off."

"At least not yet," he says, taking a deep pull.

This time he strikes a nerve, not with a bullet or battle-axe but with some thin adamantine blade of an adverbial phrase, something that's

doing damage to your idea of yourself even
after the words have left the air. It doesn't hurt
yet. But you know that it will. You don't respond
to his question but still manage to keep the conversation going.

"Do you know how much there is? You got
the formula for the strain? Chemical break-
downs? Any idea of how much product he actually has? I need logistics."

"That's the beauty of it. I've cut into this guy
about four different ways. I've got his phones.
I've got his email. I've got the codes to his security system. I just need someone to go in."

"But I don't go in," you say firmly, as you are
determined to never again get caught with your
hand in the cookie jar. "So like I said, what do
you need from me?"

"He's got eyes all around in the neighborhood, high and low. Cops. Lookouts on the corners. An old lady with a sniper rifle up on the
roof. His block is *his* block. I need his block to
be Ray Charles and Andrea Bocelli rolled into
one, for just long enough for me to make this
one move. And I need enough hands and trans-
portation to carry out all the goods without anyone seeing a thing."

You're nervous now. There are butterflies in
your gut. This sounds like some grand movie vil-
lain plot, the stuff of Bond films or the whinings
of Skeletor on *Masters of the Universe*. You get shit
done on the block, but he's talking about a
move that's worldwide. It seems too big for you.
But at the same time there's no possible way for
you to turn it down.

Your concentration targets the flat plasma screen displaying the latest in ballad music video. It's Maxwell's "Bad Habits." There are a man and woman sealed in a room. His hand to her bare ankle, his tongue to a perfect set of toes, water cascading down half-naked bodies shaped and toned by too many hours at the local weight pile.

The imagery is more than familiar. But Jenna's darker. The crease in her spine is closer to perfect as it channels into perfection. As the high kicks in, Jenna once again becomes the distraction that allows you to dismiss Josh's proposal as pure foolishness. You can get the job done, but where does it go from there?

"This is like stealing a car from inside a garage without a door to drive it through, or holding up a supermarket just to clean out all the T-bones."

"If you trust your handler, you'll know that you're here for more than just the money," he says, exhaling a cloud that encircles his head like a fishbowl.

You're already considering who you might ask to do this thing. You're already thinking about what you can accomplish with the current resources on Nostrand Avenue. Who's been locked up and who's been released? Who owes you a favor? Who can be bought? Who can sell you out? A plan and crew is assembling itself when you once again rechain yourself to the crushing guilt of five months before.

You are back in your crib, wearing nothing but tube socks, with the skinny blond dread from Queens taking it missionary underneath you, and Four Eyes, too drunk to do anything else, is rimming your anus with her tongue. Had Jenna stabbed you, your blood might have actually been the color of Irish whiskey.

She came in probably thinking from the noise that you were watching porn again or peeping something on HBO. She was more than used to the hot mess you could make of any stretch of downtime. But a threesome with thirst queens was a Mary J. Blige ballad just waiting to be put on paper. And you didn't even nut. The room had been a blur, except for your girl, standing there in the doorway, looking at her man and the close encounter of the third kind going down on the bed where she slept.

The chick giving you the rimjob took a solid jab to the face. Then you tumbled onto the floor and landed on top of your own jeans, on top of the layer of pillows Jenna kept on the bed just for decoration. By the time you were back on your feet she had blondie by the hair and was tossing her out of the front doorway. And then she was beating you senseless.

She stopped with the closed fists when she broke the nail on her middle finger. After that the blows were all open-handed, until you passed out.

"So do you think you can pull it off?" Josh asks, hogging the blunt now that it's almost down to a cinder.

"I need a day to look at all of the logistics," you say.

"That's cool. I was going to give you two or three anyway. As long as it's done by Thursday."

What is it about Thursdays? You shake hands and wander out. You take the stairs, and it seems like it's forever before you get to the bottom. Out on the street the high hits you even harder, so high that you find yourself staggering toward 125th, which is a long way to go without a taxicab in sight.

There are haloes around the streetlights. Every bulb on a passing car is a five-pointed star, like the fluorescent ones Jenna had stickered to the bathroom ceiling for the first year the two of you were together. You always took baths with the lights off, candles lit in Mason jars filled with beeswax from the lady down the street on Tompkins who had an apiary in her backyard.

You loved to play with Jenna's clit under warm water while you ran a washcloth over the heart shape of her ass, and you remember the eerie feeling that she was about to slip through your hands onto cast iron and porcelain that could've killed her. So you held tighter. You made each thrust more fluid, grinding your heels into the rubber bathmat, feeling the way she became you, that way you dissolved into her great space of being.

These thoughts give you the worst erection as you meander down the street, still thirsting for her while exiled in Death Valley. Then your thoughts go back to Josh. Your feet find themselves and you try to use the THC as a meditative tool. You start to wonder how much he really knows about what you've done. Does he have the whole résumé? Is this plan his own or is he a front for a collective of larger motives, people whom you are still unable to see?

Why are you climbing into bed with yet another stranger who you get the sense has worked the ho stroll before and might be working it now? Are you really this gullible? Or are you just high and paranoid? It's time for a drink.

You hop an M2 bus that goes all the way down Adam Clayton Powell. The high evens out and you're back in plotting mode, clear on what's being asked of you but increasingly certain that this job is one part of a larger puzzle. The bus is crowded with people, mostly men going to and from night jobs or middle-aged women, single moms, the ones that predators ignore because they're dripping with that New York realness, the kind that says that any predatory assault might not go in the predator's favor.

The only seat is across from the homeless guy taking up three chairs in total, the one who probably hasn't bathed in weeks with crusted dirt on the extremities visible from the dirty wool blanket covering the rest of him. The rear of the natural gas–powered bus hums and vibrates. It's also soothing until the dirty man with the dirty face pulls a .22 pistol, complete with empty clip, puts it to his head, and pulls the trigger. No bang. Just an empty clip. He does this repeatedly, looking you dead in the eye as if to taunt you somehow, as if he is a dismal projection of your own future.

But you do not fear him. You are good at what you do, good enough to steer past all of this. This Jenna wound will take time, but it will eventually heal. Maybe that's why this Josh job exists, because you need something to keep you going.

The bus lets you off back on 125th, a way from the A at Adam Clayton Powell. You go underground and take a 2 train toward the Village, headed for one spot in particular in a neighborhood where your face is stranger than Camus and Billy Joel put together. It's well past eleven on a weeknight, and there are only a few riders in the car. Ten or fifteen years before, a mugging might be an issue. But now, blind to any such possibility, you are a man without fear.

You're topside at 14th Street and walk down into the Village. A Prince wannabe with a matching acoustic guitar plays "Strollin' " in a crushed velvet outfit that's more Lenny Kravitz than the purple man himself. Retroactively, you will understand the importance of remembering this night, and this particular cry for help, because this is the night when it all changes, even if you don't know it yet.

"If my little girl's gonna smoke weed, I want her to smoke it with me."

The woman says this with a literal whip wrapped around her neck like a scarf, her dark brown curly locks cascading every which way.

She is short, maybe 5'4" or less, perched at the bar on hips that would remind you of Toccara Jones when she made the cover of *Black Men* magazine. Anita Baker's "Fairy Tales" is playing on the system.

As a note to the reader, you are writing this in the second person because it's the only voice where you can bear to be honest with yourself. You can tell yourself the story as if you are removed, as if the words coming out of her mouth don't automatically tell you that this is someone that you need to pay attention to, either because she might be perfectly tuned into your frequency, or she is someone you need to get away from at the speed of light.

With a clear mind, you would most likely respond to her statement with a turbo-charged rant about the problem with chickenheads and their spawn, about the piercing fear for the future that stabs you each and every time a woman says something this complicated, something this honest, something this painfully poignant when thinking of the state of things at this particular juncture.

Your watch has become a blurred circle on your wrist. But the darkness beyond the front door gives you hope that whatever might go down in here won't come to light for a long time to come. Jenna's probably flying the friendly skies with the next balding man to their next vacation space with your DNA still all over her, and you've downgraded to a woman who wants to puff with her kid.

This is round number three or four. And

you've been here for an hour, having wandered in after a brief stop at a diner on 6th Avenue for a burger and onion rings to line your belly for the drowning that was to come. You had a beer there. Just one beer. There won't be any more beer anytime soon. Beer is a waste of stomach lining.

"I don't want her tryin' no shit laced with crack," she continues earnestly, having already confessed that it takes a whole week for her to burn through a single spliff. She works in publishing to pay the bills while daydreaming of stitching stylish threads for folks like herself.

You can't fully place the exact moment when the woman with the whip actually joined you. Perhaps it was after you complimented her on the dreads coming out of her scalp and the brass bracelets on her wrists. Or maybe it was she who spoke first. Either way, the two of you are now together, now acting as one in the ancient art of bullshit conversation.

"She's five," the mother informs me of her child. "I was only 20 when I had her." There are a few strands of gray in her hair. Gray at 25 is kinda sexy. What would you look like gray?

The big 2-0. The end of innocence and the start of ignorance, that decade of false starts and delusions of grandeur that rolled up into the biggest dildo of your existence. You have to smile in remembering who you were back then, that church boy who only wanted to make his mama happy, your hair brushed forward until your scalp was raw, just so you could get those "waves."

The big 2-0. You were dead in the center of college, and that big-breasted girl with the devilish smile had promised you the world with a side of the universe. It was you who pushed her into that fling she had. Then she pushed you out the door for being everything he wasn't. Six years later you're still picking up the pieces, still mopping up tears you didn't cry for a train to the promised land that never left the station. Jenna was your second chance, and you blew it.

"I feel old," she says before she drains her latest glass of Riesling. Her eyes wear the glaze of tipsiness. But it'll take at least three more to get her full-blown drunk. Ready. Set. Go.

"You wanna come outside with me and smoke?" she asks politely, her thick thigh lightly brushing against yours. As she stands, you get the first good look at her. She's maybe a B-cup, with flesh of a honey brown and an ample amount of junk in the trunk. First generation Haitian American with dreams bigger than her booty.

She's the kind of girl you prayed for back in the early years before Jenna: pretty, uncomplicated, and not likely to make waves in the wishing well. That was what you told yourself you needed to numb you from the Mount Gay and Cokes and the repeated blow of the same party night after night, the same article with the same deadline, always made but never found fulfilling. You prayed for someone to come and tell you their dreams, to make you a meal that wouldn't be served in Styrofoam or out of a box, a perfect thigh to rest your head on when the check you needed did not arrive.

You would've done anything for that: massaged every inch of her being, put your lips to her shrine until your neck went sore, or blown your next three checks on whatever she wanted before they even cleared, all for that kind of simple girlfriend bullshit you couldn't find to save your life when you were certain that you needed it most.

Unfortunately, your prayers were not answered just then. It took two years and a 12-block move before Jenna came along, speaking Kingston patois or the king's English, depending on who was around. There wasn't a more beautiful soul in all of Brooklyn. But by then ego had already taken hold. By then that up-and-coming rapper had sent Ms. X to your room with Veuve on ice and nothing else, just to make sure the cover story came out right. By then you burned a J every 12 hours and thought like a criminal in the rap record racket. It all came out in the wash, and she was on dry detail.

The girl with the whip around her neck, however, continues.

"I keep setting the date and then pushing it back," she says after a puff from her Salem. Your Newport burns more quickly. Maybe it's the cleaning fluid that's allegedly in the list of ingredients.

Her baby's daddy has made it big out in La-La land and wants to pick up the tab for a two-parent family, a recipe for bliss equipped with a white picket fence and a platinum Visa. Of course, she doesn't want it. Because she doesn't love him anymore. And at 23, dead center in the decade of ignorance, love is all that matters. But he is only a stepping stone in her ultimate plan.

"I keep having these dreams with Denzel Washington," she begins. "I know he's like 50, but he can still give me a baby. He comes to me in my dreams and tells me how good I'm doin' in my acting classes. Sometimes I even think he flies out and has somebody videotape me when I do a monologue. He's gonna give me a part, and I'm gonna give him some, and that's gonna be all I need."

This is where sympathy and disdain dry into a holy prayer paste that you want to rub all over her cheeks and ask the Good Lord to cast the demon out of her vessel. Here she is a struggling single mom crammed into a matchbook of an apartment on a pittance of a paycheck, and there's a Prince Charming offering up deliverance on a platter, a free merge into the express lane to happiness and security squared. This is the kind of shit that only happens on OWN or in the pages of the lamest brand of Black fiction, and yet she's willing to toss it over the side for nothing more than a lovey-dovey fairy tale. There's got to be some larger fish to snag, some bigger bull to steer. You take a step back with your eyes and take a look at her inebriated aura. It's the deepest violet, so purple that it's almost blue. This Haitian woman before you is a seductress, a performer, the dancing

Twil'lek looking to be chained to her next Jabba the Hutt.

You can afford no part of this. It is the mistake of all mistakes to let this continue, particularly when any senses of sobriety are far beyond the horizon. Standing straight, in both senses, would be a miracle not unlike that leper washed clean in the river Jordan.

"Love is overrated, honey," you assure her with slurred speech, your intonation making the words smash against her like that bottle on your living floor with Jenna during the Marquis incident. Why are you back there again?

"What's that supposed to mean?" she demands before a hard pull on a square that ends up flicked onto Avenue A.

"Just what it says," you reply. "Love ain't pertinent to your survival."

"Well, I think it is," she shoves back, fully charged with vehemence. "And Denzel is gonna be with me. He *knows* what I've got to offer. And I think it's more important than anything else when you're trying to choose your partner for life. I don't know about you, but for me that's just some shit I gotta have."

You retreat. The muscles have flexed in her ample left quad. Her arm is bent at a perfect right angle as her hand rests on the curve of her right hip. It's pointless trying to negotiate with a suicide bomber.

"Maybe I've just lived a different life from you," you utter. "Maybe I just chose people that made love hard. Maybe loving me is hard."

Now you've definitely blown it. She sees the stitches and scars from the knives plunged deep within your chest. Any edge you might have had has been filed smooth. That façade of cool indifference has gone the way of sweaters with leather patches and Troop sneakers. Now she can see your pain. Now she can put her finger through that hole where your heart was when you were in the spotlight on that stage at Larry's Liquid Love, spilling volumes of empty words recited for the millionth time. She probably brought that whip around her neck to hang you with.

You await your dismissal. You expect this Haitian American stranger to suck her teeth and sashay down the block toward the closest neo-soul-lovin' nigga in vintage disco gear. You've already prepared the "Fuck you, bitch!" that will be needed to maintain your street rep as a bona fide asshole.

But she does not leave. As a matter of fact, she doesn't move at all. Her eyes compromise what's left of the shield you made certain no broad would ever breach. And you don't even know her name.

"She isn't all of us, you know?" she replies. The last of the pimp juice in your veins evaporates.

"I know," you spill in defeat. "But she was the one."

"And he's *not* the one for me," she says, emphasizing the "n." "You see what I mean?"

You do but you won't admit that you do. Because if you confess to the Black male sin of self-awareness, if you stand here and fully admit to the next girl you'd like to fuck that you hate yourself for betraying the truest love you could have ever possibly conceived, then that would be growing up. And even now, at 25, you lack the know-how to do that shit.

"I see what you sayin' and all," you reply, glazing the words with faked concern. "I mean, you got a tough decision to make."

She knows that she has you, even if she doesn't particularly want you. But the positioning is there. Her spirit guides outnumber yours three to one. Yet she's playing it cool. And you're even cooler, each of you waiting to see which move the opposing player aims to execute.

"Why is it that we never get it how we want it?" she asks.

"Because we'd find something wrong with it," you say with a clarity that even surprises you. "Because if we got what we wanted, we'd never have anything to dream about."

Her features freeze, a page taking too long to load. The tables are turning.

"What are you thinking?" you ask.

"About Brooklyn," she says.

"What about it?" you follow up. One more round and you've got her spread-eagled on her Posturepedic with the freshly changed sheets.

"Your house." She grins. Maybe you told her you owned it. Maybe that impressed her enough to donate her panties ahead of schedule. "I wanna see it."

You smile wide. She is yours, at least until morning.

The two of you abandon Open Air for the Bitter End. Along the way you pull a daisy from someone's flower bed and she puts it between her locks like a coffeehouse Billie Holiday. She giggles like a five-year-old. You grin like a dirty old man.

A woman the color of finished maple is at the mic. She gives her soul to a song called "Whispers." The sign out front says her name is Chanda. You'd buy the record if there was one.

"So, did you go to college?" she inquires. This is the question you hate answering, mainly due to the embarrassment factor that usually accompanies it. The believability of the experience diminishes with every year you age. The debutantes and gold-diggers, the feminist zealots, vegan enthusiasts, the jocks on the football team that couldn't complete a pass, and a thousand hours of lectures and losers who thought graduating from a "school of distinction" made them special.

"Yeah," you say.

"Well, I didn't. Always wish I had, though."

"You got time," you tell her.

"It doesn't seem like it."

"But you do. You're just getting to the point where you understand you. Next thing you gotta figure is what you want. If school is a part of that, then you'll go and get the piece of paper. You'll get whatever you need."

Sobriety arrives and brings the scene into focus: the basket of fried calamari and glasses of ice water, the pleather booth at a perfect distance from the stage, the trio of Asian girls across the way in short skirts with legs to die for. The clock over the bar reads 12:45.

"You think so?" she asks.

"Yeah, I do," you say with an assuring grin. She glances over at the clock.

"Damn, how long have we been here?" she asks.

"Long enough," you say.

"I wanted to see your house, but I think it's better if you see mine. My kid is at my mom's."

"Then let's go," you say.

"What's your name?" she asks.

"Kango," you say. "What's yours?"

"Mimi," she says.

The cab costs you close to 30 bucks out of Josh's envelope. But it doesn't matter. You need this. Her building is on a nondescript block on Rockaway near Ralph Avenue. There's a Wyoming Fried Chicken on the corner that looks like it's open 24 hours, a good place to sober up if this is a quick in and out.

Your tongues knot in the cab. You like the way your hands warm in the fold of flesh around her waistline. She splays her fingers while stroking the back of your neck. It relaxes you in a way that almost makes you sleepy. But that soldier down below is at attention. She strokes it. The driver, who looks Sudanese in the rearview mirror reflection, is taking glances at the show going on in his back seat. You slide him an extra 20 and almost have to carry her out of the cab. She takes your hand in the elevator while you run a finger up the inside of the denimed surface of her thigh.

What follows is clumsy. You break two buttons on her blouse and have to deal with the unpleasant feeling of your exposed erection against a metal zipper. But things get better. Tab A enters slot B. You hook your arm around one of her legs and go for broke. This is not an experience to be sealed behind plastic in an album of conquests. This is not some 45-minute thrust-fest that ends with lit cigarettes and a love theme playing in the background. This is real life fueled by real alcohol. And you black out on top of her, pants still around your ankles.

When you come to, the outline around the drapes is orange, signifying the light of a new day. She is no longer underneath you but has retreated to the bed at the back corner of the studio apartment. There are a child's scribblings on the refrigerator and fake flowers in a vase on a mahogany coffee table. There is a framed picture of Martin Luther King at the March on Washington hanging on the longest wall, and a Haitian flag on a stick pushpinned into place.

You think about leaving a number but somehow know that that would be a waste of time. According to her there's a fiancé and (eventually) Denzel in her future. There's no place for a flighty fuck after too much talky dialogue. You leave the bottom lock on and make your way past the dead bolt. On the street you take out your cell, which still has some juice, and dial the only number you trust for a quick extraction.

Shaheed is about 30 and a devout Baptist preacher who pays the bills behind the wheel. He doesn't drink or smoke and only takes to the night hours to save souls. This is why you usually call him in the mornings. He texts you that he'll be there in 20. You could walk home. But you're not going home. You haven't eaten since that diner, and your mouth is filled with the metal taste of alcohol. You light a cigarette as the first means of erasing all the damage to your insides and then head to the bodega on the opposite corner. A sign in front says "The Plantation."

The inside of the place is an ode to slavery. On the walls are old combs like the ones that inspired Eli Whitney to create the cotton gin. A master photographer has taken the framed photos of fields of wheat and cotton and corn that cover much of the wall space. There are images from the films *Roots, Mandingo,* and *Hollywood Shuffle,* as well as portraits of Fredrick Douglass and Harriet Tubman, a drawing of Nat Turner, and a mosaic collage of a slave rebellion on the entrance wall.

A 15-year-old kid is behind the counter wearing a straw farmer's hat and reading the *New York Times* like it's *King* magazine.

"What you want?" he asks, not looking up at you from his light reading. You grab an orange juice from the lit freezer case at the back and slap it on the counter along with a Reese's Peanut Butter Cup from the candy shelf. You slap down a five and he gives you two bills back, never looking at you at all.

"Have a good one," the kid says. "And stay free."

* * *

You step out and sip on your juice as you walk back to the pickup point at Ralph Avenue station. Shaheed will be along soon enough. There's that slight retching feeling at the bottom of your belly and a numbing ache around your temples that vitamin C can do nothing for. By the time you think of going back to the Plantation for water, you accept the reality that it's just too far behind you. What's ahead are proper coffee and a waffle down at Academy Diner. This will be the right way to really start the day. The dry and sticky residue of intercourse forces you to remember where you came from. So a hot shower is also in order. You regret the act, but you don't regret the conversation leading up to it. Another chapter of self-condemnation appears to be coming to a close.

You turn off Rockaway onto Fulton. Most things are still closed. Even the Dallas, a bodega exclusively dedicated to the Cowboys NFL franchise, is still completely shuttered, as is that Caribbean breakfast place on the corner that's rumored to serve the best "doubles," a breakfast device islanders line up for like they're Sade tickets. The Caribbean has been all around you for years, but you've never fully explored it. It's not that you didn't have love for the people. There are just so many different flags, and so many different sects, all of these dialects to a language you only knew through Bob Marley, '90s dancehall records, and Jenna.

But no more Jenna. These next few moments will be a Jenna time-out.

There is a cluster of high-rise columns of project buildings near the corner of Fulton and Ralph Ave. Though it's early, you can already hear basketballs bouncing off the rims and painted blacktop. A flock of seagulls flies low, narrowing into a squadron of bombers on an attack run, hovering just above the streetlights as they sail toward the Long Island Sound.

A group of dudes around your age wander out of Ralph Avenue station, appearing to be nursing hangovers, or hard luck, or both. It's too early in the week for this shit, but pain doesn't operate on a calendar or clock, nor do the arts and sciences of self-medication.

Shaheed pulls up in a spotless black '82 Cutlass that looks like it just rolled off the showroom floor. The hubcaps are chrome. And the system is booming. The Clark Sisters' "You Brought the Sunshine" rattles the speakers as the car turns left off Ralph and stops on the opposite side of the street, pointing the opposite way from where you need to go.

"No worries, dog," he says, slapping his fingers against yours over the driver's headrest. Shaheed is not a gypsy cabbie. There is no partition between you. But there are two pistols under his front seat, just in case he needs to use them.

"Who said I was worried?" you reply. "Take me over to Academy Diner on Lafayette."

He whips the car into a smooth 180 with a one-handed twist of the wheel and a little pedal.

"Was this early for you?" you ask. "I know you work late nights."

"I work when I need to work," he says. "Sleep when I need to sleep. The human body ain't nothin' but a machine powered by the Holy Spirit."

"Amen," you say.

"Besides, I get up to read my scriptures around 5:30. I time it with that mosque call."

"Reading the Bible to a mosque call?" you ask.

"Ain't no bells around here. The call to God is the call to God. What you doing up and about? Some young lady?"

"Yeah," you say matter-of-factly. "Something to pass the time."

"I've heard you say that before, brother. But how much time are you gonna let pass before you make another real move?"

"When I'm ready," you say.

"You're the most quick-on-the-draw dude I know. Seems like you lost your way."

"That might be the truth," you sigh. "There's no way you can understand."

"What do you think led me to the Lord?" he asks.

The eyes in his rearview mirror lock directly with mine.

"It sounds like you got a story there."

"I always had it." He grins. "You just never ask about it. And it's a story you gotta ask if you want me to tell."

You want to tell him to pull the rip cord and chute it all out. But you are afraid that it's an invitation to be the next candidate for him to save, which is exactly what you don't want. You have too many bad memories of churches, and too many walking nightmares about religion. You sometimes tell yourself that it's religion that put you in your current predicament. But still, you would like to hear his story.

Your lips part. Your jaw opens up enough to let the words crawl out from your diaphragm as the car crosses Fulton and Patchen. But that's also where a white '92 Aerostar and '73 Ford F-150 crash into the front and rear of Shaheed's ride, spinning it clockwise. You black out for a few moments but start to come around when you hear what seems to be the sound of bata drums. And you don't hear batas every day.

Your eyes open. Shaheed's hood is folded in half. That's when you know his shit is totaled. Shaheed's body is still, but his head is jerking back and forth like the rest of him is trapped in quicksand. The wave of shock and inertia that just coursed through you has debilitated certain body parts. You can unhitch the seat belt easily, but your legs are having trouble finding themselves. You make several more desperate attempts as a gathering of men surround the car, men that don't seem to be too concerned with their damaged automobiles. When you take a focused view out of the passenger windows, you see that they all have guns raised and pointed directly at you. The only one who isn't armed is the post-teen standing in back of the crew. He's chubby with Ray-Ban *Risky Business* shades on and he's banging on the batas like he's the crew's official theme music.

You can hear Shaheed's radiator hissing and

the engine crankcase hemorrhaging oil. If they're here to kill you, then they need to get it over with. But you don't say this, of course.

Your eyes keep opening and closing. And you don't know who's talking. But they're all dressed in amber and blue Le Coq Sportif sweatsuits that appear to be new. The last time you saw that brand on the street, Will Smith was still the Fresh Prince.

"Nabors has friends," someone says. It takes you a few seconds before you fully comprehend the statement, which at first sounds like "neighbors and friends." The lightbulb in your head goes off late. There is a defined reason for this assault. This is about that Thursday job from the month before.

If this were a film you would pull some surprise blade from your belt, slash an Achilles tendon, snatch a pistol, and get buck on every man present. But tape and sound are not rolling and the only stars present only exist because of your fucked-up equilibrium. A counterattack of any kind just isn't practical. All there really is to do is listen.

"Time for you to go home," another voice says. The sound of approaching sirens causes the gang to disperse abruptly before the trigger-pulling or stomp-out session ever commences. You don't get it. Why didn't they just finish you off?

They just walk away, leaving their wrecked cars behind. Then they disappear into the subway entrance, taking their dated sweatsuits back where they belong. So much for the coffee and waffles. So much for the final cigarette and firing squad in your dreams. Upon further review, skipping the diner might not be a total loss. You were only going there to remember last night's fuck before you began to erase it from your hard drive. This has become a habit as you've made best friends with brown liquor.

You started out at Academy Diner with your old crew, the dudes you knew from college who were up in the Apple trying to make their way as day walkers. You were in there with this Rasta girl who only ordered the fries off the menu because she was vegetarian. You were having coffee, really good Greek coffee, and she spotted some woman outside the window, a woman you hadn't even noticed. You were too busy reading some magazine or thinking about things ahead and behind. That was your problem too much of the time. You couldn't stay in the moment where you were.

"That's your type right there," she said, motioning toward a light-skinned girl of maybe 20 with Amel Larrieux hair, a short, flowered sundress, and legs like that feature model in the Justin Timberlake "Señorita" video. You glanced over at her through the diner window to see her standing in front of a stop sign while talking to someone on a flip-phone.

You weren't sure what the Rasta woman's words meant, as the target girl was physically her opposite, that type who only got the crowd hype in color-struck circles. Was she saying that you were into women less unique than she? Was she saying that you didn't love the dark and lovely? Or did she already know, way back then, that you were going to leave her for someone else, even before you realized it? You think about the oddest shit at the oddest times. Then your injuries overcome you and you tune out of consciousness and fall into liquid laced with black ink until nothing of the world remains.

CHAPTER FIVE

When you come to, you are not in a hospital bed. You are not lying on a stretcher in some crowded hallway. Instead you are in a straight-backed chair, cushioned to the left, right, and behind by hospital pillows in the emergency room of Interfaith Medical Center. The place is teeming with people, more than the norm for any Saturday night or the aftermath of the West Indian Day Parade. On the TV screen overhead CNN has highlighted in big block letters that mutated sharks are attacking Rockaway Beach residents. The animals, by-products of the heavy dumping of soy products into the Long Island Sound, have been going after African American beachgoers in droves. But these sharks are so tiny they can only inflict minor flesh wounds. Still, Borough Hall and the City Council are up in arms. Borough President Marty Markowitz swears that he's going to "get to the bottom of this." What he means is that he'll keep his show of interest up until the news cameras stop rolling.

As for the shark attacks, this is not the first time mini-Jaws and his kin have reared their heads in the five boroughs. Shark attacks tend to preclude any rise in real estate prices in overpriced neighborhoods, as if the mermen at the bottom of the city channel feel the need to make a statement about the lack of affordable housing in Brooklyn.

What you are certain of is that there will be hell to pay from the Head Wraps about this shark thing if it's still in the news by the time of the annual Yemoja festival, a celebration for the same face of God they were doing that bucket cleaning for over on Grand Avenue last night. The festival needs the ocean because it is on the top layer of the ocean where Yemoja lives. And the Head Wraps will get what they want, because unbeknownst to many, they are infiltrating everything. This is not a shady infiltration. You in no way condemn it. Their view of the world is a peaceful one, focused on harmony, community, and mind elevation.

Beaded up and draped in white on the weekends, they are your bank teller, your schoolteacher, your bus driver, etc. during the week. This camouflage makes them dangerous, as they wield a power that so few others have yet to become aware of. This is why their ranks are growing. This is why your time with them never fully leaves your mind. Something is calling you back, but you won't hear or heed it for a long a time yet to come.

The breaking news story changes. Two buses have collided at the intersection of Atlantic and Pennsylvania, and there are bloodied people rushing into the emergency room, mostly nursing minor cuts, scrapes, and a few fractures. The massive potential for a class action lawsuit against the city has everyone in the place stepping over each other to get medical attention and join the ranks of future lottery winners. You would think that someone told these over-the-top folks that the judges for the Oscars were watching on hidden camera.

In the foreground of this scene is Khujo, who is on the phone with someone who is obviously a dude. She tosses you a slight nod as she tears a fried garlic chicken wing covered in black sauce in half and starts munching on it.

"What?" She grins to the voice on the other end of the line. "I like to eat."

There are two whole wings and a side of scallion pancakes on top of salt and pepper fries. You have no idea how she maintains such an excellent hip to ass to waistline ratio while eating mostly out of Chinese carry-outs.

"Oil sheen?" she asks next. "How many cases and to where?"

There is a brief pause.

"Sugar Land, Texas? How come you don't wanna sign for it?"

There is another pause as the male voice on the other end explains something.

"Oh, so you want me to pack some of that and tape it to the bottom of the cans?"

You can't help but feel neglected. Your head is starting to ache, and something doesn't feel right in your lower spine. In your left palm is a bodega-style two-pack of Advil. You tear it open and swallow it down dry, hoping that this came from Khujo and not from the medical professionals who have left you in this chair. Then Shaheed pops into your head. Your first fear is that he is no longer among the living. But as of yet, you don't have anyone to ask. There is not a medical professional in sight.

More awareness comes to your body. You feel like a shaken snow globe. Khujo crosses her legs, denim on top of denim with green suede Pumas with fat white laces on her tiny feet. Your inner child wants to throw a tantrum that forces her to end the conversation, but you're way too cool for that. Plus your body feels like an unbuttoned shirt hanging off one shoulder. You adjust your eyes and watch her aura switch from pink to a rich blue, from the "hot bitch who don't care" to someone a bit more feeling, more maternal.

She reaches down into her bottomless shoulder bag and produces a king-size pack of Reese's Peanut Butter Cups, knowing that these will chill you out like peppermint candy to a kid trapped on a church pew. The first cup makes you feel a little better. The second is like spinach for Popeye. The aches don't end, but your outlook lightens. Maybe a doctor or a nurse will actually show up before this girl gets off the phone.

Then, like the miracle of manna from heaven, she ends the call.

"Nothin' broken. No concussion," she says, like she knows her stuff. "They say your aura took most of the hit. I wish all the news was that good."

She starts to explain a number of things that do indeed make matters worse. The first is that Shaheed is in intensive care with a broken leg and internal bleeding. The second is that Patrolman Nabors is alive and well. Whatever reason that whole thing on that Thursday had been set up for didn't work. Patrolman Nabors is still alive and Horowitz is at war with the Jamaicans, having recruited that Le Coq Sportif crew to watch his back. Horowitz wants you to do a thing for him. It's only Sam he wants dead.

Sam used Shango to throw you the job as a way to keep his fingerprints off it. And the least sunny of these three tidbits is that Shango has gone missing, like in the milk carton sense. The Le Coq Sportifs snatched him off the street around the same time those two cars knocked you sideways, and no one has seen him since.

"It might be time to do the Howard Beach thing," she explains. Howard Beach is the A train station for JFK Airport. She's suggesting that you leave Brooklyn: transfer your assets, give the brownstone to a management company to run, and then disappear.

It's a decent enough plan, but a little paranoid for you just yet. There are still too many questions lingering for you to turn tail and head for the hills. A low-level cop and some dated sweatsuits aren't enough to get you to up and quit. Racing out of dodge is black and white. What you're looking for is someone or something to color in the details.

"I told you about takin' side work that I don't get a chance to look into," Khujo grunts. "And this is some personal shit."

While there are neither angels nor guardian angels in your line of work, you travel through your memory stores for a highlighted list of the folks you have actually wronged who could have also played a part in this. You were not the man to stomp anyone bloody on the floor of some bar or club. You never dropped any corpses yourself. The aim when you got into this racket was never to get your hands dirty. Like Josh said, you draw the blueprint, get the cash, and be gone. You have always undervalued the power of your plans and, more importantly, the strength of your own aura.

You think of Gilda, but you don't want to sling accusations too soon.

"Now, I'm not sayin' you gotta be gone on some permanent shit," Khujo continues, having now emptied the takeout container of all its contents. The loud belch is coming. You can feel it like the beat of that chubby kid's batas playing back at the accident scene.

"Head to Atlantic City for a week. Hit Miami. Go down to DC and see your moms. They know where you stay at. Don't be in there smokin' trees and fuckin' bitches thinkin' that they won't kick your door in too."

And this is when the nurse shows up wearing multicolored drawstring pants and a white button-up, smacking chewing gum at a syncopated rhythm that might fit perfectly underneath Doug E. Fresh's human beatbox.

"Watts!" she yells from a few feet away. You follow her to an examination room with piercing fluorescent light overhead.

You get a look at the nurse while she makes markings on a clipboard chart that don't seem to require her to ask you any questions. She uses her flashlight thing to check your eyes for pupil constriction and then asks you about the crash. There are bags under her eyes and she looks to be in her late 40s. Given the age of most of the nurses around here, you would guess that this is her second career, a job she took on for the better money and benefits after a kid or a divorce, or both.

She doesn't look you in the eye, more at the space you fill on her time card.

"Like I told your friend, Mr. Watts, it looks like your aura protected you from most of the damage. What you're feeling is the aftermath of the impact. You must be pretty well developed to absorb that kind of shock without injury."

"I do yoga," you say.

She nods, seeming to be impressed.

"Keep it up," she says. "I can't give you much for the pain as it's not really *inside* your body, but I can tell you that you were very fortunate. The other young man upstairs wasn't so lucky, but I'm told that he's out of intensive care already. His aura was only strong enough to protect his head and neck. He's mainly recovering from the energy expenditure, but he will need surgery on that leg."

All of the mind-over-matter stuff requires a great deal of power. When you channel the energy around you to block something as deadly as the inertia from a double car impact, your battery drains right down to zero. Then you have to build it up again at whatever speed your body chemistry allows. Someone needs to write a book on this whole aura thing. It might be helpful.

Returning to your assessment of the attack at Patchen and Fulton, you know the whole thing had nothing to do with Shaheed. But these friends of Nabors wanted to make you feel it. For a brief moment you flash back to Denzel's next wife from last night and wonder what happened to that whip of hers between the bar and her couch. At one point, you were touching its coarse English leather while she stroked the back of your neck during back-seat foreplay. The next thing you knew it was gone, like it had taken off with a life of its own.

"It's not like any doctor is gonna admit you," the nurse explains, as if that would be silly. "Y'all don't get that. The main thing I suggest is that you rest. And don't do anything strenuous."

There's an ache where the back of your skull connects to your spine. The final question you ask yourself on hospital grounds is why in the hell you're paying for health insurance if this is the only "care" that it provides you while your aura does the rest.

You come back out on the main floor and

face the room full of mini-Jaws victims. There's a tall, dark-skinned dude in an off-brand hoodie and sweatpants at the triage desk. His left arm is in a cast.

"All I want is something to make this shit stop hurting," he yells, wearing the pain on his wincing face.

"We just don't give out painkillers in here," the fiftysomething woman with the blond Afro argues somewhat coldly. "That's not what we do here."

Khujo is at the other end of the room by the automatic exit doors. And she's on the phone again.

"What you mean when am I gonna come over in the catsuit again," she murmurs seductively into the mouthpiece. You're glad to not hear what whoever says on the other end of the conversation.

Khujo puts you in a cab, drops a 50 to the driver, and tells you that you'll be crossing the bridge. This is a very specific warning, not unlike her preamble when it came to the Josh trip.

"The farther away you are from what's happening, the better."

Of course, this makes you think of home, of that brownstone that is your fortress when you're not out in the mix. On that top floor, in that two-bedroom where you live and breathe, anything and everything is possible. Perhaps if you had avoided binge drinking altogether, then none of this would have ever happened.

The '98 Crown Vic travels west, taking Atlantic Avenue all the way. You pass the big public storage place at Washington, and the train yards before the Pathmark where they keep saying the Nets are going to build a new stadium. They're saying that Jay-Z is bringing the Nets from Jersey to Brooklyn. A Black man is finally going to have a piece of the NBA.

But you cry bullshit.

Something about the crash has knocked something loose in your skull. You should be thinking about Shaheed. You should be thinking about the Le Coq Sportifs. Khujo shouldn't be on the phone doing everything but touching herself with yet another mystery dude when you're in a serious crisis. That chubby kid with the bata drum was playing out a war cry, and it's still vibing underneath your thoughts like a film score. Who the fuck is Nabors and why hasn't he been on the street since that Thursday?

The car turns onto Flatbush and takes a dip downward as it travels past Ft. Greene and officially into downtown Brooklyn. You pass the Verizon building with the McDonald's at the bottom, the Brooklyn Academy of Music having come and gone a few blocks before. Then it's up the elevated stretch of street that takes you onto the Manhattan Bridge over the new DUMBO (Down Under the Manhattan Bridge Overpass), across the river and onto Canal Street.

"Where the hell are you taking us?" you ask Khujo, who looks visibly annoyed that you are interrupting her call.

"Acupuncture," she grunts, turning her eyes away from you. "You need all the help you can get."

This spa trip, of course, is not solely for the benefits of alternative healing. No one is going to be looking for anybody Black at a needling spot in Chinatown dead in the middle of the lunch rush. It's clear that your options for next moves are limited. What you need are clear motives on exactly how this particular deck of a problem has been stacked. Who's at the top? Who's at the bottom? Who's in the middle? If you could just answer any one of these questions, you could draft a plan of attack and find your way out of this labyrinth.

But your aura tells you that making any kind of offensive move is exactly what the particular powers against you are hoping to avoid. The continuous itch at the back of your neck is the most brutal of tortures. You have to scratch, again and again, as it is the only way to get through it.

When you've heard about the benefits of alternative healing, you expect them to go down in a healing environment. You envision exotic padded cushions on top of massage tables with teak frames and Eastern flutes, strings and incense setting a scene fitting somewhere between David Lo Pan's throne room and the first two hours of *The Last Emperor.* What you don't expect is to be lying on a queen-sized mattress on the floor of what might as well be a studio apartment with a 60-year-old guy putting needles into your lower back while he chain-smokes unfiltered cigarettes. But this is where you are.

"I never heard of bargain basement acupuncture," you say.

"The service ain't bargain basement," Khujo argues. "Just the location."

You've been in this cloud of tobacco and needles for just under an hour, and you have to admit that your body feels better. Your mind, however, is another story. Things out in the streets continue to get worse. Reports have come into Khujo via both call and text. Miel Rodriguez ate a hail of bullets while sitting in the White Castle drive-thru on Atlantic Avenue, a landmark you and Khujo passed by a little more than an hour before. The drug dealer boyfriend you refused to name is as dead as doing the Running Man dance at the club.

Miel is in critical condition. Now two people you know have landed in hospital beds in the same day.

"You know this ain't no coincidence," Khujo says, seated in the corner as she runs a wet rag across the surface of an almost antique CZ Bobwhite sawed-off 20-gauge double barrel, her favorite piece. You raise your head to lock eyes with her.

"You got something in the bag for me?" you ask, knowing that she's not holding the gun just because she needs to do something with her hands.

"You know I got the backup ready," she says. This is usually her Colt 1911 or a black metal Walther PPK .380.

In addition to your lower back there are needles in your left shoulder and on the right side of your neck. There has been no mystical music. Instead the last ten minutes have featured a medley of '80s rock: Heart's "Alone," Whitesnake's "Here I Go Again," and now Springsteen's "Glory Days." Jerry Springer is on mute on the 15-inch set in the corner complete with antenna and broken dial. And there is the faint aroma of Salisbury steak and noodles, a reminder of Grandad's home cooking courtesy of a foil-covered oven-only tin.

Then even more bad news arrives.

A gas explosion just killed Sam and two customers at Sam's Shears, turning half of that block to slag. Now you are officially scared. Now you know that you can't go home . . . possibly ever again. There are only two things left to do: a trip to Crown Heights to see the Twins, and a trip to Queens Boulevard for your go-bag, in exactly *that* order.

Though your face is frozen water on a windshield, these deaths weigh heavy on your skull. Though the array of suffering that is day-to-day life in the Rotten Apple affords you a certain layer of numbness, each passing second reminds you that faces you knew, experiences you had, moments you shared with now-departed souls are becoming, by the moment, more distant memories.

Sam will never provide you with hardware or line you up in his pump-action elevating pleather chair again. Miel's skin will no longer glow in the summer sunlight, sparking the looped idea that, by not being able to afford her or the lifestyle that was her niche, you had somehow missed out on something. They are gone now, and you have to accept the fact that accessorizing them in your plans is probably the root cause.

But if that's the case, then why are you still alive? Why didn't they finish you off at the corner of Patchen and Fulton? You don't have an aura that tells you the future, but how in the fuck didn't you see this coming? You are not good with emotions. This is why there is weed and whiskey and pussy, and why Jenna was such a good upgrade for the expandable motherboard that is your existence. She was the pressure valve that kept it all from overloading, both the brick wall and sweet stream that kept you in line.

Strangely enough, you don't worry about Jenna's safety. Though you cannot prove it, you know that her mother's reach is far and wide. Her moms can call on stealthy Klingon birds of prey who fly higher than you ever could. No one will touch her. But they have already touched you.

You and Khujo take the Q train toward Church Avenue, where the Twins live above a supermarket and a 99-cent store. The train car is all but empty as you head west back toward Brooklyn, the car rocking from side to side on rickety rails that make you feel even more uneasy than you did on the street before.

"This is the last time in the world to be fucking with some Head Wrap shit," Khujo grunts as she constantly peers into her bag, checking on that shotgun of hers like it's a live animal bent on running away from her.

This is when you notice your back teeth grinding against each other. This is not good. Your aura constricts like tightened abs bracing themselves for a blow. This is when the rear entrance door to the train car comes open, which officially shouldn't happen, as car-to-car transfer on the Q is limited because of the nature of the hitches between trains. But as the War Boys come charging into the car, dressed from head to toe in Kansas City Chiefs gear adorned with sewn-on feathers that make them look like a cross between a break beat–era rap crew and masked Mardi Gras Indians, you know they're not in here looking for open seating.

Their facial features are all remotely similar. They are not seven brothers, but they could be cousins; they have the same mahogany color with the same cheekbones and eyes. But the rest of their features vary: an array of noses and lip arrangements, and eyes from wide to narrow.

The gym rat pretty boy steps to the front, his 20-inch guns pulsating through his sleeves.

"You Kango?" he demands.

"Am I supposed to say yes?"

"Somebody wants to see you," he says.

These boys are kids, 17 or 18 at best. But their faces look older. Still, they could be playing hooky from high school for all you know.

"Who?" you ask. Then another one decides to speak.

"We ain't supposed to say."

"Buck one of these niggas and the rest of 'em will go running," Khujo whispers. While this may be true, a homicide on public transit isn't good for any of you.

You stand up. Six feet with broad shoulders is enough to make it clear that this could hurt for them too. Part of it is to shield the girl with the shoulder bag. If it goes bad, she can let off and you can make a break for the next car behind you. If you time it right, the train should pull into 7th Avenue station by then and you can make a break from the platform to the street.

Gym Rat pokes his chest out. "Ain't nobody supposed to get hurt," he says. "They just wanna talk."

"Talk where?" you ask.

"Prospect Park," he says. "The Drummer's Circle."

You relax a little. There is nothing more harmless than the drum circle.

"What they need all of you for if it's just to the drum circle?"

And then a third one, shorter and less athletic, takes his turn. "'Cuz they gave us $300. We on our way to the comic convention up at the Javitz Center."

"How'd you know where to find me?" you ask.

"They got an aura tracker. And she cute too."

Aura trackers are like drug-sniffing dogs. You give them a name and they can tell you where somebody will be within a two-hour window. If they're real good they have it down to 20 minutes. But it's not so effective if that person is in a place you don't know or is completely beyond borders. Most of them end up working for law enforcement or the private sector. They usually don't make it out of grade school without getting tagged by somebody. But if they keep it quiet, the underworld always finds them. You'd like to know one for the sake of your own business, but right about now it doesn't look like you have a business anymore.

"We get another $300 if we walk you over there. Don't be an asshole. See what they got to say."

Khujo is surprisingly quiet, which means she doesn't sense a threat either. Besides, Flatbush and Crown Heights are adjacent.

The Drummer's Circle is a little cul-de-sac on the southeast end of Prospect Park, near where Ocean Avenue meets Parkside. On any Sunday afternoon in spring, summer, and fall, African drummers of all kinds and types drop through to play together. And they draw a good-sized crowd. But it's not a panhandling thing. It's more like an artist showcase at Birdland or a Village Vanguard for the African drummers in the five boroughs. You can hear them long before you get there.

You never brought Jenna here. Truth be told, you never brought anyone here. When you came to the park it was to be alone, to find the right tree, or to pick up the right branch to carve, sand, and shape back at your abode, especially back when you were a Head Wrap, one of the many, a connected guy who they wouldn't open up the books for. And that hurt you.

There's tension in the air. It's mixed into the surroundings like cooked and seasoned beef into a marinara sauce. You wouldn't be surprised if Spike Lee started putting Head Wraps in his movies.

Pop used to always tell you that being self-employed was a family curse, that there was something about Watts men and them not being able to take orders. Watts men work in solitude. Watts men run their own show. These mantras were pounded into your head at an early age and caused you to look down on the idea of being summoned by higher-ups, of having anyone to answer to. Being accosted by the *Ebony Jr.* mob on the Q train was aggravating and leads you to enter Prospect Park with a chip on your shoulder.

Though you won't pinpoint it until much later, you feel like that zookeeper at the Bronx Zoo who let some killer python get loose or a whistleblower who let the cat out of the bag by accidentally leaving his microphone on. You are a ball of nerves but maintain a cool surface.

You and Khujo walk the curved path to the Drummer's Circle. And "they" are waiting for you.

They are the cast of characters from This Is Your Brooklyn Life. And these are not the kinds of folks to come out in the open to sit on benches and listen to the drums. Gilda is a regal queen who carries her signature Kate Spade clutch with a leopard pattern and soft, dark brown features. She is a walking data file of honey-sweet connections and cliques. She sits on the boards of banks and nonprofits, helps to raise support for political campaigns, and funds membership drives. She knows everyone and remembers no one, her signature salt-pepper extension braids flowing in the electric air that crackles around her. No one knows her aura class, and it's not a thing that she discusses publicly, though your guess was always 9. Anyone with good sense either kisses the ring or stays the fuck out of her way. Her full smile, whenever brought forth, is a thing of true beauty.

You know more about Gilda than anyone else here. She was your mother away from your mother, the one who saw what others didn't when you were a kid fresh out of college looking for your place in the world. She is the one who brought you in and later took you out of the game of thrones that has placed you in this particular predicament.

Baba Jameel and son Apani are a light-skinned and freckled-faced father and son dressed in white and covered in eleke beads with Aso Oke hats on their crowns. They know their shit. They believe in their one god, Olodumare, before the magic in their own hands, and make the music that brings the Divine down on the regular folks. They study and pray and sacrifice and set the tone for the family and aspiring initiates who follow them.

Mike Schmitz is a homicide detective from Crown Heights. You don't know him from the underworld. You know him from the *Star Trek* club that meets at different bars from time to time to talk Kirk, Spock, and McCoy while getting smashed on the kind of spirits you love to pour.

Marv Bowman is a portly man with an affinity for oversized satin vests and one in a million bowler hats, looking more like he should be playing piano in some Western saloon than walking the Brooklyn streets. But, truth be told, this cat is worth millions. He's refurbishing the brownstones on Nostrand Avenue on the southern side of Eastern Parkway, the part of the strip where you don't know as many people. That dude can do some damage with a pool cue and the right rack of balls. He broke you and Bonz Malone for a few dollars here and there when you used to run into him at the Manhattan halls. But he never plays in Brooklyn. That's his rule. He doesn't shit where he eats.

There are three others you don't know in cheap suits and shades. They look like secret service as they flank Will Alexander, another real estate shot caller, the dude who used to own your crib before he lost it to you in the best game of No Limit Hold'em you would ever play. You haven't seen Alexander in years. He looks old now, his 70s showing what his 60s did not. These are people who don't come out to play in the sunshine. And yet they're here, waiting for you. What does it all mean?

"We need you to leave," Alexander begins, his accent still as thick as lobster bisque. You were expecting Gilda to do all of the talking. "It's not personal and it's not your fault."

"You don't belong here anymore," Jameel says. "You've stirred up a demon you can't control. And you can't clean up the mess it's about to make."

"The fuck are you talkin' about?" you demand indignantly. "I own my house. I pay my taxes. I do what I do away from you."

"You think that this is about what we think," Gilda says, cool as a cucumber. "You think the God you serve has abandoned you. He has not. But others are coming. A cleansing needs to happen that you can't be here for."

"Jim Nabors is supposed to be dead," Schmitz chimes in. "But he ain't. His setup got set up on. And he's about to let out the wolves, the young ones, the ones we can't control."

"Then why didn't they clap me?" you ask. "They had me on Fulton Avenue. Coulda done me right there."

"It's not the roosters in yellow, honey," Gilda grins. "They're with me. That was to slow you down from a crash you couldn't survive."

"They're the B team," Apani says. He looks like he could still be walking the halls in a high school. "The Arsonists are coming."

"Then call the muthafuckin' fire department," Khujo all but screams, having been dead silent for far longer than usual.

"She's living in *your* building," Jameel continues. "But you don't know who she is. She lives between the walls, between the auras you trust the most. You can't put cuffs on her or a bullet in her brain. If you stay, she will take everything away from you."

"What is she? A spirit? A dead person? The Antichrist?" You feel like they are all speaking in riddles, dancing around something a little too important to be explained in parables.

"Then break out the frankincense and the orange peel and we can get busy," you say.

"You walked away, remember?" Gilda gibes. "You told me that you didn't believe anymore."

"This ain't the time for that conversation, Gilda," you say firmly but without disrespect, reliving the events that changed your relationship quietly, painfully. You were in her crew. You know how she rolls. You used to help her run one of her places. You helped her with jobs she put together. She once told you that you were the son she never had but that she would not be the one to put the crown on your head. That would be up to you.

This little intervention is almost dreamlike. Reality ripples like water in a shaken and sealed jar. You came here to get the 411 on why people are dead, and these game-changers, cops, and big willies are throwing words at you like it's a Sunday morning sermon.

"People I know are dead," you say, as if there is profundity in the words.

"And more might be dead tomorrow," Schmitz says, lighting a loose Marlboro. "This isn't about the body count. This is about you. Nobody's trying to keep you from working. No one wants to take what's yours from you."

"The Arsonists are coming for all of us," Apani says. "And when the time comes, we will need you to craft a plan. Architects are few and far between here."

"I live here and I'm not going nowhere,"

you say again. But this time your words don't feel as strong. You no longer believe them yourself. You know how serious all of this is.

What appear to be 100 starlings seem to jet across the sky above you.

"Go and see the Twins," Gilda says. "If you don't trust me, you will trust them. She is looking for you, and she will find you, and you have to be ready."

"Do not fly and do not take any more trains as you leave," Will says, sounding awfully sage-like for a man in a satin vest. "This will save your life."

Silence washes over this Council of Nicaea.

"Is that all you gonna fuckin' say?" Khujo demands.

"Go and see the Twins," Gilda says again.

And with that, the group rises from their benches and starts off in different directions like some twisted version of the close-out to the Clooney/Pitt/Damon *Ocean's Eleven*.

You're now wondering if that weed at Josh's crib was laced. You're wondering if the chick with the whip slipped you a Mickey you're still recovering from. You're wondering if Shaheed is okay. But most of all, you're wondering about Patrolman Jim Nabors and why in the fuck he's so important to the future of all things Brooklyn. From what you know he's just a beat cop. What could he possibly have to do with things to come?

"That's what we came the fuck over here for?" Khujo grunts.

"Apparently," you say.

"Well, they're right about one thing," she says, fishing a fresh Black & Mild out of her shoulder bag. Then she sparks it with a plastic purple lighter. "You need to see the Twins. I'm about to go get my nails done."

CHAPTER SIX

"The Twins," better known as Janine and Judith Austin, were born on July 16, 1956, in Hattiesburg, Mississippi. Destined to be children of the Lord Almighty by a preacher father named Preacher Austin, they were marked as prophets at the time of their christening. Their apartment is filled with photographs demarcating their history and service to both the choir and the usher board in a wooden church painted white with a cemetery right next to it. This church flooded every 30 years or so, when the Leaf River got angry and washed the outskirts of surrounding civilization away.

The Twins went to the same schools all the way up until college. Then Janine went to cosmetology school and stayed within the Hattiesburg limits. But Judith came to New York and learned urban decay by way of the North Bronx at Fordham. She studied history and sociology, got a master's in anthropology from NYU, and became permanent convert to the five boroughs. By the '70s she was a part of the East movement, a post-Panther collective dedicated to political expression through arts and culture. And this was where God gave her a different name and swept her up into the whirlwind that binds the dead and the living and showed her a new kind of God in that new city in the very same year Janine was ordained an evangelist in white wooden church where she and her sister had grown up.

These choices resulted in a long period of silence between the sisters: a decade of marriages to men who never met each other, cousins who barely knew of each other's existence, and the call from an ailing father for the elder twin to go to New York and save young Judith from the wiles of Satan himself. Janine went into the Apple for the rescue but failed to leave the city either. Their marriages melted away like cotton candy on the tongue, and their children came to visit the city like they'd been born in the place. The Twin sisters took up residence in a railroad apartment above the New Mexico Fried Chicken on Winthrop and never left. Those who don't mind hearing the voice of God with two different identical faces come here.

The first time you met them was at the party in Fort Greene Park. Judith, then in her 50s, would be there dancing on roller skates, zipping left and right through the moving bodies possessed by the sounds of Frankie Knuckles and

Aly-Us's "Follow Me" while Janine sold chicken and yam dinners and prayed for people on the sidelines.

"The Lord's got a plan for you," she had said when you were 22, your beard a patchy mess, forming a goatee that didn't fully connect. You were there amongst all of those beautiful bodies, girls with sculpted abs and tails that bounced like a Bootsy Collins bassline, sucking in the pheromones of the rhythm even though you hated to dance.

You were a head-nod dude. You played the outskirts, took in the scene and wrote it all down later beyond the sight lines of judgmental eyes.

"The Lord is gonna call on you to do something you wanna do," she continued. "And once it's done, He will let you finally have the love of your life. Until then you're gonna chase the tail through these crowds of harlots who done lost their way. But you will save some of them too, without even knowing it."

Though you remember her words, it's the Head Wrap twin who sticks in your mind, spinning on one roller skate with the other perfectly extended in the air like a brown-skinned Dorothy Hamill. From what you saw they were the same person in two different bodies, a shared soul that had finally made peace with itself.

There is not a whole lot of ceremony to their spiritual readings. They sit side by side. Janine prays and opens the Bible to a certain page, reads the verse, and then she tells you the story. Judith takes out the 16 cowrie shells, prays to the copper goddess Oya, and asks for Olodumare to bring revolution down upon your head. And then your story begins, played out before you like a script written just for you.

You've seen them ten times for about twenty different jobs since you wandered out on your own. And when you follow what they say, you always end up standing in the sunshine.

Janine goes through the Lord's Prayer like someone has a gun to her head.

"I got the number eight in my head. God's seven, and then one for me, I guess."

She flips open to the book of Amos, which makes you think about the father on *Good Times*.

"I will send a fire into the house of Hazael, which shall devour the palaces of Ben-hadad. I will break also the bar of Damascus, and cut off the inhabitant from the plain of Aven, and him that holdeth the scepter from the house of Eden: and the people of Syria shall go into captivity unto Kir, saith the Lord.

"Thus saith the Lord; For three transgressions of Gaza, and for four, I will not turn away the punishment thereof; because they carried away captive the whole captivity, to deliver them up to Edom. But I will send a fire on the wall of Gaza, which shall devour the palaces thereof. But I will send a fire on the wall of Gaza, which shall devour the palaces thereof.

"And I will cut off the inhabitant from Ashdod, and him that holdeth the sceptre from Ashkelon, and I will turn mine hand against Ekron: and the remnant of the Philistines shall perish, saith the Lord God."

Then Janine slams the book shut and drops it into her lap like it's made of C-4 explosive. She closes her eyes, allowing the spirit to move through her. Then they open again. Judith's face washes with an almost childlike anxiety for her turn to get into the game.

"You ever been in a war, Kango?" As if her reading wasn't the least bit dramatic.

"I had my fights," you say.

"People walk home after fights, or maybe go to the hospital. Bodies don't get buried in ditches. In fights men come back home to their women. This ain't a fight. This is a war. And you stumbled into the middle of somebody else's playground. A lot of money on that playground. A lot of people with old scores to settle. Scores older than that building of yours, feuds that are older than you. They came to you like they was your friends, like it was all grits and gravy on Sunday mornin' before church. They did that because they don't want to kill you. Killin' you turns it into something worse. What they told you was right. It's time for you to leave."

Judith wastes no time in saying her prayers in an olden form of the Yoruba language. The 16 cowrie shells hit the surface of the winnowing basket. She scrutinizes them with her hands and eyes. Each shell tells its own part of the tale.

"They been checkin' on you," Judith begins. "Adding up all the numbers. Checking all the files. You take the picture, and then it becomes what happened. That's your gift. But you ain't got no people. You ain't bend the knee. You kicked up some dust and it got in some people's faces. Took away their eyes for a while. And when the cloud settled, their eyes belonged to you. You don't see it, but you can make soldiers for an army. You touched somebody who's supposed to be untouchable. And he called in some folks that's threatening to wash away the whole thing like a river in a hurricane.

"You have to be here for the flood to happen. You have to be standing on Brooklyn soil in order for God to make it rain. And since all they want is sunny days like *Sesame Street*, quickest way to keep it happy and safe, for the money to keep flowing and the reputations to stay solid, is to keep you out of their way.

"But you don't want to give them the satisfaction, right, honey?" Judith continues. "You don't wanna go out like no punk. You wanna stand tall like a block boy. But thing is . . . you already own the block and don't even know it. But your block ain't in Brooklyn. It's somewhere else. That's the place you want to keep safe from these people. That's the place you have to protect, no matter what the cost."

This is, of course, a lot for you to take in. You woke up fresh off a sloppy fuck with Mimi, the woman with the whip, and now these two seasoned ladies you trust are trying to tell you that the sky might be falling and there isn't anything Chicken Little can do about it. This is a puzzle Sajak can't solve, even with the answers on the screen right in front of him. But if Pat walks away with the cash and prizes, then the game doesn't happen at all. Millions of dollars, legalized bullets, the power of the gods, and

everything else is somehow scared of a weed-
head from DC who wants to wish away the acci-
dental shit storm that ruined his love life.

Sam and Miel are gone. Shango is missing
in action. It's going to take more than a sacrificed rooster and a pair of pigeons for you to believe in this madness. Or did shit finally just get
real to you?

The specter of Jenna evaporates like the
bullshit idea of James Bond as a blonde. And
the Twins aren't even done with what they have
to say to you. Janine flips the Good Book open
again. This time she lands at Isaiah 30.

"And therefore will the Lord wait, that he
may be gracious to you, and therefore will he be
exalted, that he may have mercy on you: for the
Lord is a God of judgment: blessed are they that
wait for him. For the people shall dwell in Zion
at Jerusalem: you shall weep no more: He will
be very gracious to you at the voice of your cry;
when he shall hear it, he will answer you. And
though the Lord give you the bread of adversity,
and the water of affliction, yet shall not your
teachers be removed into a corner any more,
but your eyes shall see your teachers. And your
ears shall hear a word behind you saying, This is
the way, walk in it.

"Shit is about to get turned upside down,"
Judith continues. "You gonna have to fight your
way out of here. But you need to get home. The
place where you were born will save you."

"Home?" you say, as if the words are in another language. "You mean over the hill? I been
here for years."

"Five years ain't a lifetime," Janine argues. "This is not where you were born."

The prospect focuses in your mind that they mean DC, the place you claim to everyone who will hear it, the place where the accent you overemphasize originated. You are proud of where you are from. It is the place where all of your childhood memories, your sense of self, and the beginnings of your aura awareness were born. But it has never been the easy chair that felt just right. In comparison to Brooklyn, you saw your home turf as a house of betrayal.

"You need to make a new place," Judith says with softening eyes. "Start a business. You can't do what you did here, runnin' and gunnin', sneak thievin' and cryin' innocent because somebody else walked away with the prize. You gotta start over."

All of a sudden you are thirteen, cowering in a ball after they stomped the shit out of you on the recess field because you were in one of the "gifted and talented" sections and they weren't. You are kissing that big-titty girl in the parking lot of that building in Langley Park with the tongue that tasted like grape-flavored Bubble Yum. You and your mother are screaming at each other at high volume because you have the same face and voice as the man who left her behind.

Going back to that place is like the "not going back to jail" line DMX made famous in *Belly*. DC is the pit where Old Testament Joseph was cast before his deliverance. You can't chance that shit past a week at a time and all the required Christian holidays. If you go back there, you'll get stuck.

"You won't be there forever," Janine promises. "Ain't no monsters with magic powers in those parts. Go and get your bag. Stay off the train. And everything will be okay."

You drop two Benjamins in the copper dish for the Twins to split. You double the rate, unsure of when (or if) you'll ever see them again. There is a flash in the back of your mind, a tug at that place between skull and spine, and the next thing you know you are spiraling through a wormhole that lands you right back on Winthrop Street. A horn blares. A bus splashes a pool of putrid water from a puddle against the sidewalk like a wave of ocean crashing against a beach. And that is where you see them, standing on the other side of the street.

Unlike the feathered chiefs on the train, you know that this crew of seven is not looking dead at you on the way to some comic book convention. It's summer and they're in all black: black ball caps with baggy black tees, jeans, black and white retro Air Jordan high-tops, and silver chains with iced-out skulls swinging like a neck in a noose, their bandannas over their faces. They flow around the traffic like squirrels hopping from wire to wire.

You can't outrun them, so you take them head-on. Right about now you really wish Khujo wasn't somewhere getting her nails done.

Taking on a group of armed men and women does not look pretty. Every punch and kick does not snap with a crisp sound effect. Every blow

does not land. But as the look in the eyes and
the determination in the gait of your enemies
suggest, they don't want you to make it away
from them unharmed. And you don't want to
die, at least not at the hands of skull-swinging
punks.

You do not pay attention to their physical at-
tributes or the weight of their armaments. You
can only apply your own strength, skill, and the
will to survive against seemingly insurmount-
able odds. You also have the strength of your
aura, which turns fire engine red and radiates
an untenable amount of heat. Heat makes objects expand, which does things to their molecu-
lar structure. There's more blood flow. Nerve
endings are more sensitive.

So when the first guy lunges forward with
the Japanese wakizashi blade, his wrist hurts all
the more when you snap it at a 90-degree angle.
Another guy fires a .45 at your head, and the
bullet bounces off your aura and wings another
guy in the leg. You pull a pectoral muscle pushing a third into a moving gypsy cab. You try to
slap a .25 pistol out of the hand of another guy
and he gets you twice into the leg before you
flip him into the windshield of an idling MTA
bus.

Cars swerve every which way, some crashing
into each other. You can hear screams of
writhing pain and the sounds of local cops right
up on you.

But they don't all stay down. The ones who
don't have disabling injuries keep coming. And
you've got two small caliber bullet wounds in

your leg, so running away isn't going to get you too far, and the zoo erupting all around you isn't going to produce any Good Samaritan assistance. Blood is gushing out of your thigh and your enemies are maybe three feet away. This is when the miracle happens.

Khujo's sawed-off goes off louder than a bomb, and one of the skulls Supermans out of sight. The other two turn tail. You hobble and then stumble and then collapse onto the back seat of someone's SUV.

"You made me smudge my fuckin' nails," she says, mourning the ruined acrylic on her fingers.

And then you pass out.

You come to in what smells like a dentist's office. Fluoride is in the air, and the Muzak version of M.O.P.'s "Ante Up" makes you want to hurl. There's an Indian guy digging the bullet out of your leg, and Khujo is close behind smoking a Black & Mild.

"I thought you was gettin' you nails done," you grunt.

"Yeah," she says. "I was around the corner. You think I wasn't gonna stay close?"

"I didn't know dentists pulled bullets," you say sarcastically. Your leg doesn't hurt at all.

"I'm an MD too, asshole," the dark brown doctor with a beard quips. "Be lucky I used to date your friend over here."

You're trying to picture Khujo with an Indian guy. This is not to say that you have any racial hang-ups about Indians, but more of the idea of Khujo wearing a catsuit for one. But then again you don't really know her like that. Your relationship is *all* business.

"I gotta get to Queens," you murmur.

"Don't trip, nigga," she says. "We got you covered."

"What a gyan?" Richard Louissaint asks from the counter at Mugshots, a camera shop that still processes film and deals in photo-related antiques. If you're a modern-day photographer looking for an original Polaroid Land Model 95 from 1948 to hang in your studio lobby, then he's the guy. If you need prints made from that same camera, he's also the guy. He writes. He directs music videos and documentaries, and at 6' 7" and covered in locks, he's a gentle giant known across all five boroughs.

Every once in a while, the two of you get up to shoot pool or you slide over to the expensive-ass lanes in Manhattan to roll a few strikes and spares. He's about as Haitian as they come, which doesn't bother you, because for some reason or another, there's always been a Haitian in your life.

But Richard's real business is storage. And when you say storage, you don't mean lockers and closets for rent in climate-controlled buildings. Richard keeps the shit you don't want anyone else to find. Not only is he the guy least likely to talk to the cops, he's also the guy the cops are least likely to talk to. So when the time came for you to pack a go-bag, an essential carry-on with enough of everything to sustain you on outside soil, foreign or domestic, you figured he was the place to stash it. Actually, that was his idea.

"If you're gonna be in the streets in Brooklyn, then your escape plan should be in Queens. You can take the commuter rails out of the city to Long Island or head north and catch a plane or a train from Connecticut or Jersey."

Official copies of your birth certificate and Social Security card are in there, with about 20gs in 100s, a fake passport and driver's license that ID you as Charles Nathaniel Millner, a commercial fishermen with a phony license to operate a tour vessel on the Long Island Sound. There's a black Beretta 9mm with two full magazines, a copy of the deed to your crib and all the insurance paperwork, a flash drive with everything you wrote from 2001 to date, cans of salmon, a box of blueberry crisp protein bars, an unopened pack of boxers, a bag of tube socks, and a North Face bubble coat and brimmed skullcap just in case you needed to make a move for Canada. Under pressure you would rather try for Canada before trying to head back to DC.

"What happened to your leg?" Richard asks, noticing your limp. He tends to notice everything.

"Día de los Muertos," you say. "I had some skulls after me."

This confuses him. "Aren't you the guy that stays out of the spotlight?"

"Why do you think I'm here for my bag?"

This news flash hits the Gentle Giant like a ton of bricks.

"For real, son?"

"Fo' *real*," you say.

He takes a good look at the outside windows, as if he can somehow clock whether or not the place will get swamped.

"I'll be right back," he says and darts down the narrow hallway lined with old film boxes and unopened camera equipment from 20 years before.

He isn't gone 30 seconds before he's back with your black leather backpack, covered in dust. He drops it on the counter like he had to go through hell and back to get it.

"Where you been keepin' that shit since the last time I was here," you ask.

He shrugs his shoulders.

"Stuff moves around. You lucky I hadn't left it in one of my other spots or in the locker out on Staten Island."

"You go out to Staten Island?"

"I go everywhere, Kango. Trust."

"I owe you any extra?"

He waves you off like the very idea is an insult.

"Only stay gone as long as you have to," he says.

You blow dust off the bag and wipe what still clings to it off with your bare forearm.

The sun is low in the sky, out on the street. A kid drives a basketball to the hole and takes flight to slam it through the hoop like he was born to do it. There is the smell of sizzling lamb from the falafel cart on the corner down the way. A pair of bronzed legs struts by, the attached head and torso, complete with hair weave, held in a near headlock by a boy a little shorter and a lot heavier than she.

You remember all of these details. You burn them into your brain because this is when it registers that you won't be here tomorrow. You can't be. Bodies on Winthrop. Bodies on Nostrand Avenue. A coalition of bigwigs has told you that your time is done . . . for now. But you need at least one more night. You have to go back to the house one last time. It isn't rational, but it's something you have to do.

Maybe there are more skulls waiting for you there. Maybe there's a whole battalion of cops. Maybe Shango will be sitting on your front stoop with a story. It doesn't matter. If you're gonna go to bed for the last time, it might as well be in the only place in town that you actually own.

Your house has a history, one you often bury from yourself while living in a cloud of weed and whiskey. What kind of brother blows into town at 21 and ends up with his own crib in less than a week?

Your address is 132 Hancock, the fourth one over from the big castle-like one on the corner. The front face used to be grimy until you made it a point to have it sandblasted at least once every year or two so the sunlight bounces off it in the right way. You spent the money to keep the window treatments in order. You finished the floors yourself with the help of a few different dudes who owed you favors. Looking back on it, you could have had a show on HGTV. You could have had a lot of things, but living in a hood where you had no history clouded the need for any kind of excessive ambition.

Your boy Jet had told you about a card game at the back of the bar on corner of Putnam and Nostrand, right next to the North Dakota Fried Chicken and the Duck Down Records bodega, where DJ Evil Dee used to spin on Sunday afternoon while O.G.C. ran the waffle iron and cooked chicken sausage on the griddle.

You were staying in a rooming house off Myrtle and Lewis, sleeping in a top bunk a good six feet above the bottom one and doing things with Top Ramen that should have gotten you on the Food Network. The guys at the table were all islanders, real inside players. Alexander and his crew were rumored to have a big pool of money coming in from offshore, a 24/7 laundromat for dudes who made Pablo Escobar come off like a used car salesman.

They had money to burn and made their dough off the books or by cooking them for others. What better thing was there for rich Black men to do than blow their money on trying to take it from each other? It was known to be an open game. The buy-in was only a grand, but there was fear in who you as an outsider were playing against. These dudes were sociopath Rastas. Win the wrong hand and some dude standing behind you either chops your head off or suffocates you with the plastic shopping bag.

You were nowhere near card-shark status. And you were not some kind of poker master.

You didn't think that you were big shit because you'd seen *Rounders*. You came up in a family of dudes who only played spades, tonk, and bid whist. Poker was just a game you knew the rules to. But the most consistent part of your personality was discipline.

When you learned something, you took it apart and memorized the pieces inside out. You stayed in your lane and played within your limit until it was time to take your balls out. Ten Benjamins was all that you had in the world. You were fresh off the Chinatown Express bus thinking that the town was going to bow down and knight you just because you thought you were dope.

Jet had actually mentioned the game as something you needed to stay away from. But à la Kanye, you were a college dropout with something to prove. So you went and dropped your whole life on the green velvet like you had a steady check coming in. If you lost it all there was still that C-note in your sock, the age 21 version of your current go-bag.

Four hours later you had 20 grand in chips, a nice buzz from the 5-Star Barbancourt they were serving on the house, and one opponent remaining, one William Alexander, then age 65: part-time drunk, full-time degenerate, and respectable player in local real estate. He owned eight houses in a ten-block radius and another twelve within the borough limits, not to mention the club where Jelly would later found her yoga class.

Word was that back in the day he had a different name and he used to run heists, which
led to his connections to the faceless men now
funding him and his homies. And when it came
to cards, word was that Phil never lost. Never.
He'd been using the take from that little card
game to fund the pair of broads he had on the
side from a wife with a face made for radio.
Money for sex. Pussy for an aging man who slept
in a separate room and only looked at his life
partner through reflections on mirrored sur-
faces in fear of turning to stone.

It's important to reiterate that you were no
Phil Ivey or Chris Moneymaker. You were not
born to be seen on close-ups wearing dark
glasses or a brim pulled down on ESPN, putting
six figures in the middle like it was beer money.
Your life was on the line. And that's probably
the only reason that it went the way it went. You
had run your chips up to 40gs. The plan was to
check and raise him until he had to go all in.

Even if he won, you would still have enough
to walk out with a few years' rent money and
your dignity intact. You were looking at a basement apartment down on Lafayette by the art
gallery not too far from the Amphitheater.

That was when he threw it on the table. You
knew what a property deed looked like. You
could practically draw them from memory after
all the Xeroxing you did back when you worked
for Marion Barry's Summer Youth Employment
Program back in the day. Four stories with a
brand-new roof and all of the original wood still
intact. Market already had it at $150 grand. A

$150,000 house for a 20-something kid sleeping on his boy's couch ten blocks up.

Looking back, there were plenty of questions that you should have asked. Why was he throwing out a $150K piece of property in a 40K card game? If you were, at best, the luckiest player in the world, why in the hell didn't Alexander and his crew call it an early night? It was almost like he wanted to get rid of the place.

But all you saw was a brownstone. Sitting there, face-to-face with men who you knew were as serious as that Jermaine Jackson single, all you could think about was the big moment for your young-ass ego.

He knew that you would play to win. And all you knew was that he had enough property where he could afford to let this one go. You thought that his sole purpose in life was breaking you, turning the lights out on the Yankee boy that was fucking with his mistress money. Or maybe he'd already ordered a batch of soldiers with iron on their hips to put two in your head right after the last card fell and leave you for the rotties in the yard behind the bar to feed on.

The river was an ace, which gave you a royal flush. He had a pair of jacks. You can never forget how he just sat there staring into space, his eyes dodging between you and the dealer, who looked like he was due to catch a Singapore caning if he ever dealt a deck that way again. All the other guys who had been at the table had either gone home or were out in front throwing back shots poured by Sam Malone with a perm, their toasts a prayer for the young buck's demise.

Alexander just sat there blankly for the longest five seconds of your life while you scanned the dimness for something to counter whatever weapon this dude was bound to pull if the cards announced you as the winner. The cards fell. Were there a DJ in the house he might have played Jigga's "U Don't Know."

You won. Or at least you thought you did.

"I'll have it empty for you by end of the week," he had murmured. "But don't come here again."

You didn't listen the first time. But he forced you to hear him today at the Drummer's Circle.

The last thing you remembered of Alexander, at 65, was him parting the thin fabric that separated the player's club from the bar. The fabric rippled in the rush of air. And then he was gone. A few seconds later a light-skinned dwarf in a lapel-free suit gave you your dough in a thin plastic shopping bag. You held the deed tightly in your hand, afraid that somebody was going to snatch it from you. The dwarf showed you to the rear entrance, right next to where the rotties were dead asleep. You slithered into the pitch black of the alleyway, watching your ass all the way back to Lewis Avenue.

Seven days later the place was as empty as he promised it would be. Keys were in an envelope with your name on it taped to the window on the front door, though you'd never given him your name. There were 16 rooms and three baths with a yard in the rear. Everything you owned barely filled a corner of the living room in the apartment on the top floor.

It was April of 2001 and you finally had a home. All of your mail came to the same address. You got a credit account at the chain hardware store. Next thing you knew you were waving to Ms. Johnson across the street, the fiftysomething lady in the red windbreaker who seemed to know everything. You got nods and pounds from the ever-changing boys on corners, and the undercover jump-outs whose job it was to keep them in chains. Wolves and shepherds sealed into the same pen. And then you got to know Raheem, Wes, and Michele.

It didn't take long to burn through the dough you won. So you picked up some tenants, good working Black people who just assumed you were an underemployed neighbor who smoked too much weed and had live parties every New Year's. The rent went to a PO box and complaints went to Jet in exchange for 10 percent of the take. The rest of the time you were either doing "favors" in the street or pounding away on your old-ass laptop, trying to tell your own story by writing it in the second person. That way the truth about who you were always belonged to someone else.

It's well after 8:00 when you're standing on that street off Fulton between Nostrand and Bedford whose name you can't remember. There's a quiet crossroads there, a little cluster of houses bordered one side by the Foot Locker and all those other stores on the strip, and on the right by a massive 99 Cent Store, where anyone with a 20-dollar bill can form a junkyard band of items that will either cease to function by the time they get them home or add to the hoarder and clutter problem that's killing Black aunties and grandmas worldwide.

Standing there, with a new moon in the sky, you find yourself thinking about Josh, and his big plan, and how you completely dropped the ball on crafting yet another perfect scenario. Khujo hasn't mentioned it either. But in the mix of all that's happened since the sun came up, a thing like Josh stealing some specialized strain of weed wouldn't have exactly made the front page.

You've got the Beretta pressing against your hip inside your jeans, creating this clammy feeling between iron and flesh. There are lights on in the shaded windows overhead, and the sounds and music and people are barely contained by brick and mortar. This is world unto itself.

There is the outline of an elderly woman on one of the rooftops, her elbows leaning against the ledge, the long barrel of her Remington M24 visible from a few stories up. That's Madge. Word has it that once upon a time Madge was special forces in Vietnam, part of a special unit of women that rocked the shit out of the Viet Cong in the jungles in an operation that was allegedly known as "Nair and Neet."

Wes used to say it was bullshit, that Army intelligence didn't have any "broads on the payroll that didn't type and take notes." But Madge is up there every night, watching her block like a hawk. Josh knew who she was. And so did you, even though you kept that to yourself while he was rambling on and on like an egomaniac in a blunt-filled haze.

She's up there all the time. Rumor has it her grandkids bring her dinners up to her. She has a cot up there and a portable TV, and she's got a boyfriend 20 years younger who does all the cooking and never leaves the house. But as it's the corner's job to tell stories, you don't necessarily know if any of that is real. You're just standing here to steel yourself up for the slow walk around the corner to Bedford and down to Hancock to say the last of your goodbyes. You nod up toward her, your face illuminated by the streetlight. She fires a shot in the air with her .45 sidearm and the shot echoes for a half mile in each direction. Then you start toward Halsey and turn left.

With all that's happened, and all that you're expecting, it's a disappointment that your sector of Hancock Street is dead. As you travel west toward 132 you see the flickering of TV screens in open windows and take in the smell of home-made pizza coming out of someone's kitchen and the garbage cans that need to dumped. Rats dart across property lines like the dark shadows of restless spirits shuffling underneath the ground. You treat each step like it leads to the gas chamber. But death is not waiting for you on that front stoop. Instead there is an old man cradling new life.

Steve Kemet is a throwback to an older Brooklyn, a Black Panther Wakanda kind of Brooklyn, where all is righteous and upright and Black people rule supreme. Born out of the movement that got choked out by heroin and the feds, he is the embodiment of neighborly wisdom, a walking book of quotations that has the right set of words for those who need them. And he's sitting on your front stoop holding his sleeping infant daughter by way of a Jamaican girl named Carrol who is young enough to be his granddaughter.

"Streets say that you're leavin'," he says. "This isn't your fault, you know?"

"Yeah," you say solemnly. "I know."

"It ain't about fightin' either."

You sigh.

"Heard that already too," you say.

"I would come up and chief one with you before you roll, but the missus is out with her girls. You gotta let a young girl be a young girl. She gave me Assata. And my baby is my greatest blessing. You need to make a baby."

"Not here," you say. "Not now. I lost my woman."

"Like there's only one womb in the world? Like you didn't do what you did because you were looking to make a change? Before you go in this place and think it's all over, you gotta know that what's ahead is way better than what's behind."

"It don't feel like it," you say.

"That's Black man's ego talkin'. You ain't Tupac or Biggie. You gonna walk this earth for a long time to come. To be honest, I think that's what scares you. That's how you got all of these people shook."

"But there's all of these pieces to the puzzle that I just don't get," you say.

Then your consciousness jumps again, and you're sliding into Jenna's ocean, feeling the strength in her thighs clamp around you at the top of the morning. You want to drift off into that memory. Can it be that it was all so simple then?

"You ain't a cop," he continues. "You ain't in the machine. You don't keep the gears turning. Instead, you take them apart. Remake them to your own will and desire. But you do it without oil or grease. Surgery without none of the anesthetic or crafting tools. You rip hearts out of chests before they can feel it."

"Nah, that ain't what I do," you say.

"That's not what you *think* you do," he says. And then he stands, a cue that his words for you have come to an end. He steps to the side, a stone rolling away from the entrance to your tomb. His baby girl comes awake as he stands down the sienna-colored stairs. Maybe it's finally time for you to wake up too.

Certain things come to you that you hadn't considered before. Did Tola, the son of Ms. Orgi in your first-floor unit, pass his tae kwon do green belt exam? Is she still struggling with insomnia and the graveyard shift all at once? Are you going to need to bleed her radiators again because of that blockage in the line that sparks up right around Christmas every year?

Do Jay and Connie in the two-bedroom on the second floor with the toddler ever smell all the herb you puff or lose any sleep because of you and Jenna's torture sessions? You have been a shitty landlord, so caught up with yourself up on Mount Olympus that you didn't stop to think about other people's lives. It was either about getting away from it or getting away from your pain. Those were the only reasons you ever did anything.

You step lightly as you climb the stairs, remembering the click clack of Jenna's wedges and the scent of her all over your face. You tell yourself that you might swing by the salon in the morning to say goodbye. But what good would that really do? What is there to say that hasn't already been said? As you reach the top of your landing, you see that the front door is ajar. You draw your weapon and flip off the safety, uncertain of just how many there might be on the inside. There are no lights. Whoever is waiting can apparently see in the dark.

The door comes open and you enter in that tactical cop stance. You hit the switch and find Khujo snoring on the couch, one hand inside that seemingly bottomless shoulder bag of hers. So you playfully kick the couch, and she jumps awake, her black .380 Walther pointed in the opposite direction of where you're standing.

"How long you been here?" you ask.

She tucks the gun away, yawns, and stretches, her nipples visibly erect through the cheap black bra underneath her wifebeater tee.

"Ever since I realized your dumb ass was

gonna have to say goodbye to this place. Plus I wanted to make sure your leg was still okay."

You take a seat on the blue papasan across from the couch and feel the fatigue take hold. There's a jar of weed behind the speaker doubling as an end table next to you. You're about to reach for it when Khujo interrupts.

"I already got one rolled," she says, pulling a phat blunt from her magic pouch. She lights. You sit to next to her on the sofa to make the session easier. She takes a deep hit while you relight the half-dead stick of sandalwood in the incense holder in the corner.

"Vishnu says you're gonna need gauze to change that dressing before you go to bed and at least twice a day after that," she says.

"Then I'll hit the drugstore in the morning," you say.

Then she reaches in the bag and produces a pack of gauze pads and tape.

"I got you covered," she says. "You know that. I made a call to Josh to try and square that job, but the number was dead. Had my dude up on Morningside try to run by his spot and give him a message, but nobody answered. I'll stay on it, though."

She passes you the sizable L and you take a deep but guilty pull, trying to blame your sins on weed when the herb was merely a masking agent.

"Cool," you say. Khujo knows everything you're not saying.

"This shit ain't the end of the world," she says. "You were super hot. You needed to cool off. That red aura shit you pulled with those Muertos was bold as fuck."

"You act like I think it through," you say. "I just react."

"You only needed me for that last one," she says, taking the blunt back. "I'ma put you in a car outta here and all of this will be in the rearview."

Khujo and Jenna were like oil and water. They rarely had anything nice to say to each other but hugged and kissed like they were best friends when the cameras were rolling. You and Khujo kept your distance out in public, but folks in the know knew. You had this barbecue in '03, right after you first got your crib decorated and put tenants in the place. You had the gas grill set up down in the courtyard with the carne asada marinated in Merlot and black pepper over fire with veggie burgers and balsamic veggies on skewers for the vegans and vegetarians with five gallons of rum punch in the water cooler jug. You were doing it big, high on life, high on Brooklyn, high on the quarter of hydro big Jet had brought through as a housewarming present.

You and Khujo had just done your first job for Gilda over on Myrtle off Lafayette, a complicated smash and grab on a guy dealing in antiques, which hadn't gone as expected but landed you your first chunk of cash since the Will Alexander game. Jenna had braided your hair in these micro-thin cornrows that everybody was sweatin' you for. Khujo didn't sweat anybody, and even she was impressed.

"That's tight work," she'd said to Jenna as a

compliment. But Jenna saw something else. Maybe it was the length on Khujo's poom poom shorts, or the low cut in her top. Maybe she figured that the two of you had fucked, even though that was never your thing. But Jenna came out of her mouth with words that started their feud.

"You never gonna get it. So don't try so hard."

The music on the box stopped. Girls and dudes getting their mack on felt the temperature drop until everyone could see their breath.

"Hey, Jen, cool out," you said. "That shit ain't nice. You said Khujo is peoples."

"*Your* people," she had said before heading upstairs for a good hour or two until Khujo bounced. Khujo played it smooth. She finished her drink and poured another one from the cooler like retaliation was beneath her. You always respected that.

"She gonna undo herself with you," Khujo said, low enough for only the two of you to hear. "And I'ma be there when it happens."

That was the beginning of it, and she had been right. Khujo was still here in the crib on your last night, and Jenna was long gone. You never saw it as a triangle until 25 made you wise. There ain't room for two straight women in a straight man's life. Sooner or later somebody's number comes up.

You snap your fingers and Sade's "Is It a Crime" starts off the mix. You think about that Middle Eastern–looking dude in the video riding in that London cab. Or was it 42nd Street?

You were never sure. He just looked cool as shit with this whole complicated emotionally un-available persona. It seemed like that's what all the fine ass women wanted: a man who could never give them what they asked for. So you be-came that, whenever it suited you.

"I'ma miss you," Khujo says. Now you know the high is hitting her heavy. "I manage a few folks, but—"

"Yeah," you say, cutting her off before she says anything that makes you think of staying and standing your ground. The Twins have spo-ken. The Five have said their piece, and you can't survive another ambush like the Muertos just hit you with. But if you wanted to be a tough guy you should have conjured Kool G Rap to play instead of Big Forehead Girl.

It's an awkward moment. She gets it. And you get it, given that mess on Winthrop, though any bodies have been peeled off the street by now. The cops have closed the files and moved onto the next incident in Negro theater be-cause that's just how it goes in Brooklyn.

You finish the blunt and listen to the sounds, and the two of you find yourself drifting off, leaning on one another like fallen domi-noes as sleep overtakes you. Then you have a dream. This is your last dream in Brooklyn for 15 years.

You are standing on the top floor of your crib. It's the way it looked on moving day: blind-ingly white walls, sparkling tall windows, olden creaking wood full of splinters and nicks. The skinny blond dread and the busty geeky Head

Wrap are there. They are standing in the north-east corner speaking French to each other.

"What are you saying?" you ask.

Then Shango materializes wearing a black Armani suit with a white and red striped tie and fire axe cuff links.

"You act like you don't know the language," he says. "But you do."

You look out the window and the streets begin to fill with ocean water. Burning meteorites fall from the sky, setting rooftops ablaze. Lightning flashes. Then there are 100 Muertos, their faces covered, their diamond-encrusted chains swinging left to right like pendulums in the still air. They are armed with every weapon imaginable: baseball bats with nails driven through them, Japanese katana swords, AR-15s, Uzis, slingshots, hand grenades, zip guns, naval depth charges, and that glass-encased nuclear device from that movie *The Manhattan Project*. And they all clearly have you marked as the bullseye.

Your aura blazes a dark green, hardening into something like Teflon. There is a Beretta in your hand. And you are ready to go, as usual, expecting to be overrun by the onslaught.

Then hands grab you from behind and pull you through the glass, which turns into a sugary sweet candy powder that gets into your mouth as you plunge into the rising fresh water. People are still walking the streets underneath. They are driving in cars. They are taking their kids to school. The world continues, even though it feels like you (and only you) are being drowned. You look up at the surface as if it's heaven and not the edge of hell you were just delivered from. But something tells you that there is another way.

When you jump awake you are no longer in that apartment of yours. Instead you're somewhere in the middle of the New Jersey Turnpike, in the back of what appears to be an Audi sedan. Oasis sings "Don't Look Back in Anger" on the driver's stereo. And there is a woman at the wheel, smallish and slender with a big poof of a wavy black Afro. Her face is as Ethiopian as they come. She has Tracee Ellis Ross's eyes.

"I'm supposed to take you to Union Station in DC," she says. "Your bag is in the trunk."

The back of your head aches.

"How did I get here?" you ask.

"A girl walked you down the steps. Real cute, smoking a cigar. She said to tell you that you couldn't do it alone."

Khujo's shoulder bag is a metaphor for the woman herself. She thinks of everything and has it packed and planned out before it's even a lightbulb in anyone else's head.

"What's your name?" you ask the driver.

"Biseat. Like Biz and it. Go back to sleep," she says before raising the volume on the song. And you do just that.

CHAPTER SEVEN

You don't go out much anymore. This is not because people don't invite you or because you're tied down with wife and family or some debilitating disease or an embarrassing weight gain. The truth is that you don't get out because you know what you're getting out there. You know all the interactions and can predict them within the first 30 seconds of meeting people. It's like when you used to tell people that you were a writer. The first thing they always ask is "what kind?" The once two-person conversation transforms into their verbal personal memoir about how they always wished that they could write a book, as if you had chosen to endure the creative process specifically to live out their dreams and not your own. So you stopped talking about it.

But it wasn't much different when you started

telling them that you owned a restaurant. The first response now is "Oh, what kind of food is it?" And the second follow-up has something to do with how brave you must be to take on a business that fails most of the time. It's basically the exact same conversation with the switching of a few minor nouns and adjectives. It seemed like the conversations people were having with you were the talks they really wanted to have with more accomplished versions of themselves. What you wanted to do was meet new people and have new experiences, disbelieving the universal fact that most people become boring as fuck once they either achieve their desired station in life or reach the capacity for the number of folks depending on them for life, support, and survival. Carpe Diem is an extra-credit course that barely keeps enough students in it to stay in the catalog.

So you gave up on people. But you didn't give up on yoga. That first class you took with Jelly was the kind of low-cost luxury that just can't happen in a gentrified city like DC. But now people aren't doing it to strengthen their auras or align their chakras or any of that. They're doing it because it makes them look cool and mystic and shit while they model tight pants and tops on Instagram to show off their six-packs and tight racks.

The yoga classes in DC are mostly all white and in parts of town where you don't like the air quality. Either you're the only straight Black man in there who has to endure the stares of mostly white women who seem to be either in denial about secretly wanting to fuck you or imagining you in a hoodie, skinny jeans, and pulled-down snapback so that they can want to clutch the purses they left back in the changing room.

Or maybe it's not Black and white with token Asians thrown in. Maybe you make it through an enjoyable journey of movements only to end up at the juice bar next door where you listen to the vacuous nature of conversations about vegan chicken wings smothered in organic mambo sauce or how they just don't understand what makes go-go music such a big deal because there are too many drums or not enough woodwinds playing in the background. Or maybe more than all of this, you've just become a grumpy old man at 40 who finds the best thing in life to be his job. There's no shame in this, of course, as your real job isn't running the Queen and Country. You still do what you were doing back in Brooklyn. But you keep it far away from where you rest your head.

Your grandma passed and you moved into the maternal family house over on 34th Street in Hillcrest, the one you self-published that book about that nobody bought. You converted the attic into a home gym and office space. That's where you do yoga now. You've got the charts on the walls and all the Vedic, Yoruba, Congolese, Islamic, and Christian mysticism texts that you might need.

Your aura is stronger than it's ever been before. But no one knows. You learned from dumb-ass Tom Cruise's mistake in *The Color of Money*.

Don't show off what you can do to the world. They'll either take advantage or try to take out the competition. It's just that simple.

This house you inherited was a godsend in that it provided you the equity you needed to get the loan for the restaurant, which gave you a way out of having to plan heists for a living. You heeded every word the Twins told you to the letter. You gutted all the hideous furniture and transformed the two floors into someplace respectable that you could bring the occasional date to. But you only date about twice a year, treating the courting process like most do dental checkups. For six months at a time you load a woman into the bedchamber for a concussion and leg-bends and call it a wrap. This is not said to be in any way sadistic or misogynistic, but the truth, barely discussed in these times of diversity and accountability, is that some women rather enjoy being dominated. Pulling their hair and applying your larger weight, size, and strength to theirs in an erotic and aggressive manner can make them pour like a canal down there when done properly.

And once you have a partner for such things, you can partake in all the coupling-esque activities that don't require you to go anywhere or to attend the functions that full-blown relationships require. Living in exile changes you in that way. Fifteen years go by, and part of you is still hanging on to that last high, that last night in that crib you still own, that still pays you in rent and robs you in liabilities like the rising costs of heating oil, property taxes, and increasing number of gentrifying assholes on your old Brooklyn block.

You haven't been back since but spend too much of your limited online life celebrating birthdays through Facebook like you're still living the life. Brownie took a shiv inside for some prison bullshit about a stash of Hostess Twinkies stolen out of the wrong man's cell. But he survived.

Miel Rodriguez has become, of all things, a Pentecostal evangelist who you hear looks more like a Mexican Nell Carter than the fine-ass chick you used to flirt with. Shango is still missing. Ain't nobody seen that man since the day before you left. And that's all you really know about 15 years ago.

When you and Khujo link up on FaceTime, it's mostly to listen to her complain about her girlfriend and how she wants to fuck all the time. Khujo coming out as a lesbian was about as surprising as how fast free fried shrimp and wings go on the table at a house party. She's still your point of contact up top, still plugged in to what you left behind. That's why you can't talk to her but so much. It's easier to put that dude you used to be in the rearview, while still holding on to the lessons he taught you.

But today is not a day to roll yourself in salt. There is a job on the table courtesy of your new handler, Avery Graves, a light-skinned pretty boy who sleeps in a shirt and tie and knows how to do things with a smartphone that make hardcore hackers look like your auntie getting excited about knowing the lyrics to last year's radio hits. What's even worse about that metaphor is that kids don't even listen to the radio anymore.

As was previously mentioned, there is a job today. But you have to go to the Queen and Country to learn more about it. So you hop into the Audi A5 in a plain white tee, plain black cap, some Levi's straight legs, and a pair of camouflage Adidas low-tops. You take the curve down Good Hope Road near the Anacostia Arts Center and then that last right before you hit the freeway and you're there, a nice and neat bar and grill stashed between the Black-owned bank and the two-screen art house movie theater.

The Queen and Country was a five-star place in a three-star neighborhood. Then the neighborhood changed. White folks had been living east of the river en masse for close to a decade, but they weren't walking the neighborhoods or spending money close to their houses. They had yet to fully penetrate the culture of a part of town where dudes used to jump people at the bus stops for exercise. It's still possible for your patrons to come out of your place having digested the best meal of their lives only to lose their wallets to a pair of fifteen-year-olds armed an ice pick and a spear gun stolen from the boating goods shop over by the library, Chinese carry-out, and heart-attack fish place on MLK near Talbert. But they still come to see you. And you're doing pretty okay.

"What it do, Buster?" you say to the bartender/maître d', a fiftysomething Gulf War vet who looks about ten years younger. A former truck driver who did six for armed robbery, you hired him here as a part of the convict rehab program you sponsor. You take guys with records who you find trustworthy and put them to work, helping them find matching funds to start their own businesses. But Buster doesn't want his own business. He just wants to be the bartender and maître d'. You respect the hell out of that and love him like an older brother.

"Makin' that money, Slim," Buster says, a nicotine patch clearly visible at the edge of the bicep stretching the fabric on his white short-sleeve dress shirt gift-wrapped with a loosened skinny necktie.

"Your boy's in the back," Buster winks. And you know he means Avery.

Your converted closet of an office has a 30-inch plasma on the wall, where Avery is engrossed in a game of *Assassin's Creed*. You know this because it's the only game out of the staff pile that he plays well. But before you get to him you pass the restaurant kitchen, a griddle and two-oven, eight-burner operation run by Jaime and Rafael, two Salvadorian cousin line cooks you recruited after they came home from a five-year bid for breaking into a string of ATMs using the company service manual to relieve the boxes of their goodies.

Butchie is the chef. He did ten for a gun charge and parole violation but can cook his ass off. It's Butchie who makes the food what it is. He is currently busy sprinkling diced ginger, garlic, and sea salt in the huge pot of kale simmering on one of the burners. Jaime, 5' 3" and 180, short and squat, and Rafael, 5' 9" and around 160, are plating two carry-out orders of shrimp and yellow polenta grits sprinkled with bacon and diced shallots, the Queen and Country's undisputed brunch-time favorite.

Avery thinks a lot of himself. You know this because he speaks of himself in the third person.

"Avery is killing this shit," he says, knowing that it's you because no one else comes into your office when you're not in it. You're concerned about the job he's there to offer you but find yourself distracted by the idea of the curried goat and peppers over couscous Butchie had you sample the night before. You love it, but it might be just a tad too exotic for the folks you serve. But you also trust the chef. And as he told you that his great-aunt Marion suggested the dish to him in a dream at the top of the week, you're willing to give it a shot. Still, every time he's tried it out he finds something missing, a phantom element that keeps it from the oneness he's looking for.

"Avery doesn't know why you spend so much time in this place when you can't actually cook," he says, continuing his spree of onscreen murder and mayhem. "With what you do, you could easily—"

"We don't talk about that in here," you interrupt. "But it's called a cover."

"Your books are clean as a whistle and you got no sheet," Avery explains like the attorney he is not. "There's so much work here that we can be taking advantage of."

"Not where I live, man," you say plainly. "I've

been telling you that for five years. Besides, you wouldn't be here if you didn't have a job for me."

He kills the power button on the console in the middle of the action and spins around to face you with a smile.

"How about 60K for two days' work? And most of that is travel."

"Okay. You got my attention."

Before proceeding into the details of this particular job, you feel the need to revisit elements of your past that took place before that fateful Thursday in Brooklyn 2005, when all hell broke loose and you ended up ejecting to your natural habitat by way of Divine suggestion and a 7-on-2 street fight that should have killed you. While yoga develops aura, your usage of that aura of yours began long before you ever set foot in Jelly's yoga class.

God parcels out a mixed bag of tricks to his babies. And after 400 years of slavery, oppression, suppression, and exploitation within almost every system there is, most Black boys feel like God's personal gifts to them are limited to athleticism, dick size, and musical ability. While you were blessed to luck up in at least two of these areas, you learned at an early age that you also excelled in a third, which was revealed to you in November of 1992.

While you, Jamison "Kango" Watts, could not bench-press half a ton or speak things into being just by thinking hard enough, you could walk directly into the office of your principal, Dr. Leslie Plummer, and reclaim confiscated goods from her desk while she was standing in the room, and then leave without her ever knowing. You were equally adept at smuggling yourself (and the occasional female schoolmate) into off-limits rooms and classrooms for window-fogging make-out sessions after school and during the early morning breakfast service. While they might not have all necessarily been the cheerleaders or the promiscuous sexpots, you judged with your heart, and those you chose fit comfortably within the shielding properties of your then-silver aura rather nicely.

Of course, you weren't actively aware of the whole aura thing at first. You dismissed the changes in color around you as optical illusions. You just thought that you were slick. You kept a B average, stayed off the MPD's radar, and tried to keep as small a footprint in your world as possible while Willie Clinton was getting raked over the coals for using no stealth whatsoever in the when, where, and with whom he chose to get his dick sucked.

You dotted every *I* and crossed every *T*. You never drank or smoked a thing until you got hit with that horrible case of senioritis in the winter of 1993 and coasted through the rest of high school like you were surfing down a sheet of ice on an incline. Then you went to school in Atlanta and realized, at 19, your lifelong dream of finally falling in love with a girl. This was a shiny and happy experience in the very beginning, but toward the end resulted in repeated bouts of heartbreak and general disappointment that led your inner nice guy to take a hike toward the distant meditative shores of what corner boys Raheem, Wes, and Michele would refer to, many years later, as the "fuck it point."

This fuck it point arrives in a young man's life when, free of things like premature fatherhood and prison, he decides to throw the straight and narrow to the wind and give in to his baser instincts. Many arrive at this juncture because of personal rejection. Others hit this wall as they embrace the realization that every system and organization worth anything is required to have at least three gaping assholes who want to make your life difficult just because you have talent.

The pothead showboat you became in Brooklyn was a direct reaction to the collective of said assholes who had stood in your way from your days in the sandbox to the neighborhood crew wars and those years in DC, where girls only judged based on how many kilos you moved or the number of other boys you beat, shot, or scarred in the name of the blocks and corners you shouted out in the stormy waters at the center of every go-go, before the bodies dropped in the parking lot.

You came to learn the lay of the land in "Soufeast" DC during the twice-daily walks you took with your Cocker Spaniel/Lab mix named Blackstone from 38th Street to Alabama Ave. to Penn Ave., to Southern, and then back to 38th again. Sure, Nancy Reagan had armed you and all the other "children of the future" with the power to "just say no" when offered anything other than a prayer book or a few dollars for washing a car or raking leaves in a yard. There was money in the crack game, and applications required neither résumé nor interview.

You only managed to survive that era via an addiction to cable TV, your Nintendo controllers, and parents who rarely ever let you go out in the street once Maury Povich and TV shows like *City Under Siege* had officially declared that the way of the gun was here to stay. And yet you still managed to learn the rules of the streets as one close enough to them but never actually in them until you arrived at a much earlier training wheels version of your fuck it point in the summer of 1992.

You wore the mask of a sucker-ass nerd, which you have to admit, kept you away from the battalions of street soldiers trying to shoot real pistols sideways, like the ones on TV, and consequently sent stray bullets out in the world like flyers under windshield wipers. But neither your parents nor Nancy Reagan could save you from the natural discovery of who you were and what you could do. Your aura was always there. You just didn't know about it. Most people didn't back then, especially not Black folks who had to work twice as hard to acquire any kind of knowledge that might possibly put them ahead.

Then you saw a scene go down right in front of your eyes, a transaction between two dudes begging to be caught slipping that you just couldn't pass up. Hand-to-hand exchanges happen in the hood a million times a day. And this is not just because of the illegal drug trade. In general, it has more to do with the need to mind one's own fucking business in communities where things of material value are in lesser supply. If you have anything new, whether it's jewelry, Jordans, an Easter suit, one of the 100 types of electronics that the street will relieve you of if you're dumb enough to bring them out in the open, or anything with four wheels that doesn't have a rust problem, then stealth is a most necessary part of doing the do.

These particular men on a winter afternoon, clad in a suede shearling coat and a leather Avirex jacket respectively, were in front of the grimy-ass apartment buildings across Pennsylvania Avenue just below Fort Davis Drive. Though it was wrapped in paper, it was not "paper bag money," meaning not a collection of crumpled bills stuffed into some corner store sack. This was fresh-from-the-bank money.

You could smell the ink on that new linen from right across the street. You had never missed a meal in your life. You didn't live in the projects. You were not married to the game by older siblings or an uncle or father that had decided to pass a life of crime on. You just wanted a taste of what it seemed like everyone else had. You wanted your moment.

Daniel LaRusso's moment had been kicking a blond bully in the face with a technique that would have gotten him beaten senseless anywhere but in the movies. Larry Davis was sick enough of dirty cops that he took on nine of them in his sister's apartment in the Bronx and lived to tell the tale. Rayful Edmond had literally owned DC and had a crew that everybody knew by the earring in their ears. On the flip side there had been Martin, and Malcolm, Mandela, Huey, Harriet, Angela, and all the others that you knew because you were a Black boy raised to read books. You did not fight. And you did not shoot. But you wanted *your* moment. So you took it.

Your silver aura would stretch and shrink unexpectedly. It was a surprise guest that would turn up to wreak havoc when you least needed it to. You would almost be right up on that girl you liked in the junior high hallway and it would yank some other dude in between the two of you, the dude that would get her pregnant or the dude that would hurt her so that, when the time came, she couldn't hear the words you were trying to say to her. It might completely abandon you when the time came for you to block that loose basketball that would eventually collide with your face during those intramural volleyball games in junior high.

Your aura seemed determined to alienate you from the cool-kid cliques that you wanted to be a part of the most. But what you didn't understand about that fledgling shield of yours was that had you done what you wanted, the consequences might have gotten you killed. Now back to that sloppy-ass handoff you witnessed less than half a block from the DC border . . .

You knew the dude in the Avirex from the Scouts at St. Timothy's Church. He was a full-fledged Scout then who had been the first in Troop 1650 to earn the infamous Totin' Chip badge, which gave him the right to use knives, axes, and wood saws on camping expeditions. You were still a Webelo, somewhere between a kid and a middle school kid. You knew that this dude, Yameen, lived in the building because your parents had dropped him off there on one of those station wagon group rides where the cool parents take all the kids with parents who don't drive where they needed to go. You had a pair of cool parents. The directory had his last name listed on the fourth floor.

You had made note of the time the sloppy hand-to-hand took place and came back daily during your dog walk to see if you saw him out there again. You were only curious at first. You looked at it almost like a science experiment. It only took two days for you to see him on the block in front of that same building. People in the hood are especially predictable. The truth of all truths is that they have very few places go to, especially when they're too young to have places of their own.

That's the thing about juvenile criminal acts. They have to be kept secret not only in the streets but also in homes controlled by parents with all-access passes to every nook and cranny of the walls you sleep between. As kid crook you have to rely on a parent's apathy or distraction, or the convenient combination of both. A voice at the back of your skull just told you to follow the guy. And that was what you did.

The buzz lock on his front door was bullshit. You narrowed that silver aura of yours until it felt like a second skin and eased a paper-thin slice of energy between the latch bolt and the door frame. And then it opened like you had his key on your ring.

You climbed the stairs a good 60 seconds behind him and clocked the designated door by the way the echo came down the staircase. You learned then that you could hear better when you focused your aura around your ears. That complicated eye at the center of your forehead gave you a strong enough notion of the way you should go.

The next thing you knew you were standing right in front of unit 301. But this time you didn't aim to turn the dead bolt on the other side of the door. This time you measured the length of the door frame, pictured yourself on the other side, and then literally walked through solid matter. You skirted past the Totin' Chip dude while he sat on the couch watching a tape of *Rap City* on BET. The door to his room was open. Focused, and both scared and thrilled by the rush of it all, you continued taking invisible steps toward the bedroom, a cubbyhole that featured posters on the walls for Ice-T's *Power* and *Rhyme Pays* records. Next to the twin bed and a beanbag chair was a cardboard box filled to the brim with stacks of cash.

You didn't know what the money was for. You didn't know where it came from. And you really didn't know why you were doing any of it. But you lifted two of those rubber-banded stacks, eased them into your back pocket, and phased back out the front door into the hallway, where you almost fell to your knees from the exhaustion of the effort. You could hear your own breath bouncing around the brick chamber of the apartment corridor and the levels below.

It felt like you had run five miles, but you hadn't broken a bead of sweat. You felt hungry and tired and out of sorts, but fear shuffled you down those stairs and out in the street, where you'd tied the most loyal dog in the world to the bus stop sign. Blackstone was sitting there, waiting for you, loyal and happy, when you came back 20 grand richer.

You never saw the Avirex kid again, but there was a fire in that building three days later that turned its insides to ash. An elderly lady died inside in her hospital bed and a bunch of other folks lost their homes. Your parents mentioned something about it at the breakfast table before you all took your separate routes to school and work. They said it was arson and the building owner was a suspect. But even then, at barely 16, you knew better. This training wheels version of the fuck it point had helped find your higher purpose. It allowed you to circumvent questions of morality that might have kept you in therapy for weeks in prior incarnations.

The following summer, Charles Cheyney, a Howard student who lived on Fort Davis, had gotten a job as an office assistant to a private eye who mostly handled divorce cases. In exchange for answering phones and picking up lunch orders, the private dick taught him little tricks of the trade, like how to cut into a phone line from the switchbox on the outside of the building. While this was only supposed to be used for company business, Cheyney smelled bread in it.

And somehow you got in on the hustle. But this wasn't an aura thing. This was learning the nuts and bolts of bare bones investigation.

You and Cheyney used to be the first dudes up at Lee's barber shop on Saturday morning to get your hair cut, and you were both addicted to the cop and private eye shows like *Remington Steele* and *Hunter.* He used to watch reruns of *The Rockford Files* with his mom. You watched the same show with your dad. Somehow this vague connection turned the two of you into partners for a single summer.

You would figure out who lived where, and if you could find the box, you'd open it and cut into their lines on the late night. You learned about deliveries of valuables, and high-end cash exchanges sent through coded advertisements in the *Washington Post* classifieds. The folks doing the talking were easy candidates for cuffs and the gavel the minute anyone got them on a wiretap. At the end of that summer Cheyney ended up transferring schools after he took too much from some dudes who tolerated too little. Gordon Gekko in *Wall Street* was a liar. Greed was *not good.*

After '92 and all the mess left in your wake, you vowed to never commit a crime yourself again. Your career in personal theft had totally become one of convenience. That 20gs got spent as slow as molasses in order to avoid suspicion. That was a lot of money to burn and you don't really remember what you spent it on without drugs, a car, or pussy. Or maybe something else had happened to it altogether.

Now, after that considerable flashback, you find yourself standing sitting in front of Avery in your office at the Queen and Country, because now, almost 30 years later, there is still more valuable shit worth stealing.

"I don't know the specifics," Avery explains. "But you gotta get in there."

"And in there is where?" you ask.

"I have no idea," Avery says, distracted as he answers texts on his iPhone XIV. "But she wants to meet you to talk about it."

Face-to-face meetings are rare in 2020. There is too much concern about connectable associations. If you based identity on social media profiles then you might have done jobs for the same ten people 100 times. All that mattered was that the cash transfer went through and that nobody dimed you to the cops or more frightening federal bodies if something went off script.

The whole point of Avery's cut is to keep things impersonal.

"What's her name?" you ask about this new client, as curious as the cat who got himself killed.

"Jalana," he says.

You freeze in your tracks and remember the feeling of cool linoleum under your biodegradable mat 15 years before. You think of Guinness. You think of calypso. Then it all comes together in a flash.

"Jelly," you say, your face curling in a smile.

"What the hell is that on your face?" Avery jokes. "What happened to that permanent old-man scowl?"

Jelly. This has to be a good thing. You *know* this is a good thing. It has to be a good thing, because there haven't been a lot of truly good things in a long while.

"I'll upload the files to your box tonight," he says.

And with that Avery heads for the exit and you head for the kitchen, where you find yourself surprisingly pleased by the plating of Butchie's rack of lamb sprinkled with fresh basil, blackened garlic chips, and a light dusting of kosher salt and cracked black pepper. Your favorite part of being a business owner is watching repeat customers take in the wonders your brand gives birth to.

Not unlike in crime, the Queen and Country ran like a machine because all your people have their skills filed to the sharpest point. They all learned food and drink in family kitchens. While most guys in the city had gone to culinary schools or come out of programs like Job Corps, your squad picked up everything they knew the old-fashioned way. They'd started off snapping green beans and pulling kale leaves off the stems. They'd fried chicken and fish for church fund-raising events and made sloppy plates of gumbo and beans and rice, fried wings with mambo sauce, and steak and cheese subs dripping with mozzarella and provolone, all for their own families. They took pride in their precision and consistency. But most of all they loved watching their plates get cleaned. That was better than all of their paychecks combined.

The three ladies at the front of your house

are equally responsible for the Queen's expanding field of milk and honey. LaTonya and Taren are the eye candy double threat. Emily, the Tropical punch Kool-Aid redhead, is a light-skinned mother covered in tats from neck to breastbone, a single mother who is taking classes toward a nursing degree. Just under 5'3"and skinny as a rail, you imagine her as the type who would have literally shown her ass at the front of the stage during DC's go-go heyday.

LaTonya is the other side of the coin. Halfway through med school at 24, she's read the Bible cover to cover three times and can always be spotted with a book in hand on her breaks, even the ones she takes for cigarettes. This week's volume is Susan Isaacs's *Long Time No See,* which she'd picked up because it has the same title as a Chico DeBarge album she's been running into the group as part of the staff music playlist.

Taren keeps a quiet eye on everything. The best waitress there is, she knows what you want to eat before you do. And she has the lovely ability of pushing folks toward the more expensive parts of the menu. And last but not least is Frances, who handles the books and inventory from the room in the back that no one visits. Nothing on her face screams 52, except maybe the voice that came from between her pursed lips.

A savant in all matters of color and order, Frances is known for alphabetizing her own kitchen spices twice a year and going door to door in search of people willing to sign whichever her political petition she's carrying at the time.

These are your people now. This is your family. Though they might not know it from your cool surface, they are your stability. They keep you in line. They have allowed you to start over. It's not uncommon for you to spend half the day standing in the kitchen doorway or out on the restaurant floor, admiring the work that you do together every day, whether the place is packed or empty. The Queen and Country is the only thing in your life that has been completely permanent. The rest has been locked boxes and stray pieces from a puzzle begun long ago, still unfinished.

"It's been over 14 years and you're still fixated on Jenna," the therapist says. She is not Dr. Melfi from *The Sopranos*. There are no crossed legs wrapped in nylon to divert your attention. She is a mother of four working out of her basement in Congress Heights, just a few blocks from the Congress Heights Metro station. And she looks like a TV mom, traces of sultriness and feminine wiles painted over by time, responsibility, and commitment to one man, the guy in the tuxedo next to her in the white dress in the 8x10 on her desk.

You started coming to therapy to "get it all out," the crust and cobwebs that had taken up the back room in your mind, places you'd smoothed over long ago and left to dry. Something deep inside you pleaded that you need to jackhammer it up, to cut away all the stagnant and cancerous layers and pour a fresh foundation. Therapy helps you. It gives you a chance to breathe. You think of that water filling up the streets in your dream all of those years before. Like in that dream, you didn't drown. You just didn't surface in Brooklyn again.

"Not Jenna," you say, "but the space she left behind."

"What do you mean by that?" she asks.

"Before her I always kept the door open. I was always ready for the next thing, knowin' that it was gonna be better than what came before. But then I got caught up in myself, and I didn't pay attention to that."

"When you say that, you mean the other women you cheated on her with?"

"It was two at the same time. One night, but I threw away something that I could never seem to get back."

"Have you tried? There have to have been other women in all this time since."

You have the answers ready for the questions. It's not as if you have trouble expressing yourself. Paying someone to process your secrets seems safer than divulging them freely. There is a bond and an oath to protect you from some tirade of vomiting e-blasts on Facebook, from the surprise attack tags of your ex—she and someone else posing like perfect prom dates on Twitter. There are no photos of born and growing children to mask the inevitable decay of love into hate. Everything around you in the world screams that nothing lasts. So why bother? Isn't it easier to smash and grab a few fistfuls of meaningful quotes to drop into your next creative work?

"I go out," you say. "I get to know women. We spend time together. But they don't fit right in my aura. It's like I always know that the thing is doomed from the start."

"Isn't that a little defeatist of you?" she asks. "Auras can do a lot of things, but they in themselves can't tell the future."

"Some do," you say. "But mine doesn't. Mine does other shit."

"Being a class 7 has its privileges," she explains. In the last decade the National Institutes of Health have begun to track aura development within children, which has led to a classification system determined by a combination of blood type and a groundbreaking sensory reflex test. The rankings go from 1 all the way up to 10. The 10s usually end up in cells of various varieties, are always people of color, and are usually gunned down by the police. Freddie Gray was an 8.5. Sandra Bland was a 7 like you. Trayvon was a 9 just coming into himself. George Zimmerman was a 1. Ones don't even feel the ground shake during earthquakes.

"Yeah, but it has its drawbacks too," you explain. "You don't end up fitting anywhere. You have to make places for yourself."

"So did Jenna leave a space behind because she was the last person you truly committed to for more than a month or two?"

"No. She understood me. She wanted me to

live when a whole lot of people wanted me to die."

"You're referring to the feud that caused you to leave New York?"

"No, this was before that. The whole Gilda thing was about money and ego and a problem over another woman, something small that got real big real fast."

"Well, those problems are a dime a dozen." She snickers.

"Yeah," you say. "But that ain't what I'm here for."

"You're here for your life," she says. "Therapy isn't a to-do list."

"I just don't want to hurt anymore," you say. "I'm sick of being in pain."

"And the pain is what motivates you to stay sober?" she asks.

"The pain is what keeps me on target until it doesn't hurt anymore."

"It shouldn't have to hurt in order for you to live a balanced life," she says.

"You're right about that," you say. "It has to hurt because there's a part of me that needs to keep hurting. That's the only thing that's keeping me alive."

There's a red undertone to the almond color of your therapist's skin, like half of your Grandma Ally's sisters, like Kaya Fontaine in the seventh grade. You imagine her at 18 or 19, rail thin and bright eyed. Some graduation night roll in the hay transformed into procreations, plural, that start to cry whenever the nipples run dry. You know that she got her doctorate in psychology after 9 years of night school. She's proud of that, because she was dedicated, because she stayed on task and target. It's the one accomplishment in her life she can't smother under her perfect shield of professionalism and is prominently featured on her business website.

"I've calmed down a lot," you say. "I have a business now."

"You had a business then. What changed?"

"I came home," you say. "Back then I was using people, people from somewhere different than where I was from. They were pieces on a game board, and I made moves with them until it caught up with me."

"You can't take responsibility for those deaths, especially after all the time that has passed. You can't be in control of everything."

"I know. But I try."

"Maybe that's the cause for the disaster that brought you back to DC. Maybe you couldn't let go of a certain wheel."

"I knew the car was going to crash. That's why I got out."

CHAPTER EIGHT

The tension starts with some underling saying, "We shouldn't give 100K to no niggers."

And that, of course, is when the guns were pulled.

The hallway is long and narrow. Gilda is standing in front of you and three other guys. Standing in your way are ten white men, also young, also angry, and also armed. You are all willing to die in the name of the flag you wave. But Gilda is the counselor here, the peacekeeper. The neckline of her top plunges toward her cleavage. Her print skirt wraps tightly around her hips. She is a middle-aged woman at the center of men with far more physical prowess. This teaches you the power of women, Black women in particular.

"Now, we're all going to walk out of here," she says. "But that's not because we have to. I have no problem putting holes in any one of you white boys that wants to play this shit like we're in a Jim Crow country. That is over. The price we agreed to is the price we agreed to. We have what you asked for. You have our money."

The white boys look at each other, then at us. Then they hand over the bag.

"He doesn't speak for us," their leader says, bending the knee. "I do."

There's a tree at the top of the hill that was once two trees. You can see its history at the roots. They started as one but they split into two, pieces of the same whole that would never meet again. At 21, sitting in her basement, her flawless face surrounded by brick and flawless things, Gilda once told you to find a tree like this one where you stand. The one you found was in Prospect Park in Brooklyn.

This one is next to the Anacostia River, with the perfect view of both the Douglass Bridge and the towers of exorbitant condominiums that form their own skyline between the river and Nationals Park. She told you to find these places, to use them as conduits for energy and spirit to come together as one. These are the places where you make decisions. And you are here to discern the meeting that has yet to take place.

You are cautious about anything that has to do with Brooklyn, paranoid even. You think of Shaheed, and Sam and Miel and the Muertos on Winthrop, and all the years shrink into a single thread that has yet to snap. But when you last left her, Jelly was of light and not of the darkness that nearly took you under. Like Khujo, there was never that thing between you and her. She's always been married, and now they have a kid. Happy units remain off-limits when you're a dude with an aura that tends to kick doors in for you.

Jelly taught you the basics of yoga. She taught you how to stretch your spine, how to arch your back in the cobra with the soles of your feet pointing to the sky. She showed you how to be one with gravity as your arms and shoulders lift the rest of your body toward the ceiling. She showed you the face of a god who was concerned with more than the amounts in the church collection plate or who was fornicating before they got married. Jelly showed you your own power in a way that Jenna couldn't.

You are good for blowing off a lot of client meetings after a visit to the tree. While there, the world around you hints at things. Maybe a few too many park police cruisers roll past while you're standing there. Maybe some lady taking five on one of the benches on the runner's path looks over at you for too long, and that makes you worry that the meeting to come is being surveilled or that you'll be stiffed on the second half of your money. You don't take chances if things don't feel right. And that is always a good thing.

You never want to come out of an elevator and find another set of Muertos waiting for you in the lobby or on the corner across the street.

The sun is lower but still bright in the sky.

The warm breeze makes 90 degrees feel like 80.
It's time to head back to the crib. You need to
get dressed.

"What kind of food is this anyway?" the young
and drunk white couple, underdressed and barely
standing, ask their plastic-encased menus. In the
old DC they would never be in an Ethiopian
spot on U Street. But, truthfully, in the old DC
there wouldn't be an Ethiopian spot on U
Street. There were only three back in the day:
Red Sea, Meskerem, and Fasika. That was it.
Now the Ethiopians have more of a stake in this
town than the Head Wraps do in Brooklyn.
There are joints all over the place. But you
come here because this was where you and your
homie Chips used to hang.
    Ethiopian and Eritrean women mostly date
their own. Their faith is a sect of Christianity
with a history unlike any other, and thus trying
to cut into their culture is like trying to make
your way through a jungle with a butter knife.
You and Chips would come to lady-watch and
drink and to dap up all the cabbies and drivers
whose faces you started to know when you went
drinking in Adams Morgan on college breaks.
Now it's a little more expected for a brother of
your demographic to hang in the spot, even
more so now that the city's more of a latte than
Chocolate. The drunk couple drones on.
    "Can we even eat this? Do they have vegan
options?"
    They are lucky that this is a weeknight and

that the crowd isn't there for the band and the dancing that comes with Saturday nights, when the place is for the culture and not just for the exoticism of menu. When you show up on Saturday night and you weren't born under an East African flag, you know how to stay in the rear and keep your mouth shut. These two don't.

The drunk white kids have voices louder than Ric Flair and Michael Buffer with a microphone. If this were the '80s or even the '90s, this pair wouldn't get service at all. And that generation of white folks in this city would have understood their rejection, seeing that the odds were against them in a place like this. But these skullcap and wifebeater-clad cretins, disrespectful of the food and the culture and only in search of a plate to soak up the various liquors in their gut, could file a lawsuit. And said lawsuit might create licensing problems or some investigative story from Channel Four News. So the owner back behind the bar keeps his tongue on safety and keeps the waitress unhappily serving their table. She has lovely legs underneath the fine translucent fabric of her skirted uniform and can only roll her eyes as they mispronounce their orders even though the phonetic spellings are printed right next to the dishes on the menus.

Jelly walks in wearing stretch pants and a Danceteria T-shirt with the neck scissor-cut so she looks like a caramel Jennifer Beals in her 20s, even though she's well into her 40s now. And she's wearing high-heeled Japanese getas, which make every step look like she's walking a tightrope. She doesn't need a *Star Trek* phaser to stun.

"You up and disappeared on me," she says. "You're in class every day and then you're gone without a trace."

"I left a trace," you say, as your Jamie on the rocks arrives. You gave up the cloud but kept the anvil.

"Yeah, you did," she says, knowing enough about what you used to do. "But you still could've made a call, sent a text, an email maybe?"

"I dumped everything," you say. "Dropped all my social media accounts for a while. I just wanted to start over."

"But you didn't really start over." She smiles. "You just came back home."

"What brings you here, honey?" you say, cutting to the chase. You smile. Her aura is golden and shimmering. She orders a veggie sambusa. You order the lamb tibs in the spicy sauce and the cabbage, lentil, collards, and salad, small sample size sides that used to come free with the meal before the neighborhood got so pricey.

"Did you read the stuff I sent Avery?" she asks.

You visualize the file fanning open three-dimensionally from your tablet, a Tony Stark gadget turned into 2020 tech, as it had the night before. Three antique books: a Bible, a Koran, and a copy of the Atharvaveda, the definitive text on Hindu sorcery, each over 100 years old.

"Praying to the Many-Faced God?" you joke.

"Each is older than this country and vacuum sealed in a titanium case that you need a four-digit code to open."

"I did my homework," you say, though the truth is that you barely browsed it all until the tree in the park gave you its okay.

"Why me?" you ask.

"Because you're a Class 7 who knows how to move without being heard. These boxes aren't easy to get to. And the people that have them are Class 7 linebackers."

If you were a dog, this is where your ears would have perked up. While your aura is fluid, more liquid than solid, hardening only when needed, a class 7 linebacker can fall ten stories and get up without a scratch. Bullets never get to them. Fire doesn't touch them. These guys make millions of dollars a year without ever needing to carry a gun, train in a martial art, etc. Their biggest weakness is that their auras are so heavy that they can't float. Kick them into a 12-foot swimming pool and it's over. And if you can't get them in water, then you have to get to their food.

With these things being said, you don't fuck with linebackers. That's for the more aggressive daredevil types. Class 6s are known for getting dicks hard and slits wet over fierce challenges. But you aren't a six. Jelly can already tell by the hesitation that you're on the fence.

Your food arrives and you both begin to nibble, more focused on the business now than the plates you ordered.

"I told Avery that it was 60, but the job pays 120K. I'll transfer 60 into your account tomorrow and book the flights myself."

"Flights?" you asked. You haven't been out of the country since high school.

"You really didn't read everything, did you?"

You throw your hands up in surrender. "You got me."

"It's important that you go through it all, like every page. I sent everything for a reason. Because there's something else in Brooklyn that I need you to get."

"You know I don't do Brooklyn," you say.

"It's not that you don't. It's that you're waiting to get called back. The Asanas are calling you back."

You know "asana" to mean a relaxed position that you sit in during yoga, like a lotus or a half-lotus.

"It's more than that," she says. "We formed a group a few years after you left. The Head Wraps got out of control."

"From what I hear they're still out of control," you say.

"I *need* you to do this for us." As if this is some movie, like you're her savior and not an entry guy who runs a jack move every now and again for old time's sake. "You're the only one who can."

"Why do you say that?" you ask with a mouthful of spicy lamb.

"Do you want the job or not?" she asks.

It's not like Jelly to dodge a question. So this

is when you freeze. This is when you stop feeling slightly flirty and cynical and feel that fear that washed over you on that last night in Brooklyn. This is when your appetite does a David Copperfield and starts twisting in knots.

This is when you feel that twisting in your sacral chakra. It begins to tremble and pulsate like the speakers in LL's "Boomin' System." It's like someone just destroyed a Voldemort horcrux, like an unveiling of Dorian Gray's hidden picture.

"We need all three books," she reiterates. "We know where they are. But we need you to go and get them."

"Who is your information coming from?" you ask.

"We figured it out," she says. "I've been working on this for the last nine years."

"Class 7s? Titanium boxes? This ain't no neighborhood shit."

"But it is about the neighborhood. It's about saving the neighborhood. We—"

"Who's we?"

"We have an aura tracker, a remote viewer, a few other folks, and me."

You've never known Jelly's aura type, or what it does. It's not always a thing that comes up in conversation. Sure, you may see the color shifts, but when you're not sure of how familiar you are, it can almost come off like asking their favorite sexual position out of the blue.

"What does your aura do?" you ask her.

The music seems to rise. The clinking of

glasses and the scrape of utensils on porcelain sends a chill through you. A high-pitched hum fills the room.

Her eyes bulge. She hears it too.

"Go through the window!" she yells.

"What window?"

In less than a second the window next to you comes down in a million little pieces and the warm summer breeze rushes into the restaurant. Then the bullets start to fly.

You know the men outside the window, even though the last time you saw them they were boys in Kansas City Chiefs gear. Now they're wearing Brooklyn Nets jerseys with muscle tees underneath and are packing H&K H45s. A hand grabs you by the ankle and pulls you through the floor underneath you. Your skull slams against a steel beam as you tumble onto hard concrete. Everything hurts.

"Sorry about that," Jelly says, looking like her pulse is still even while you're seeing stars. "There were three different bullets headed for your dome. The bump on the head was the best alternative."

In layman's terms, Jelly saw all the different probabilities into the given moment with bullets flying and chose the one that kept you both alive and the least injured. She is what they call a Slot, short for "slot machine." Slots are usually Class 5s or Class 8s, depending on their levels of intensity. Your head hurts and your knees aren't what they used to be. The gunfire has stopped, but that doesn't mean you two are in the clear. You feel that ache at the back of your skull, the one you haven't felt in a long time. Your aura grabs hold of her, and the next thing you know you're in the alley behind the restaurant.

"We need to get off the street," you say.

"No," Jelly says, finally looking a little shaken. "You need to get to London."

A cab drops you and Jelly off at the Embassy Inn in Dupont Circle, a part of town where the Brooklyn Nets squad isn't likely to show up with guns blazing. You enter the building lobby quietly and slightly shaken. Things have been quiet for so long that you've forgotten the power of adrenaline. The fight-or-flight response doesn't happen much when you spend your days managing people who are trying to stay out of jail and not end up back in it.

Jelly's suite is on the fifth floor, a nook of a one-bedroom packed in between two double-bed suites.

"Why didn't you get a bigger room?" you ask as you step into a spot so tiny that it could have been something out of *Alice in Wonderland*. Her suitcase is in front of the made bed. There is a yoga mat rolled out on the floor with a pillow at one end and a pair of portable virtual reality towers on either side of it. With little piece of 2019 tech, she can actually transform her tiny room into a Buddhist temple, a projection of her own yoga studio, or even the beach before a great wide ocean. But for right now it's just you and her in this little shoe box.

"How's your husband?" you ask. She is polite

and speaks highly of him. But you can tell that something is wrong. The focus of the small talk is their daughter, who is 18 now and a freshwoman at Spelman, home for the holiday break.

"When the kids grow up, the marriage serves a different purpose," she says. "In a way there is more room to breathe. In another way there's too much space to fill. How come you didn't get married?"

"I missed my window," you say.

"Or are you keeping that window closed?" She grins.

"I don't think this is the time to talk about my love life," you say.

"Why not?" she asks. "The danger is done for now."

"I didn't think that you would be so calm about bullets," you say.

"There's no need to stress about what you already saw coming. They were just trying to keep you out of Brooklyn. There were no casualties at the restaurant, just a lot of property damage. A waitress got shot in the stomach with no permanent damage to her internal organs. Two male customers were winged in the shoulders. One broken ankle, one dislocated shoulder and a panic attack."

"How do you know all of that?" you ask.

"We're thorough," she says.

She reaches into the pocket of her suitcase and produces a blond envelope with your name on it in thick black marker. You open it up to find a pair of plane tickets for the following morning, a fake passport under the name of Todd Antwone

Shaw of Philadelphia, Pennsylvania, complete with a photo of yourself you don't remember taking, the key to a safe deposit box, and a few thousand crisp UK pounds wrapped in a band.

"You can't miss that flight," she says. "What's set in place is super solid. You can't miss a beat."

"And what am I supposed to do again?"

"Go home. Actually read the package we sent you. Follow the details to the letter. You won't sleep on the plane, so you'll have plenty of time to review things."

"And what are you gonna do?" you ask.

"I'm going back to Brooklyn," she says. "I'll see you there."

"But you just got here," you argue, with a certain whininess in your tone. You feel shaky, like a Marine about to head into some uncharted war zone with limited intel. You want to talk to her more, suggest that the two of you find a bar and continue that talk between the two of you that got interrupted before you had the chance to pay the check.

"It will be better after this," she says, telepathically informing you that she needs you to leave the room, that she has some other purpose that can only be executed in your absence.

"How do you know that?" you ask.

"Because I've seen the future." She grins. "And you're a part of it."

Two hours later you can see the cop cruisers all over U Street from 12th to 10th. As crime in the city is sparse, a shoot-out like this one will be combed over until morning, from DNA and shell casings to the lipstick prints on tissue found in the ladies room. As you appear to have been the target of the Brooklyn Nets ambush, it's not too intelligent to be anywhere near the scene. Any tickets on your car will be eaten by your consultation fee. You call a car on your phone with 5 percent of the battery left, and take the long ride back to Hillcrest.

And then you dream.

You are sitting in Huey's Café on Halsey and Lewis. Gilda is sitting across from you, her signature line of cleavage forced into the V of her neckline. Her jumpsuit is leopard with a matching cap, and her hair is long and the perfect shade of gray. The place is empty and neither of you are speaking. Then a little girl walks in, a child of maybe 9 or ten, tomboyish with her hat pulled low over her eyes looking like Blue Ivy Carter, her hair braided in cornrows that spell the name "Keisha" on her scalp. She is twirling small knives in each hand. Her eyes are on fire as if there is some raging furnace within, a soul engulfed in turmoil.

Two others enter behind her: one the Black grade school version of Pinky from *Pinky and The Brain*, the other a gay kid dressed in all red from shirt to socks to special edition Jordans with a kind of candy paint finish. He walks with a cane, limping slightly as if the injury is new and not particularly debilitating. They all stand next to Gilda, who wears a kind of pride on her face, as if these are your replacements. You don't feel fear. You don't feel intimidated. You just feel sad that those getting pulled into the game only get younger and younger. And the only thing you feel sorry about is that she got you at all.

You come awake 30,000 feet in the air with that wind tunnel sound from the ventilation system all around you. The flight out was early. You didn't shower or shave. You just grabbed your bag and the envelope with the fake ID and tickets and called a cab to take you to the train, which you took to Reagan Airport.

You spend hours going over everything in Jelly's file before you drift off again, even though Jelly said you wouldn't sleep on the plane. Apparently her predictions aren't always perfect. But, then again, no one's are.

There were about 30 pages in the holographic file, three-dimensional squares hovering in midair within the safety of your own home. But on the plane you plug in your VR goggles and wireless earpieces for the sake of discretion. There are three scheduled stops in London. The first is to a safe deposit box at the Picasso hotel in Bloomsbury. The second is a security storage spot in Brixton, and the third is the offices of the man who employs the linebacker 7s at 3 Minster Court on Mincing Lane.

What you'll be doing inside the office building is unclear, but you know that there's a simple security desk at the front with a passkey turnstile that your aura can easily phase through. Once you get up to the 15th floor you'll have two linebackers to face—one posted at the front desk disguised as a receptionist and a second as Phipps's personal assistant in the office adjacent to the one with the wall safe—and a third whose identity the intel doesn't confirm. 120K is a lot of dough. Pulling this off is going to be deserving of every penny.

You go through the specs again and again, committing them to memory as you know that you'll have to leave the data card it came on flushed down a toilet or melting in a fire somewhere. It's better to trust your own head than to rely on somebody else's notes.

CHAPTER NINE

"**H**ow can I be of service?" she asks you, her French manicure tapping against the brass placard with "Concierge" on it. This is not the London you remember from '01. But then again, why should it be? Nineteen years is a long time.

The woman's question is a complicated one, particularly because she is fine as fuck: early 30s with seductively pouty lips, three-inch heels, and her permed hair in a pageboy clipped just above her ears. She reminds you of a darker Diahann Carroll. There are things that you need to consider before answering. The first is where you are. The second is why you are here in the first place. The third is the way the short wool skirt (a little less than a half-inch above the knee) tightens around her thighs and ample backside when she waltzes over to the desk where you are patiently waiting. "Service" has more than one definition in your dictionary.

The concierge is at least 5'11" to your six feet. The two of you would be neck and neck with her calves on your shoulders. The South London accent with a tinge of Barbados doesn't ease the potential erection in your jeans. Nor does her Nutella complexion. But the small gold-set diamond on the proper finger of her left hand makes the decision easy-peasy. Right about now you need to stick to the script.

"I left something in Box 67," you say with an eager tourist's smile. There is an itch underneath your stubbly chin, so you scratch.

"This way, Mr. Shaw," she says after matching your passport with the list on the holographic tablet she holds in her hand. You follow her down the corridor, just beyond the front desk area. The carpet is blood red. Her hips sway in two-four time as they travel the ten yards to the security door. There is a touch-screen keypad just above the knob on the gray titanium surface. She types in seven digits with lightning speed. The muscles in her forearm flex.

You follow her inside to the wall of security boxes on the left wall of the vault. There is a bare granite-topped table at the center of the room, obviously placed there for the convenience of reviewing box contents.

"Do you have your code?" she asks politely.

You nod. You find Box 67 and enter the code, 191926, from the files you've memorized. The box springs open, revealing the tiny box inside. You don't have a lot of time. The real Todd

Shaw will be here within the hour, expecting to find the box that you're about to steal. No aura tricks have been needed this far. All you've had to do is play it cool and remember the fake name they gave you.

"If you need anything I'll be out front," she says, practically slamming the door behind her without another word. You check your pits to make sure you didn't skip the deodorant or something. And there is the remainder of a peppermint Altoid between your tongue and teeth. So whatever's bouncing around that thick baby blue aura of hers has nothing to do with you. Maybe she just wanted to do her job so that she could keep it. She is married, after all. What difference does it make?

You take the box, which is the size of a tin of mints and made of the same thin metal painted black. And then you're out of there. Phase one is done, more than worth the 12 hours and the fresh and clean 60K sitting in your account. The dull pain at the center of your skull screams that you need to sleep. But there will be no rest for the weary. The next move is to get back into the streets.

The Picasso is a boutique hotel, an inn that is a living ode to the master cubist. A man of 50 with thick snow-white hair and a beard to match leads a post-teen waif with a streak of purple on the right side of her blond shoulder-length hair toward the elevator bank at the rear. Twin boys chase each other around pillars tattooed with cubist images, each armed with a Nerf foam dart pistol. An unfortunate bellboy with the Côte d'Ivoire flag tattooed on his neck takes a soft dart to the eye and earns himself a folded bribe from a parent for his trouble. And the concierge, the former object of your lust, wears a personal grin as she whispers something sweet into the house phone against her ear.

You tell yourself that you will see her again. But you have no idea of just how soon. You try to think of some worthy excuse to force another conversation with the fine-ass woman with the pageboy cut in heels, but you hit a wall. And then you hit the streets.

"I need a cab," you murmur to the doorman out front, whose overcoat is painted as Picasso's *Guernica*. The last of that pesky peppermint almost slides out of your mouth along with the words. The doorman, who looks somewhere between 30 and 40 and as pale as the Pink Panther, looks at you like a joke that wasn't funny.

"Are you a guest here?" the guy asks.

"Sometime this week," you say, emphasizing your impatience for any kind of prejudice when you're on the job. The look he gives you back says that he don't want no problems. Then he rolls his eyes to say that he isn't a full-on punk either. With men, everything is a dick-measuring contest.

Your driver flags the black-on-black Chrysler waiting for its turn in the cab line, and it pulls up from its parking space at the curb. This particular model of Chrysler, the 300C, is basically a Rolls without the impossible price tag. You had no idea that people bought American in England. You still can't get over the whole driving on the left side of the road thing. The doorman gets the peace sign as a tip as you close the rear door behind you.

"Where to?" the driver asks into the rearview mirror. His eyes are dark and beady, and he's wearing a red plain paddy cap. His teeth are a riddle even the great Sherlock Holmes probably couldn't solve.

"Brixton Hill Self Storage," you say as you place a crisp quid through the small window in the Plexiglas partition. "7 Weir Road."

"Twenty-five to thirty," he says, like a man on military time.

"You don't use the apps and Uber like most tourists?" he asks. His accent is Irish. You watch a lot of BBC America.

"I lost my phone," you say, just as it vibrates in your pocket. Luckily, he can't hear the buzzing inside your pocket. You will check it later.

It's a quiet ride, even with evening traffic heavy in both directions. From a passing car, with no audible accents this could be New York, or maybe even parts of Chicago. You have to remind yourself that you're in an entirely different part of the world. What feels like fatigue weighs heavy on your eyelids, and they close. This is when you see the concierge, standing at the same desk with the same jacket but a different blouse. Then your eyes open again and you smile to yourself. Jelly apparently doesn't know everything about this trip.

Things are bothering you, and they have nothing to do with the job. You are thinking about the restaurant, about the water heater the plumber says is due to die in less than two months that you don't feel like replacing. You think about Frances's complaints about your health insurance plans and about the occasional tendency of the place to smell like after-hours sex due to Buster's occasional late-night escapades on company property. As a live-in caretaker for his mother, he needs another place for his "dates."

You think about the quiet and still consistency of 15 years left undisturbed by anything that reminded you of Brooklyn, of Jelly, and of the questions unanswered in the first book of your existence. Most importantly, you think about the freedom that came with no new Jenna's no-pitter-patter Tony Terry lovey-dovey stories to share on your Instagram like all the other suckers out there.

You think about all the dudes whose lives have changed because you stayed in one place and stopped with all the high-flying daredevil shit so that you could become a respectable businessman. The jobs you've done with Avery repping you have been simple, cat-caught-in-a-tree shit in comparison to the raging infernos of your past. You didn't fear those bullets from the Brooklyn Nets. Even those who got hit will live to tell the tale.

What was it that made you go along with that fucking exile all those years ago? There was something you knew, before the Twins, before the Drummer's Circle and the Kansas City Chiefs on the way to the Javitz Center. But you still can't admit it to yourself.

Then the cab lets you off at Brixton Self Storage, and you plant feet on asphalt thousands of miles away from a life you built that was just enough to keep you free of suicidal boredom. You're starting to feel the foundation of your cover life rattle like the vibrating tracks before an oncoming train.

The storage space is the color of McDonald's arches, and just as busy. As you already have the locker number (13306) and passcode (2742) memorized, it's a quiet two-story elevator ride to achievement. You're already counting how you're going to spend the money in that account. Maybe it's time for a vacation. Maybe it's time for your next six-month-long fling, complete with some trip out of town. Sure, Puerto Rico has had hard times since the hurricane, but maybe New Orleans, South Beach, Rio, or even Cuba. The US embassy there might not be the best destination, but from what you've read and seen in the virtual world, it's fuckin' beautiful.

You arrive at the climate-controlled third floor. Music is playing on the system overhead. Of all things the song is Rockwell's "Obscene Phone Caller." There's irony in the fact that you're listening to a Black guy from Detroit faking an English accent while you're actually in England. You can hear your footsteps traveling solo down a corridor. Then you make a left turn, and then a right, zipping past hundreds of portals being rented by strangers who only partially speak the same language as you.

You're expecting unit 13306 to be some

massive monstrosity with a big metal pull-down door. Your worry is that it might be booby-trapped somehow. Maybe the door is rigged to a tripwire attached to a grenade. Maybe there's some kind of poison on the door handle, which is why you'll slip on gloves before you punch the code in. But it ends up being one of the tiny cubbyholes above the larger locker units. So it takes another minute or two for you to wrangle one of the steel ladders on wheels from a few aisles over so you can finish the climb up and reach the box you need to get into.

You punch in the code and find a leather Adidas messenger bag with the coded titanium security box inside. The weight seems right for a large olden version of the Good Book, but your job is not to authenticate, merely to bring it back to Jelly and these yoga superheroes that are paying you. With the bag slung over your shoulder you are filled not with satisfaction but with anxiety. This was just too damn easy. And you know it. You climb down the ladder and push it back where you found it.

You look to your left, and to your right, up at the ceiling, and down to the floor. It appears that you are safe. But as you start back toward the elevator, you retrace the trail of bread crumbs left clearly in your mind: a right and then a left and then that corridor with the fire extinguisher. And then you should be home free.

But then the lights overhead start to flicker, and you hear that shrill, high-pitched sound that you know all too well. It's the sound of another charged aura, something with a spinning directional signature. You do not expect to see the 12-foot shadow come out of the wall and tower over you. It is a thing indescribable in scientific terms. It has weight, and mass, and humanoid form, but is still in some senses a ghost.

It comes charging toward you down the narrow corridor, the electric charge in the air turning the overhead bulbs into David Lynch–style strobe lights. The music coming out of the speakers now changes over to classic hip-hop, Mobb Deep's "Shook Ones (Part One)," a robbery anthem if there ever was one.

The entity takes a sweep at you with a massive clawlike hand that scratches both metal and concrete, creating sparks and smashing stone along the way. You duck, slide between its legs, and keep toward the elevator. It turns and comes after you. Its feet pound against the linoleum tiles. Your fight or flight response tells you, à la Tina Turner, that the gods don't need another hero. It's time to get to the fuck out!

There is no time for the elevator—you have to take the stairs. But as you kick open the entrance to the stairwell, you feel that tug at the back of your skull, the one you haven't felt in years, a part of the machine that is as indescribable as the class 7 bubble you live within. And without taking the stairs, you are standing in the middle of the crossroads out in front of the storage space.

A Mercedes-Benz truck swerves by you, as do several other cars. Your heart is pounding as you make it to a corner. What you saw in that space is no longer in sight. Part of you wants to dismiss it as the stuff of delusions and hallucinations. Then you see the hole explode out of the side of the storage space, raining chunks of concrete down on the world below as that clawed phantom menace takes flight and then slides into a slit of nothingness in the sky up above that causes three or four auto accidents all at once.

A woman screams. There is the eruption of sirens from some kind of fire and rescue. A block of Brixton has been transformed into momentary chaos, and for once you don't know what the fuck is going on.

You dip into an alley between two buildings and find a wall to lean against so that you can catch your breath. The cell in your pocket buzzes again, and when you take out the iPhone 15, Jelly all but holographically jumps out of your pocket.

"Get off the street," she says in sports bra and yoga pants, a wall of mirrors behind her. "I'm sending you the address to a safe house!"

Jelly's tiny chiseled frame is replaced by a white screen with black letters identifying an address on Elmo Road in Shepherd's Bush. The most important magic of the day will be finding a cab, but as a magical Negro it's not as difficult as you might expect.

You wave an electronic passkey in front of the code box, and the apartment door comes open. The place is a spick-and-span one-bedroom that looks more like an Airbnb than a fortified bunker.

You try to call Jelly but it goes to voice mail. You send Avery a text but you get an automatic reply that he's in the movies and he'll get back to you.

There's a picture of a Colonel Sanders–type plantation owner playing banjo on the wall above a leather sofa, and a tray of candy and snacks, along with bottles of water in the fridge. There are frozen, organically grown and hermetically sealed gluten-free vegetarian dinners stacked in the freezer and biodegradable fresh linens in the tiny-ass water closet with the tank on the wall and the hanging chain lying next to it.

You try Avery again. You get nothing. You try Jelly again, and it does the same voice mail dance. This space is not your home, but at least it's quiet. You take off your hoodie, remove your shoes and socks, and find a clear space on the center-stage carpet in front of the upholstered couch. You close your eyes and you breathe, expanding your aura outward until it gently kisses the corners and walls that border you on each side.

You try to process what you have just seen, something larger than you, stronger than you, a thing that destroyed not an idea, plan, or arrangement, but an actual physical place, something that tore a hole through matter normally strong enough to hold men more dangerous than you. You are in another country, holed up in a safe house owned by parties unknown. The only thing for you to do is something unexpected, something completely unrelated to the given drama/trauma. You activate the clean smartphone specifically designated for non-task operations. You shower and shave. Then you arrange for a car.

Standing on this street in Shepherd's Bush, the King's English firing off all around you, you take a glance at your reflection on the mirrored glass announcing the Toodles grocery. You've had on the same hoodie for close to 24 hours. Underneath is a tee that shows Darth Vader in a criminal line-up with several Imperial Stormtroopers, an ode to Bryan Singer's *The Usual Suspects,* and tapered jeans. You could be some hip-hop hooligan, a cretin, another Black man on the bus fresh from a job where he isn't respected in a world that shows him no love. This idea in your head requires a different dimension, the reflection of someone who hasn't spent his life on the streets of Brooklyn and DC east of the river.

Using your new phone, you identify a men's clothing spot called Drake's, which is a block west of your destination. Then the car arrives. It's dark now, early evening, but luckily you should make it before closing time.

Astrid, your saleswoman, appears to be Swedish. She is a shadowy brunette with pencil-thin eyebrows and a tiny tattoo of Snoopy behind her right ear. She takes your measurements and leads you to the high-end racks. You avoid the blazers with high button counts. All you want is a solid black with a matching shirt, tie, and shoes. Twenty minutes later you walk out wearing the first choice out of the three you try on, along with a pricey white long-sleeve with a razor-sharp collar, a pair of black Kenneth Cole slip-ons, and a pair of silver eagle cuff links from the Robin Leach collection. No tie.

Your father once told you that "a great man must have at least one pair of gaudy cuff links." And these are yours. You drop the hoodie, jeans, and boots you came in with in the fitting room garbage can. Then you exit the shop, cross the busy intersection and walk right back into the Picasso Hotel humming the string line to Isaac Hayes's "Walk on By."

The concierge is standing exactly where you left her. And she's wearing a different top underneath her blazer.

"How can I be of service to you?" she asks you, apparently not recognizing you from earlier. This time she flashes you a smile. And it is a smile that you actually believe in. You are a very different man from the one she saw earlier in the day.

"Is that a wedding ring?" you ask, pointing to the small sparkling stone on the proper left finger. As dark as she is, she still finds a way to blush. She always takes a deep breath before she tells the truth.

"It helps our single male guests to keep it business." She grins, lifting her head like a proud lioness.

"So is it the pub or the bistro?" you ask. "They're both a block away."

A line of needy guests is slowly forming behind you. They are speaking German, or Swiss German, though at this point you don't know the difference.

"Excuse me?" she asked.

"Was I not clear? Where am I taking you when you get off? To the pub or to the bistro?"

"Are you a guest here?" she asks. Your bravado rattles her. Men don't normally speak to her this way, at least not men who look like you. You're too polite to ignore. And nothing about your body language says you're a threat. Her face goes from "Can't you see I'm at work?" to "What spaceship dropped you here?"

"Not at all. But you should *still* answer me."

And just like that she lowers her shields and powers down the photon torpedoes. Then she smiles. A tidal wave of impatience from those behind you hovers over the conversation, but she makes them wait. You are the current customer, after all.

"You a football boy?" she asks.

You are thinking touchdowns and field goals. She is thinking men kicking a ball in shorts and jerseys aiming for a World Cup. This tiny bit of confusion has little effect on the final outcome.

"I know how to play the game," you say. "So what's it gonna be?"

"Why can't we do both?" she proposes.

"When do you get off?" you ask. She glances at the clock on her desk.

"On the hour. Fifty minutes."

You smile like a cereal box champion.

"Then I'll be back in an hour. You ladies are always late."

"You're getting us mixed up with the Italians." She grins.

"We'll see," you say, as you start toward the main entrance.

That tidal wave of people behind you turns out to be elderly Germans seeking directions to the closest McDonald's, and they are pleased to have her attention now that you're gone. You have an hour to kill.

You exit the hotel for a second time, and your phone comes alive. It's Jelly. Her holographic projection is the size of a matchbook as she sits in her living room. A college girl is next to her on the sofa, drowning out the world with earbuds and a touch screen. Her nipples show through the sheer material of her white boy tee.

"You got it?" she asks. You nod.

"Change of plans. Dead stage three and get that book back to me in Brooklyn. Don't stop in DC. Get here as fast as you can. Other half of the transfer goes through when you touch down at JFK."

"What happened?" you ask. "Why the switch-up?"

"Somebody else is back in town, and they need you here."

"There's something I need to tell you."

"Let me tell you something first," she says. "It's not Gilda. This has nothing to do with Gilda. Get me that book and I'll tell you everything else."

She ends the call like it's the end-of-act cliffhanger on a TV drama. And then she leaves you there, back in London. You try Avery again and finally get him. It's an audio only call. He's driving; the camera on his phone isn't picking up enough light for a hologram.

"Avery speaking," he says, obviously munching on something crunchy.

"Where the fuck have you been?" you ask.

"I fell into some pussy," he says. "Some sexy BBW Jill Scott shit."

"That's TMI," you say. "Look, there's a change of plans. I need you to hold the place down for a few days. I have to go straight to Brooklyn."

"What about the stuff you wanted me to send you to handle those class 7s out there?"

"That's on hold," you say. "Just keep the place cool and make sure Buster doesn't have any broads in my office."

"He's got no time for that. Place is swamped. Kevin Durant rolled through for his niece's b-day. The place is wall to wall but the fam has it handled. You're good."

"Damn, Kevin Durant?" you say, proud that the Queen and Country is apparently on the rise. "How in the fuck did he hear about us?"

"When you got it good, people know," he says.

"Do me a favor and set up getting that water heater replaced. And give everybody $50 bonuses for the night. Tell them I'm proud."

"Well, aren't you big daddy?" He laughs.

"Since the day you was born, you said. I'll holla."

* * *

"There's always some arse on the job," she says as the two of you are walking into the pub. "Some fucking guitar player throws a bottle of Cabernet against the suite wall while I'm telling him that there's a noise complaint, and it spills all over me. This is why I keep a change of clothes in my bag."

This explains the change in blouses in your aura vision. Then a hostess walks you to a table and you pull her chair out for her. And then the real conversation begins. The concierge has a name. She is Rena.

"My mother's from Leeds," she explains later, between bites of prawns grilled Hunan style. "My Dad's from Cameroon."

Rena Stallworth had been born in Tottenham to a family that breathed and bled "football." The highlight of her recently departed father's existence had been winning a radio contest that got him a spot as the fan guest announcer for a single period of a Tottenham-Dundee United match. It was the only time in his life that he completely overcame his fear of speaking in front of people.

"Sounds like you're a Daddy's girl," you remark.

"I am," she says. Her smile is a sad one.

You ordered three different things: the fried prawns, two fried soft-shell crabs, and a vegetable dish with snow peas, mushrooms, and bamboo shoots that you felt should have come with more bells and whistles for the price tag. Chinese is one of your favorites. But what you're having across the pond is nothing like the Korean-churned bullshit that you've snatched out of revolving Plexiglas for most of your life.

"So what happened to you?" she asks, pointing to the faint scratches at your right temple, apparently shrapnel scars from your run-in back at the storage place.

"Haters," you say.

"I hope you have fans too." She smiles.

"More than I give myself credit for," you reply, bringing the line of inquiry to a close. Any more specifics are guaranteed to end the evening early. And that is the last thing you want.

Outside of Jenna Ann Campbell, you have spent too much of your life as dude stepping lightly through minefields of chickenheads and damaged day walkers in need of either therapy or a good sit-down with their daddies. Rena is classic . . . like the Harlem Renaissance . . . like '64 Mustangs, like the first time you heard "Protect Ya Neck" through a decent system. That accent, coupled with the slender jawline and chiseled cheekbones isn't what makes sitting across from her so comfy. You just wanted to listen to her talk. She is Eve before the Serpent. But are you Adam, or the Serpent?

"I love watching things burn," she explains an hour later, while lighting a clove. You've paid the check and walked her across Bloomsbury to Silbey's, the pub she mentioned at the hotel. The match in her hand is practically burning her fingers before she blows it out.

Darren Fletcher scores a goal against Arsenal, and the pub is on its feet. She is three-quarters through her second pint. You nurse your Jameson, so caught up in her excess of cool that you kept forgetting to drink.

"Soccer's like baseball to me," you explain. "Eighty minutes of fuckups and then a whole lot of hype over scoring one point."

"Think of it like chess," she says, running her finger along the edge of her glass. "It shouldn't be easy for good warriors to catch a good goalie sleeping."

"I'll try that," you say, unsure of whether you'll ever really take the time to watch a game again.

The Arsenal fans in the place are drinking more heavily than usual by the time the second half peters out. The final score is 3–1, Manchester United. The two of them were the only customers left after the match was over.

There's that point between man and woman where the trajectory of what's ahead is clear. It's not a matter of if it's going to happen, but when. And as she knows that you're only in town for a little while, questions of both momentum and sacrifice come into play. But with you, safe sex is always a given.

"You wanna get outta here?" you ask.

"That depends on where we're going," she says.

"To get you clean," you say.

You are apparently on a roll. You dial up a car. But what shows up isn't the luxury BMW identified on your phone's service screen. You walk out of Silbey's arm in arm to find a black '89 Audi with a low-hanging muffler idling directly in front of the pub entrance. The passenger-side window comes down and the immediate area is engulfed by a cloud of mid-grade marijuana. The face behind the cloud is the color of macadamia nuts and speaks with a thick Jamaican accent. Under any other circumstances you'd tell this guy to take a hike. But appearances can be deceiving, and you're are having too much fun to care.

"Shepherd's Bush," you say, handing over the quid up front. "But we got some stops to make first."

"Whereeva, wheneva," he says. "Me name Junior. Let's ride."

The first stop is a late-night grocery, where the two of you buy coffee, a box of condoms, and a fifth of Jameson. The second is a coffee shop called Angie Stone's just a block from the safe house. Rena goes in with nothing but the playful switch of her ample ass and returns with a dessert box gift-wrapped with a purple bow on it.

"How'd you know about that place?" you ask.

"I used to shag the owner," she says matter-of-factly. "Free dessert for life."

"Di pum pum!" Junior shouts, as if he were in on the conversation. "Di pum pum rule da world!"

Things go from civilized to downright violent on the other side of the apartment door. One of her heels knocks that painting of the Col. Sanders–style plantation owner sideways.

Your tongues knot. Her bra and panties are a matching burnt orange. It's almost like she knew what was about to go down when she got dressed this morning.

You tell yourself that things shouldn't be moving this fast. Somewhere between third and fourth gear you start to question motivations and angles. This can only lead to trouble. Does she know why you're in London or what you are here to acquire? Whose payroll is she on? Are you about to fuck your way into a jack move in progress?

But then she puts her hand to your face in a certain kind of way, and the higher part of you gives you that reminder that this is different than all that you've done before, that this is all a part of the plan. That's when you let go of something, that something that keeps distance between you and the rest of the world. You drink her well dry. She gets to the center of your Tootsie Pop without biting. She calls the Lord by at least three different names after you enter her.

She bites your neck. You lick the crease of her spine where it fans into the apple below her waistline. She claws at the chiseled flatness of your abs, gripping at the strength in your arms like some sort of quality inspector. You climax so loudly that there are pounding fists on the other side of the wall of the safe house. You laugh to yourself, thinking of the Maxwell song. But in London it would be "bobbies" or "barneys" or "nickers." This joke to self is silenced by the fingers she slides between your lips.

"I thought you wanted to get me clean," she

says, her torso heaving with an infusion of your sweat.

"Yeah," you huff, your heart still racing. "But I had to get you dirty first."

Within minutes you are drawing the bath. There is both pink salt and olive oil in a kitchen cabinet. She makes coffee in nothing but your suit jacket, sprinkling cinnamon in with the freshly ground beans. Then she tops off the finished cups with healthy splashes of whiskey.

You find your way into the water first, your mind fast-forwarding to the morning ahead. You made a point of getting Junior's number for the ride to Heathrow on the other side of dawn. But once she climbs in after you, submerging her sculpted frame in front of yours, you hope that the time will pass slowly. She hands you a cup of whiskey Joe. She feels like home as she leans back against you. The warmth of her and the hot liquid brings beads of sweat back to your brow.

"What planet are you from," she asks.

"A galaxy far far away," you say.

More rounds follow on the other side of pat and dry. She is out cold by midnight, the workday and your adventures having taken their toll. Sleepless, you put a blanket over her and start erasing all evidence of the interlude. You rehang the plantation picture, gather her clothes, and lay them, folded, on the chaise next the bed. Then you scrub the tub and coffeemaker.

You are nervous, guilty, anxious, and all at once alive. But you tell yourself that this is merely an excess of energy in the afterglow, your aura charging you up for what's ahead. You cannot focus on this woman. You have an item to deliver and questions that you need answered, and responsibilities that must be upheld. You cannot live in another country, and as wonderful as she is, she could never live in yours. There are no fairy tales in America after four years of Trump. And there is no future for you and Rena.

You don't want to leave anything behind in the morning. You want her to feel like she's been in a dream. You will leave your number, though. If it's meant to be, she will come after you.

Fatigue finds you around 2:00 a.m. You send Junior a text on the non-op phone and tell him to pick you up at seven. He confirms. Then you hang the suit, shirt, shoes, and hand-washed boxers before you lie down next to her naked. She smells like Marc Jacobs and sandalwood, a scent as soothing as pure lavender.

CHAPTER TEN

The thing about being a Class 7 is that it announces itself before you ever have to. Every thing and person your aura touches walks away with your signature, your energy fingerprint. Head Wraps are trained investigators on the other side of things. If an aura tracker can find you in this world, they specialize on the other side; there things both end and begin before we ever really get wise to it. People come to them by referral and also because at any given point a Head Wrap clique can be in need of something.

You can need a Class 3 to get you into a door that won't open or to find a way into something that no one is expecting. You can need a Class 5 to help you get pregnant, to sort out your love life or help you to make moves in business. Class 8s tend to have the bird's-eye view of the whole deal. But 7s are action-oriented. They give birth to shit, or they kill it. Alexander ending up short one brownstone had turned a lot of heads, heads you didn't know in a part of Brooklyn you'd landed in like you'd fallen off a truck.

So your name was in some people's mouths. And once it's floating in the air, the Head Wraps sort through prospects with a different sense of time, grabbing things out of the ether like autumn leaves falling from trees.

They needed a plan for a job, a special job for you, something that would become routine. Ronnie Motley dealt in antiques. He imported a lot of weird shit from West Africa. Weird in this case meant mystical shit, objects charged with special energies, old energies, things that altered outcomes. What he had sitting in a literal bank vault underground were five masks, each hand-carved by a craftsman from a dying family. With one of these masks you could literally become another person. Put one on and it was basically like trading your DNA for someone else's. While you're wearing this awkward-ass piece of wood, you are some guy from 300 years ago. His body becomes your body. His knowledge becomes yours. They are the best escape money can buy. But Gilda's crew had a problem.

Their best boy, a guy from uptown, had left the ranks to start his own thing. And they were under the gun. Then your name came out of the ether like it had been uttered out of the evil witch in Snow White's mirror. And the next thing that flashed was you, Khujo, and a bunch of other men in black with covered faces in a minivan headed over to Gilda's compound near the neighborhood, a literal island fortress sitting in the middle of the East River that nobody fucked with.

"This shit ain't for you," Khujo said. These were the first words she ever shared with you.

The other dudes in there had their headphones on, or earbuds in, or were so gassed up on the dollar amounts Gilda gave out to her best and brightest that the last thing they wanted to listen to was anyone with an objection.

"This is cool for them," she continued. "But it ain't for you. Because they don't want you. But they can't get rid of you."

"How you know all of this shit?" you asked.

"Because I *know* them and I *know* you," she said calmly, just before lighting up a Black & Mild. "And you're a 7. Sevens get attached to shit."

You barely understood the numbers at that point. But you liked the way she carried herself. She talked like a dude but looked like a bona fide winner.

You nodded, but then the van stopped, and they walked you all out onto this rickety-ass pier. You could hear the river rushing under you, that splish-splosh of dirty H20 moving every which way. And Gilda was standing out there in leopard-colored ballet shoes and an orange sweatsuit with a yellow cap pulled down over her signature gray mane with the perfectly trimmed edges.

"You're gonna do great things," she began, pacing back and forth like it was some battle speech. "You're gonna help me lead my revolution. And when it's gone, you'll have what I have, a beautiful home, and a commitment to service, and a better sense of the world than your mamas and daddies could give you on their best day. But first you have to pass a test."

There was no warning for what was to come right after that. You didn't see that the plank you were walking was really a trapdoor. With the whip of some invisible wand, the panels came out from under you and you all fell into that nasty-ass water. Looking back, you came to understand that the exercise was meant to kill any linebackers on the spot.

Your aura held you in a transparent sphere that brought you to the surface and had you sitting on the water Buddha-style in exactly the same way that she was. Everyone else was either coughing up the river while treading water or soaked on the shoreline, including Khujo, who was pissed.

"You fucked my shoes up," she said, as she took both Uggs off to squeeze them dry like some character out of *Looney Tunes*.

"You'll get new ones," Gilda replied over her shoulder.

"She with you?" Gilda asked me.

"We met on the way," you say.

"Stick with her, then." She smiled. "She'll never disappoint you."

The next thing you knew you had an order of chicken tamales in front of you at Taqueria on 7th Avenue. The place is packed with white faces and far from the prying eyes of the local competition. It's just you and Gilda. She is in her mid 40s at this point and wearing a Chanel jacket, a Tiffany charm bracelet, and jeans.

"So how would you get in," she asks, having described an abandoned bank vault at the end of a tunnel running a secret course within the walls of the MTA's subway system. Built nearly 100 years before, the only access point is through the basement of a plain bodega near Lafayette and Nostrand. The bodega itself is guarded on the outside by a few guys with guns in contact by two-way radios. Challenge number one is that the bodega is diagonally across the intersection from a police station. Challenge number two is that there's only one way in and one way out via the front door of the place, which leads to a padlocked stairway with a ladder climb three stories down, followed by a 50-yard hike to the security-coded door in front of the vault itself.

"I ain't know shit about getting a safe open," you said. "But Khujo can. Her aura is only a class 2, but she can get into any box. And I can get through the doors. But in and out of there is all on you."

"I have the people," Gilda says. "As long as I believe in your plan."

You thought on this then, munching on your tamales and sipping a more sour than sweet squeezed lemonade, your nostrils taking in Gilda's scent, the chatter of the crowded restaurant all around you. You think about the bodega and the corner that it sits on. And then you compose the most oddball configuration of events in your mind, a scenario that can only happen if the audience that is southern Bed-Stuy completely believes in your play.

Your plan requires men who have no problem with violence, two thieves with considerable stamina and skill, and, perhaps most importantly, an almost suicidal reliance on the continuing rivalry between FDNY and the NYPD.

You explained things to her in broad strokes, outlining the needed resources, the time of day and the amount of time needed. You talked until your throat was dry, selling it to her like a Hollywood pitch. It is a tongue tickling the edges of her labia before your suck on the figurative clit. The problem for you was that all roads to success relied on you trusting her and in her not treating you as an expendable asset. She told you there was one week to plan it all. You told her that the very first thing she would need was a hacker.

The first move was to pay reliable and sane homeless guys to take camera phone pictures of all the movement around the place to ID employees and get a sense of the work schedule. The second move was to cut into the phone lines and have a dedicated person listening in for any juicy chatter, which Gilda was glad to do herself. On the designated day you would give seven kids a few bucks each to go into the bodega and wreak havoc: shoplifting, vandalism, whatever tickled their dysfunctional fancies, just something that would force security to react. The reaction was two guys who could've given Shrek a run for his money.

The girl behind the counter was 100 pounds soaking wet and barely old enough to vote. And the floater guy, who basically never went farther than a block away from the building, was just as manageable. From Ronnie Motley's point of view there was no need for some massive security force to protect valuables already in a safe.

There was a tactical 12-gauge behind the counter and a six-camera security system covering the front, back and rear of the spot. You hired the two guns to go in with ski masks on like all they wanted was cash out of the register. The big muscle caught bullets in legs and guts, but nothing fatal. Smoke grenades, courtesy of an off-duty cop from Richmond, were popped, creating the illusion of a store fire. All 9-1-1 calls on that block were jammed, courtesy of our hacker. Then a fire truck painted to look just like a local engine pulled up with you and Khujo on board.

The two of you went into the smoke with gas masks on, tools in backpacks, and a fire axe. The two hired guns left as you entered, having left a trail of bread crumbs for you to follow in the form of fluorescent glow sticks on the floor. You hacked the lock off the door to the basement with the fire axe. Then you located the tunnel access panel on the basement floor and scaled down the ladder three stories in the dark. The lights on your helmets guided you along the 50 yards to the security door.

As class 7 auras cannot phase through iron or dense metals, the rest of the deal was Khujo's show. She shorted out the panel on the security door and activated the factory manual release to get it open. Then she went to work on the safe, which she cracked well within the plan's three-minute window. You pulled the big vault door open, grabbed the masks off a shelf, put them in bubble wrap, and stashed them in your bags. Then something told you to call an audible on the play.

You were supposed to go back up the ladder. But something said that it was better for your health to ditch the fireman gear, phase through a wall closest to the subway tracks at the Bedford/Nostrand G station, and then fight through the muck between the tunnels and a service entrance underneath a ventilation grate to get back to the street. Had you gone back the way you planned, you would have run into a B team led by a dude you would meet a few days later as Doughboy, a Fort Greene chubster who just happened to be the right person's nephew. A fix was in that would have robbed you of what you'd rightfully stolen. But you didn't go that way, and you delivered the masks to Gilda as agreed. She paid you $1,500 against a piece of the take from the fence.

Gilda gave you a big proud mama smile and told you that it was all good and that it was time to celebrate.

Drinks were poured at Night of the Cookers on Fulton. Platters of fried wings and catfish with greens and yams. Shit-talking reigned supreme. You were respected. You were part of the crew, newly ushered into a brand-new circle of trust after a lifetime of your circles ending up smashed.

You found yourself smiling proudly. You slapped hands and were pulled into hugs. Gilda held you tightly in her embrace, enough to stir emotions down south. You had a win, and you had money in your pocket. But you still needed a day job to cover things for Uncle Sam and the old ladies in the streets whose opinions mattered more to you than the crooks' did.

"I'll get you something, baby," she had promised. And she always kept her promises. Life in the Golden Sphere was a completely different way of living, something your years at that bougie-ass school in Atlanta hadn't prepared you for.

You didn't have a block state of mind when you moved into that cramped little college dorm room, or when all the little ex-debutantes and nouveau-riche daddy's girls put a hand or stockinged toe to your crotch beneath the tables at the campus snack bar. It had been all too easy.

You didn't miss Chocolate City in college when you used to sit under that elm tree behind the English building and write stories in your notebook about all the shit you'd seen (from a distance). You weren't afraid to talk about the hour you spent inside Club Kilimanjaro when they stabbed that poor dude to death and then passed his corpse over the crowd to leave it stumped by the doorway. You dipped out of there right after the body dropped outside and still made it home in time for curfew.

You had a pager that only got a few beeps a week, which wasn't even enough to justify paying the monthly bill. It wasn't that you were fronting. It was that you were excessively sheltered. You didn't need your aura to save you. That's what Mom and Dad were there for.

The natural step after college was for you to go back to DC, get a job in the government, get fat by 30, and kick out kids for a wifey from around the way who had a phat ass and made real good fried chicken. And you tried that way, for six whole months. The only thing an English degree could do for you was to open the door for you to teach in a system where they had to pat the kids down before they came into the lobby. Or you could have worked at one of the two main newspapers. And there was grad school, which you were way too cool to do because you were sick of people telling you how to write and how to be successful when they were still renting their place in the world and not owning it.

You were a rebel without a cause, a young "nigga" (though you never heard or learned this word at home) angry at the world over all the adventures that hadn't happened. Life was a wash because you weren't living out a Death Row Records fantasy or fucking girls in high volume just to keep your stats up for the corners and boys' clubs. The worst things that had happened to you were getting jumped in front of a group of girls you knew in Chinatown and your cousin Teeny getting hit with 20 years for holding the wrong dude's dope.

So after the graduation money had turned to ash, and the mold in the air of your Aunt

Sarai's basement kept you sneezing so much that you could barely sleep, putting your nuts on the table in the Rotten Apple seemed like a pretty good bet. You were tired of walking the same blocks and Metro stations daily. You were sick of seeing the faces change and the game stay the same. That card win in the game with Alexander proved to you that the future was due north, and no one could tell you any different.

The second incident that should have told you there was a problem happened after the Dunbar deal. Gilda got you a day gig as a barback at a spot called the Tramp Stamp on Franklin and Lafayette. The job was really basic stuff, perhaps more basic than what you were built for. You emptied the change out of the pay-for-play pool table, poured the brew when it got busy, and took orders for the in-house cook, who was dealing coke on the side and barely knew how to work the microwave. Mike could talk for an hour about the time he moved a whole kilo on a road trip to Lincoln University, or three hours straight about his two years as a dealer up in Laurel, how he had an '89 Porsche Carrera for a month, and how he'd rented out a whole floor of rooms at the Brooklyn Holiday Inn, as if those were the credentials for being a kingpin.

Mike's life as a piss-poor cook was all steak sandwiches and chicken nachos but no gravy. Once you have the gravy, you don't want to give it up.

The front woman for the place was a sista in

her 50s named Cece. Half black and half Italian, she prided herself on having seen every episode of every Black sitcom ever made and was known for using quotes from those shows and working their scenarios into general conversations, when she wasn't complaining about her nail work, her weave, or the deficit the place was running at. But she drove a Mercedes E 320 and wore $300 hosiery.

There was a river of gold running underneath everything Gilda brought you in on. She never seemed to fail. No one ever saw her sweat, and her world treated her like God himself had kissed her on the forehead each morning. The convivial charm in her nature gave both the impression that she could do no wrong and that she was not a woman to fuck with. She was a door that would never be kicked, one that didn't need a knocker. Respectful taps and hushed, even tones were the only things she responded sweetly to.

Cece warned you that every room in the bar was under surveillance, and that thus, any theft on your part would be detected and dealt with accordingly. You were to open up at noon and close at 11 on the dot. Your days off were Sunday and Monday.

But it was a good gig. Your checks came in the mail and were always on time. Any difficulties were to be addressed by Gilda's attorney, one Nicole Stevens, who had offices in Chinatown and her number printed on your check stubs. You made the nightly drops at the bank around the corner without incident. If anyone was sick, a call was made to an answering service and a temp replacement sent over, usually someone who appeared to be fresh out of a halfway house. Deliveries always got there on time and any problems with the equipment were repaired the same day. You'd never known of any place that ran that smoothly. And it made you and your aura suspicious.

"Sometimes you have to nice people to death," Gilda explained over Shrimp Po' Boys at the bar.

"There are lot of men who tried to have me before my husband. These were rich men, powerful men: politicians, ball players, millionaires. But what I knew was that they were just looking for a horse that they could train, a pony that they could walk around the ring to show the world that they'd snagged a thoroughbred. They weren't looking for partners. They were looking for trophies. I'm not a trophy. I don't need trophies. Horses are put down all the time. Jockeys and trainers have long careers."

She was trying to tell you something about the way things work, about how you get ahead by recognizing the value in your position. But when you're young, you can only judge things based on what the herd has to say. Sometimes your fangs and claws are sharper than others. Sometimes you get ahead of the pack and it rubs the seasoned players the wrong way. These things cannot be avoided. But at the very least, one should understand them.

* * *

You were made assistant manager exactly one month later. Then Cece took an extended "vacation" to run another Gilda-affiliated spot in Miami. She left you the keys, a box of bank deposit slips, drop envelopes, and a folder filled with info on all the supply vendors the place dealt with. You had gone from barback to frontman in less than two months. It was your very first promotion out in the real world, a step above skipping that grade in elementary school, something beyond the framed diplomas you kept in a desk drawer just in case you needed to interview for a desk job.

"God be with you." Cece had grinned on her way out the front door, speaking as if she knew something that you didn't as you watched her flabby fanny bounce out the front door less than two hours before the joint opened. Concern number two arrived on a certain Friday evening not long after that.

Delante Darby was known as DD. Charles Brown was known as GG ("Good grief," because he fumbled a touchdown pass that lost the championship when he was playing at Erasmus High). They came in with Pelle Pelle coats, sweater vests with no shirts, and do-rags, looking like candidates for a DMX entourage.

You figured that they had come in for a quick beer and a shot or to holler at the hoodrats who clung to the red vinyl booths at the rear. These were the only two things anyone ever came into the Tramp Stamp for anyway.

"You Kango?" DD asked, as if he hadn't said

your name back to you a bunch of times before. Your aura clenched up like a fist.

"What do you think, DD?" you asked. That was when you saw the butt of the Glock being pulled out of his waistband.

You couldn't get to it in time. The bullet bounced off your aura and shattered a light fixture before Meechie, the bouncer, beat him to a pulp and fed him to the cops. GG could have qualified for the US 200 meter dash team the way he dipped out the front. Gilda was at the spot in less than an hour, looking like a concerned parent at a PTA meeting.

"What the hell happened?" she asked you, almost as if it were your fault.

"They came at me. Me and Meechie stopped them. One of the lights in the ceiling got shot out."

There was a tiny bit of a grimace on her face, an expression you had yet to notice even though you saw her pretty often.

"You're not into anything I don't know about, are you?" And this was the truth.

"I work for *you*," you said confidently, proud to be waving her flag. "But they knew my name."

"You got a name now," she said. "You're with me. Get used to it." Then she talked to the cop milling in the back, who took a report so bullshit that he actually scribbled "for bullshit report" on his notepad. And then it was over, until you took a trip to Candyland later that night.

Candyland wasn't far from the corner of Eastern Avenue and Kingston, the perfect place for a strip club. Word was that back in the '90s you were more likely to witness a shooting than get a lap dance. But it was all behind you when you strolled in for a few shots and a clear view of the scattered ass.

There was a trio of East Indian dudes around your age perched at the table closest to the stage. There were five dancers on five different stages, the stages each having a square width of a few coffee tables sandwiched together. The one farthest to the left had her black hair cut short as her pendulous breasts swung to the sounds of Juvenile's "From Her Mamma." To the far right was a super-light-skinned girl with small breasts, long legs, and more tattoos than you found attractive. There was the white girl (because there's always a white girl). She didn't have the best breasts or ass, but her thighs were thick and she wined like she knew what she was doing, turning and twisting and dipping not only for the dollars, but also, in some way, for herself. But your eyes were on the main stage, which was about twice the size of the other two.

There were two poles and one woman on each of them. As you may have noticed, you have a thing about twos. The dancer on the left was about 5'6" and chocolate brown, with an intricate tattoo of a massive dragon crawling down her left leg with a pair of ass cheeks toned in a gym. The other was dark and pretty but a piss-poor dancer. What any real connoisseur will tell you is that it's the eyes that matter more. Hers and the dragon lady's are big and dark, her locks pinned into a crown worth of African American royalty. You were 100 percent certain that she was the one for you because she was the one selling the best con.

You notice the influence of at least 17 different yoga positions in her routine. In another life she would have had Ailey written all over her. But instead of her paying in sweat, the sweat was paying her. Your aura created an arc between your palms and the stage, funneling singles to her like some kind of magic fountain. But you could tell she wanted more. Strippers are salespeople peddling the product of themselves over seductive beats until they are down to nothing.

This was the woman you wanted in high school but always watched vanish into the passenger seat of some drug dealer, or some ball player, or some guy that had way more game than you. In Candyland, your cash evened the odds. You earned their submission with each trip to the bartender in search of more ones, still destined to go home alone but willing to eat the facts in favor of the taste of grand illusion.

The white girl was wearing a strawberry-blond wig. She had angel wings tattooed on muscular though clearly less-developed cheeks, her bikini top slated to be removed as soon as the cash piled high enough. You folded a twenty the long way and rested it just below the flyaway stands of synthetic hair flailing every which way. The green linen slid down her spinal column. And then she gave you a wink.

In this moment, with the speakers rattling, the Ethiopian waitress ogled your near-empty seven-dollar Corona and came over to enforce the two-drink minimum. Then you sent her away with an order for a double shot of whiskey, knowing that she would bring back Black Label because they didn't have Jameson behind the bar.

You dissolved further into a hot bath of fantasy. The hustler's wife at center stage became the country girl peeled naked in your bed just after Sunday service, the smells of yams and greens and fried croakers overpowering the sex in the air. You imagined matching rings on your fingers and her reminding you of her former life right after you praised the Lord in unison. How many babies were made after just the right sermon between lovers who shared faith before their bodies?

You imagined your hands on those round hips, slamming into her, the 100-degree heat and humidity melting the two of you into one. She would bite the palm you placed over her mouth like the ripest of peaches. You wouldn't want the imaginary kids to hear. You liked the pain. You would concentrate on it as she came, her body quivering in that eye-rolling moment where she met orgasm on the road to the Promised Land.

She was your mother and all the women in the book on your phone in one sweeping gesture at once. And in your fantasy, she had been bred for this purpose. And then the curtain came down, and you were busted back to being just another paying customer.

She moved her attention to a couple to your left. The woman was watching the ass. The man was watching the eyes. And he was holding the cash. She had them both. And she wasn't really even trying. For some reason she was crawling toward you on all fours, her silver heels adorned with spikes that reminded you of Superman's Fortress of Solitude in the Richard Donner incarnation.

You came to Candyland to escape from the complexity. You came there because it was the place where you didn't have to wait for the lawyer to show up at your crib when she needed what she described a "thug lovin'." You had one drink and then another. No water chasers. No food. Your primary focus was devouring the grand menagerie and forgetting what you do for a living, an obvious disappointment for the high hopes your middle-class parents had for you.

The song changed, and as your fountain of ones had run dry feeding of all the sistas onstage, it was the white girl who led you by the wrist up to the VIP area. It was only a $20 buy-in; Candyland was not the most prestigious of establishments. The next thing you knew, she was literally inverted in your lap. You were talking to a pair of spread legs.

"How you doin', boo?" you asked her. She glowed with perspiration. Whatever she was wearing had a fruity scent.

"Not as much money in it now," she explained. "I just do it because I'm good at it."

When asked, she confessed that she was 30, apparently ancient for a woman in her profession. You asked if she had a man. She said that there wasn't one. You asked if you were her type and she said that she would date you, because you're respectful and calm and unlike most of what she gets from the night to night. Then the songs ended and you were out a Benjamin. But you also left with her phone number.

You were in a business of relationships and a city full of people, but you didn't have a lot of friends. You were running with a crew, out a lot of nights and doing a lot of grunt work for reasons that were above your security clearance. She was a dancer who read books, who was into movies, and cooked better than you, and made you sit on her couch and take shots with her, and she never asked you to do the dishes. And you forgot that she worked at Candyland. And you forgot that people knew your name enough to pull out semiauto pistols to try and take you out.

"You ain't never dealt with no other dudes in Gilda's crew, have you?"

She looked away, appearing as suspect as the killer on a bad whodunit show.

"No," she said. "Doughboy and I were just friends."

You chose to believe the lie because you wanted to keep getting laid. Your ego even dismissed the fact that she compared your dick to his in an open conversation.

Had she told the truth, you would have broken it off and brought it to Gilda to make sure there were no problems. That was your mistake. You were living on Mars and not Earth when this man of the Pillsbury persuasion was waiting for you when you made the late-night creep out of her crib on St. James.

There weren't a whole lot of words between you. It was more like vague threats. He had seniority. He was such and such's nephew and she was tight with Gilda, which meant that you needed to watch your step. You loved your job and would have done anything to smooth the shit over. But you didn't see much when you looked at him, just a Class 1 who knew the right people. A boxing bout ensued.

The dude had a good 5 inches and 50 pounds on you, but you tagged the shit out of him. Class 4s always go for the jugular. Windshields broke. Garbage cans got rattled. It was Craig versus Deebo, David versus Goliath, and no witnesses to say who had swung first.

You wanted to kiss the ring, but in those months with her she felt like the only thing you had, and it was gonna take more than somebody's hype man to bully you out of the only place that you'd called home as a grown man. You broke his ankle at the fibula and swole one of his eyes shut. He broke two of your left ribs and gave you a concussion. Then the cops showed up and put your both in cuffs and separate squad cars. And that was it.

Gilda didn't fire you. But she did change the locks to the bar, and Meechie told you not to show up for work. You got a paycheck in the mail for a month, and then they stopped. That was when you knew for sure that you were on your own again. You didn't know if it was him or Gilda or both. You were hurt and paranoid and determined that the best move was for you to keep your distance. As long as it didn't turn up on your front doorstep, then it didn't exist.

That was when you and Khujo started doing your own thing. That was when Hancock and Nostrand became your place of business. That was when you started making the plans but leaving it to others to carry them out. It was safer that way. No feathers ruffled. No birds in the grease. And neither of you ended up with the white girl. You forgot until you had to remember.

Leaving Gilda without a pink slip felt like a punishment messengered direct from God's office. You didn't see the blessing to it all until you were back in your own city, running your own place and keeping what you did with your aura between you and Avery and a handful of others. Now your flight is making its descent toward JFK. Now you're going back to where all of this began 15 years before. Unlike the Bible you carry, there is no casing protecting you. And you know for sure that no one, absolutely no one, has forgotten who you are. And then you make the mistake of all mistakes. You start thinking about Jenna again.

You know where she is and you know what

she does and you know that she's married and has three girls and three different salons and a brownstone in Clinton Hill. There is no way that you will allow yourself to visit her, even though half of your being is screaming in a shrill soprano that you should.

CHAPTER ELEVEN

"Anything to declare?" the customs agent asks as you reach the front of the snaking line that now ends at the escalators.

You shake your head after handing him the appropriate forms. He seems to think nothing about your overstuffed shoulder bag and the metal case in your hands. Maybe this is because you look ridiculously good in a suit, or more likely that since you're neither vibrating, screaming, nor packing firearms, you're no threat to the United States of America.

JFK has changed in 15 years. It's all automated screens and holograms. In a few years even your food will be virtual or somehow pumped into your body via Wi-Fi. But with all the crowding and regulations since the Collective, a terrorist regime, blew up Newark Airport in protest of Donald Trump's second term, you're just happy to have landed free of fireballs and gunfire.

You are expecting Jelly and are maybe even hoping for her to be in something sheer and yoga-like again. At this juncture she is the only person you know who understands the world you're living in. You need to tell her about the shadow monster in London. You need to tell her about Rena and the night you had and all the worries that you have about being back in the five boroughs.

But you don't find Jelly waiting for you on the way to the baggage claim. The person holding the magic-markered card with your name on it is Shango, who, though now in his late 60s at the earliest, has shaved his beard and appears to have aged further in reverse.

"Kango!" he yells, with the Brooklyn bellowing all through his voice. He pulls you into a hug that is uncharacteristic for the man you knew, the man rumored to have disappeared on the same day that you did all those years ago back in '05. You are happy to see him.

"Last I heard you had a bag over your head somewhere," you say before he motions for you to tone it down.

"Not here," he says. "It doesn't take much for us to end up on a watch list."

You move casually out of the airport and into the parking deck where a GMC SUV is idling in a space underneath a beam tattooed with a red exit arrow. There's another unexpected face behind the wheel as you climb into the rear passenger seat. Brownie has turned all that was phat into muscle. But you can see the years on his face like circles in the stump of a chopped-down tree.

"'Sup, Kango," he says, puffing on a freshly rolled J. As weed is legal in New York, puffing outside an airport isn't an issue. He doesn't seem happy to see you. He just knows who you are.

"A lot of shit has changed around here," Shango says as Brownie shifts the ride into reverse. "It's still Brooklyn, but it ain't."

Brownie takes Conduit Avenue to Atlantic, and the first thing you notice is the height of the buildings. Brooklyn is now littered with skyscrapers, almost as many as you remember in the island borough across the river.

"All the bodegas are gone. They make the buildings taller and more narrow," Shango explains, "so they can use all the real estate in between. Nothing I didn't see coming, but it makes parking a bitch. You either have to use the underground garage that connects to all the subway stations or park on the outskirts and take a car in."

"So where we headed?" you ask. "How's my house?"

"The same," Brownie says. "I check on it. Khujo checks on it. But there's some people you need to go see first."

"Like who?" you ask.

Shango turns around in his seat to look you dead in the eye, flashing a mouth full of perfectly polished implants.

"Like our borough president," he says.

"You're joking, right?" you say.

"I am not," he replies. "The last time you saw him there was a blunt in the air."

There are bike paths all over. Some are elevated and others run parallel with the streets and intersections. Food trucks, carts, and stalls seems to be on every available piece of sidewalk, too many for any one person to be making a profit.

"The franchises own those now," Brownie explains when you ask. "The fast food joints buy them out so that they can stay open and save face. You can order stuff from the street guys and then eat it in their restaurants."

"But how can they get away with that with the health departments?"

"Maybe not anywhere else," Shango says, taking a pull off of Brownie's J. They both offer the weed to you but you wave them off. "Here the health inspectors started disappearing."

You barely recognize Flatbush Avenue south of Grand Army Plaza. A good chunk of it has been eaten by the Romulan spaceship-looking Barclays Center. Long gone is the cheap furniture place where you bought that first platform bed that you and Jenna split in half. There is no more Modell's or the Dunkin' Donuts, but Livingston and BAM look the same. The strangest part is the way cars cut over one lane to the right or left and literally sink into the mechanized entrances to the parking garages Shango had mentioned.

Brownie cuts from Livingston to Joralemon to Court Street and pulls right up to a city valet parking area. He scans his ID over a holographic kiosk, and the kid in the red jacket drives the SUV into its own sinking hole. The first question in your mind is "Who in the fuck would give Brownie a security clearance?" Your question is answered one elevator ride, two metal detectors, and one DNA sample later.

Joshua Bandoola Alexis has done a lot of things since the last time you saw him in Harlem. And his secretary is a tiny Czech girl in Jacques Molino spectacles who is quietly singing along to the Drake song on her stereo. According to the brief holographic biography playing in front of said receptionist, Josh made over ten million farming marijuana in Massachusetts, Colorado, and Maine before becoming a campaign strategist.

He managed to make it for over a decade without ever being photographed or mentioned in any kind of press as he funneled resources into various red and blue state campaigns, remaining as bipartisan as possible while bringing the right people together and making all the right connections.

But when you see him after 15 years, about 30 pounds heavier and with salt-and-pepper hair doing the moonwalk, you're at a loss for words.

"I bet you didn't expect to see me here, huh, Kango?" he asks as you and Shango take a seat. Brownie posts up by the door, doing his best impression of a Secret Service agent.

"Can't say I did," you reply. "I owe you two grand."

"No, you don't," he says. "That was just to wet your whistle. Had you done what I wanted you to do, then you probably would've brought the Arsonists out of hiding sooner."

"The Arsonists?" you ask, confused.

"I guess you wouldn't know about it unless you knew about it. Your old neighborhood might as well be Mars," he explains. "The Head Wraps are on the ropes. You got these young kids fucking around with all this fire magic. Explosions with no explosives. They're taking it to the streets like it's some kind of Che Guevara revolution. They want to bring the old Brooklyn back. They tag a building with an image of the Notorious B.I.G. and then it goes up in smoke, even with a full cop detail all around it. Thing is, most of them aren't even old enough to remember Biggie."

"So what does that have to do with me?" you ask.

"They want you to come out of hiding," he says.

"Why?" you ask.

"Because somebody is telling them to," Shango says. "Somebody who wants you back in Brooklyn. Shooting at you at a restaurant and nobody gets hit. But in less than a day your ass is in London chasing down what they can't get."

"I got the book," you say.

"Yeah, and you'll get all three," Josh says as if it's a given. "What you don't know is what the books do."

"Very few people do," Shango adds. "Each book is like a decoder wheel. They're all marked up to create a coded list of coordinates to open a portal."

"Okay," you say, less than convinced. "I've been gone a long time, but from what I know, nothing opens portals but lasers and bulldozers."

"But you did see that thing in London, right? The shit that's all over YouTube. The ten-foot shadow that vanished into thin air over Brixton? It opens its own doors in *this* world. What the coordinates create are a different opening, a wormhole moving backward fifteen years in time."

"Excuse me," you say. "I don't smoke weed anymore, so I know I'm not trippin'. But what the fuck are you talking about?"

"You know how I know it's real?" Shango says. "Because I've been through one. I've been going through them a few times a year since the last time you saw me, looking for shortcuts back to 2005. The Arsonists want to go back and stop the whole real estate revolution. They want to go back in time and prevent the Brooklyn real estate boom from ever happening."

"And Gilda's caught up in this?"

"Just as much as you are," Josh explains. "The Dunbar job. The masks you stole. She used five of them to create five separate identities. She backstopped them with photos, Social Security numbers, shell corporations, the whole deal, and then stole the money to buy it all out from Brooklyn. She literally owns the city now, with every Head Wrap in existence filling their bellies with crumbs from her table."

"This is a lot," you say. "I know what I saw

and I might even be willing to believe in this portal shit, but time travel?"

"Everything is a circle, man. Everyone you touched before you left got either killed or elevated. Everything got brought into order. People like those Twins you used to see are billionaires now. Out of sight. Out of rotation. They're not looking for $20 tips to tell the future anymore. They're holed up at the top of the Brooklyn clock tower looking down on everybody else.

"I have to see this to believe it," you say.

"I know you do," he says. "I know you have to find your way here, get plugged back in. But the minute you hit the streets is when it starts."

"Why me?" you ask.

"Because Jim Nabors has been chief of police for four years, and he's been trying to run all the Head Wraps out of New York. He's using city codes and ordinances to outlaw their practice, which is cutting the worlds on the top and on the bottom off from all the people who know how to really read energy.

"They can't just be doing this shit out in the open," you say. "I mean, the Constitution and the Bill of Rights should keep things from getting out of hand."

"You're talking like you ain't lived through the last 40 years, like you don't know the history of shit, like what you know how to do is as normal as sweet potato pie on Turkey Day."

"Look, I got paid to bring something up here."

"Yeah, you want your money and you wanna go home," Josh snarks. "You know that song by heart, don't you?"

You want to tell him to go fuck himself, but he is the borough president and you are in his office, and he's probably right. But you have a different vantage point now. You live somewhere else. You have people to look after, not street people either, a family.

"There's a lot of history you need to find," Shango says. "Because if you don't believe it, then the shit you do won't be real."

"Why give a fuck about time travel? Why not let the kids just do what they want to do?"

"And have the world change all around us, with most of us not even realizing that there was a shift. And don't try and say that this is a white people problem. When are you finally gonna soldier up and do something other than get laid and paid?"

"It worked for Doug E. Fresh," you say. But no one in the room laughs. That voice at the back of your head calls you an asshole, and you can't really argue.

"I wanted you to come here first so you could know that you have a friend in a high place. I can get you out of anything under kidnapping or murder. I can get you a permit for a weapon. I can get you access to most of the info you're looking for. But I can't be on the street. The street has too much on me now. And I'm too visible. Truthfully, if this goes right, you shouldn't set foot in this office again."

"I need a drink," you say.

Brownie laughs, breaking his silence. "We were expecting that."

"Wes, Raheem, and Michele still around?" you ask.

Shango grins. "Things ain't changed that much."

Frank's Bar and Lounge in Fort Greene still stands, though there are fifteen stories' worth of condos on top of it. It was declared a historical landmark after the Fulton Street Massacre, when 100 Black protesters took refuge there and held out. The Alt Right declared war on Black Brooklyn and were allowed to run rampant by the NYPD as a revenge act for the payout on the Central Park Five civil suit. You, Shango, and Brownie now drink where Black people died just a few years before. The developers wanted to level the place, but Josh and some other folks apparently took a stand. The bartender is the same, with that same loose-fitting doll hair wig that shifts to the right and left when she turns her head. The damn thing really needs a chin strap. She's slow at the bar and now in her 70s—it might be time for Miss Mable to retire.

"You keep acting like this doesn't have anything to do with you," Shango says after taking the last of his shot of Hennessy to the head. His eyes are bloodshot, like he's on the verge of breathing fire. "But it's all about you and all about us. Maybe you walked out of that basement. Maybe you told the Head Wrap to go to hell for your own reasons, but that doesn't mean that you don't have the knowledge, that you ain't a muthafucka that needs to do something other than rob and steal and move through walls."

"This shit feels like peer pressure," you say. "I ain't Huey Newton or Malcolm."

"But you can get the right doors open," he says. "You can help keep these books away from the Arsonists."

"Why didn't I just leave the damn Bible where it was?" you ask.

"That ain't for me to answer," Shango says. "That answer lies with you."

There are no pretty girls in the place. And there is no DJ, just a holographic jukebox with a holographic remote strapped to Miss Mable's wrists. And it's playing LaVern Baker's "Soul on Fire," a track so old school that you weren't even alive when they cut it in the studio.

"Where's Jelly?" you asked Shango, ignoring the subject. Your back is to the front door and your reflection in the bar mirror is warped, so you don't see her when she walks up behind you. But you know she's there.

"Damn, nigga, you got fat," Khujo remarks. You are 15.6 pounds heavier than the last time she saw you. And she would be the only one to notice.

There are many strands of silver in the massive Afro bouncing above her shoulders. And she's wearing a vintage motorcycle jacket that makes her look a little like N'Bushe Wright in

Dead Presidents. All she needs is the face paint. She takes a seat on the stool at your left, and a whiskey appears in front of her that Miss Mable did not pour. She hasn't been to your side of the bar in close to 20 minutes, which is slightly annoying because you could use a refill.

"So how much you tell him?" Khujo asks Shango and Brownie, as if you're not sitting right next to her.

"He don't believe us," Brownie says, taking a sip of his ice water with lemon.

"So the Black power revolutionary change they predicted didn't happen, huh?" she snorts, throwing a comical fist up in the air. "I didn't think it would. We just gonna have to push him along. But he'll stop fronting when she show him the setup."

"Who's getting set up?" you asks. The three of them laugh like you're the punch line.

"It's not a thing." Khujo smiles. "It's a place."

Everything at the corner of Franklin and Fulton is different. There is no Popeye's, or the Jamaican place doubling as a health food store and weed spot. The laundromat, the 99-Cent Store, and the Goodwill are all as extinct as the bones of some pterodactyl suspended high above the patron floor of some dinosaur exhibit. The condos are 20 to 30 stories high, but if you strain your neck looking upward you can still glimpse the thick clouds concealing the quarter moon in the night sky.

Franklin Avenue station is now a multilevel compound made of transparent aluminum and recycled steel. The sidewalks are thin, while there are two lanes for bicycles and four lanes for traffic. Under the elevator train tracks traveling all the way down Franklin Avenue toward Williamsburg, you sink Brownie's SUV into an underground space and then climb the thin spiral staircase back to the street across the street from Franklin Library and Media Center, another building that has maintained its former façade while being surrounded by the clean, homogenous gadgetry of a brave new world.

"What the fuck is this?" you say to yourself.

"This is the new Brooklyn," Khujo huffs. "Ain't it grand?"

You travel down the pencil-thin alley between the library and a subway exit to find an iron door with a retinal scanner. Shango puts his eye to the device, and the huge door swings open, coldly welcoming you all to whatever awaits on the other side.

The first thing you pick up on is elevated heart rates and raised breathing, like what an aerobics class might sound like without the loud music on top of it. The lighting down the short corridor is limited, only two bulbs, one in need of a change, flickering overhead. Then you enter a wash of light that's a cross between a library and a martial arts dojo.

A massive white boy in his early 20s with a baby face swings a metal folding chair at a tiny woman of 4'11" holding the warrior one position. The chain breaks into pieces against her hunter green aura. A hefty thirtysomething brother in a wheelchair sits before a massive hologram mainframe monitoring video surveillance, data uploads, and downloads and is flipping through pages upon pages of text written in what appears to be Aramaic script. And Jelly and her child are at the center of the room, going through a basic series of sun salutations.

"These are the Asanas," Shango announces, as if you asked. "Like I said before, the neighborhood done changed."

"This ain't everybody," Khujo says. "A few folks are still out and about."

Jelly and her kid interrupt the series and come over. The little girl looks just like her. The last time you saw her she was barely two, playing with one of those gadget boards they give to toddlers to teach them all about their senses.

"You don't remember Kango, Nubia," she begins. "But he was one of my very first students."

"Is he who we've been waiting for?" she asks.

"He's going to help us," she explains before she turns to you. "Did you bring the book?"

You hold up the metal box under your left arm like it's nothing particularly special.

"Come over on over. I'll introduce you to everyone."

The "team" is introduced to you one by one, but you don't make note of names. The big metal box is handed over to the dude in the wheelchair who speaks like her and was born and bred in the Stuy. Such is not the case with the white girl and little Indian chick. Shango and Brownie are too quiet and Khujo isn't saying much at all. You were expecting something else when you came back here. Maybe not a parade or some kind of embrace as community messiah, but the architects have built a world on top of everything you knew before. What was once your home has now become a part of history. Are you history as well?

So many things have been said to you that seem incredibly ridiculous. It's a common fact that every human has an aura level, but all of this talk about portals and young pyros looking to burn down the world so they can bring back an era they weren't even there for? But the rabbit hole of your thought process travels even deeper.

Your mind doesn't feel any different than it was at 25. But you are no longer the dude who does pull-ups in his apartment bedroom doorway or who eats nothing but greasy takeout because he knows his metabolism will solve everything. You are so haunted by all that you've processed so far: Your very last client in the Brooklyn game is now a borough president. Shango is older but looks younger. Brownie is trusted by people more powerful than you with responsibility that you yourself would have never given him. And Khujo used to be your main girl, but she's been living life day to day without you for close to a generation.

And there's this heartbreak that still hurts, not just the ghost of Jenna and your mistake, but despite all the time that has passed, DC is still grounded in what you grew up around, even with all the people of color living on the outskirts instead of being pumped through the veins of the heart of the city. The place where you live, the house you still own and collect rent from, is less than two blocks from this underground lair where you currently stand. The smell of some serious ground coffee beans hits the air, a living metaphor for the reality at the pit of your gut that somehow inspires nausea.

"You cool, dude?" Khujo asks as she steps into your field of vision.

"I don't know," you say. Then the white girl speaks.

"He didn't expect the changes," she says. "He misses his home."

"You don't have to speak for me," you argue.

"She's an empath," Jelly interrupts, putting a hand on your shoulder that you allow. Her energy melds with yours while she winces. "It's intense. You should sit down."

A folding chair is planted under your ass and you fall back into it. This group named after yoga positions forms a loose circle around you, reminding you of a ring shout or a Baptist prayer meeting or that time at the parties back in the day when the DJ would put the house cuts on and the best dancers would enter the center to freestyle.

"You can't be afraid," she says. "They will know your fear. It's their fear that draws them to you."

"Who?" you ask.

"The Arsonists," Shango answers. "They blame *us* for this."

"But we didn't have shit to do with real estate prices," you argue. "We were just trying to get our money right."

"You had the eyes to see it but you didn't know how to use them," Jelly says. "There was a chance to stop Nabors. But you left town."

"He ain't really have a choice," Khujo argues. "I was there. We weren't some kind of army. We weren't even the street soldiers."

"All they know is what they hear and what YouTube tells them happened. The rappers didn't even rap about it. They were all so caught up in the champagne and the record sales, and they thought that part of it was gonna last forever."

"Is this a fucking PSA? When does the voice-over come in?"

"This is serious, Kango," the little Indian chick chimes in.

"And what the fuck do you know about Brooklyn," you all but yell, becoming the biggest hypocrite in the room because you were never born there. You had no more claim to the town then than she does now.

"I don't want to upset you," she says. "But you're important to us."

"What's your name, girl?" you demand.

"Fatima," she says, "and I was born in Bushwick."

"He's taking on more feelings than he should," the white girl says. "He doesn't have a frame of reference. He's traumatized."

You need this little intervention to be over.

"Look, you got your fuckin' book! Now I want my fuckin' money!"

You are now aware that the words have come out at megaphone volume, that the depth and intensity of your voice have sent a literal shock-wave through the room. Right then you just want to beam back to Caramel City, where you run your fucking restaurant and nobody both-ers you. The problem is that that life doesn't do anything for you either.

"I would tell you to calm down," Shango says, "but this is part of the process. You're back here after all of this time, but you ain't a slave on a ship. You can go where you want and do what you want. The clock is ticking on this thing, but no one has taken any rights away from you. If you walk out to that door you came in through, none of us is gonna stop you."

"Anyone could have taken a key out of a book and locker, but nobody else could get past what you saw in there."

"What's so special about me?" you ask.

"You know him," Khujo says.

"I know the ten-foot-tall shadow monster," you say. "Lemme guess, we went to high school together? This is bullshit!" Then you pop up out of the chair like a gopher out of a hole. Then you start for the door, following Shango's ad-vice.

"Whatever you do, don't go home, dude," Khujo yells after you. "That's the biggest mis-take you can make."

Other words hit your back like arrows. But your ears are underwater now. You need a drink. You need a smoke. Maybe you need to chase some more answers. But whatever answers you thought you'd find in Brooklyn are not in this library, in this block, or in this futuristic dystopian version of what used to be a regular-ass hood. It's time for you to go back downtown.

CHAPTER TWELVE

It hasn't all changed, but it's even more of a struggle to see all the stars in the sky. You travel north up Franklin, past the monstrosity of a new transit center, squeezing down the narrow gully between the rows of never-ending condos and luxury apartments. The Brooklyn Armory still stands, but it's been encased in some kind of bronzing, not unlike what parents used to do with baby shoes. It is now another piece of history to be observed by the millennials who now sit on the throne that used to belong to you. There is a statue memorial for Eric Garner, Sean Bell, Amadou Diallo, Yusef Hawkins, and a number of other police shooting victims. It's made of solid granite, a fountain that creates the illusion of a stream of water jumping from one victim statue to the next while four stone NYPD officers stand with their guns raised, even though Garner died in a choke hold. In this Brooklyn the facts no longer matter, only the general and vague idea of things that used to be.

You should not be wearing leather casuals with a thin sole for this kind of walk. Your feet will hurt soon, but in truth pain is the least of your worries. You turn onto Atlantic, moving away from the Stuy. Traffic is gridlocked for miles in both directions, backed up like a sink with a whole onion stuck in the drain because of that whole Barclay mess, which now broadcasts holographic highlights from the Nets game inside and announces concerts to come including Stevie Wonder, a St. Lunatics reunion tour, and the white Jack Johnson, whose name you always treat as stolen from the Mos Def Black rock enclave, though this is not the truth. It's your own prejudice that makes you want to hate this Wonderland of new, until you finally start to rub shoulders with the old.

You are standing in front of Barclays itself, glaring over at the Pathmark supermarket where you used to shop for steaks and fine seafood because the offerings in the old neighborhood sucked. The grocery itself is still the same, as are the Target shopping center and the Brooklyn clock tower, which is no longer the tallest and most visible edifice in the borough.

Instead of P.C. Richard there is a rollerblading rink with an island at its center featuring a performance by none other than Meshell Ndegeocello. You would think the show was free if you didn't see the electronic turnstiles where a spiraling line circling the place struggles for standing room only. That woman has made a mint off "Faithful" by now, and the soundtracks, and the ringtone, but you still try to imagine her early on when she played for the go-go bands back in DC, or when she did that show at Roseland where she didn't even hit the stage until 1:00 a.m. And people stayed, and they loved, not because she sold the most records, but because she could play her ass off and she was always herself and that was always enough to feed her in times fat and slim. You wished that you had been that kind of an artist, that what you did at the open mics and in the grimy-ass studios and for the those few little papers and blogs you wrote for had mattered enough so you didn't have to steal for a living, or help other people steal, whichever shade of those realities you choose to embrace in the given moment.

The acoustics are good and the muted hologram flashing on and off every few minutes gives an added accent even though the sound system is small and the passing traffic on Flatbush Avenue makes the acoustics shitty. You wonder why she's playing a roller rink when she should be at the Brooklyn Academy of Music across the street. But for all you know, that whole thing might be a coffee bar on the inside. The food truck and stalls are barricaded from traffic on the other side of the concert. You can smell grilled marinated beef, pork ribs, lamb, and raw vegetable kabobs on the meat-free grill that make up the majority of that fleet at the corner of your field of vision. You would only come down this way to shop or when you and

Jenna wanted ice cream or movies to rent of whatever the hell you couldn't get back there. Now back there is no different than here. And you just don't know where to go. But you have to press on. You start toward the Manhattan Bridge, telling yourself that you'll turn onto Tillery and cross the Brooklyn Bridge into Manhattan, though your feet are fucking laughing at you. You can't run that far. So you take the right onto Dekalb instead and go back into Fort Greene.

On your way up Dekalb, with the hospital and Fort Greene Park on your left, you see the building where Carol's Daughter, the natural beauty supply place, used to be. On top of it is the bed-and-breakfast where you and Jenna would rent rooms every once in a while because it had this ridiculously large claw-foot bathtub in it. She'd go down to the store and come up with these jars of salts and packs of candles and you'd just chill in the hot water in the dead of winter, the whole second floor to yourself, with the lady who ran it bringing up your meals. There was no weed, but Jenna would bring a bottle of Appleton Estate and her iPod and the two of you would go to town.

"Kango?" a voice asks. You can't believe Chee looks so much the same after so many years. He was in this underground group Oblique Brown and they had this song called "Four More Years" that you used to love.

He was nice, the first Indian dude you ever knew who could flow. Had a doctorate but still made tracks for his fans. You always respected that. He pulls you into a hug you might reserve for family.

"Yo, I heard a rumor that you was ghost," he begins. "Like really ghost, like dead. You and Shango just up and disappeared on the world."

"Well, it wasn't no conspiracy," you say. "We ain't do it together."

"Nah, I've seen since. Him and those yoga muthafuckas be keepin' the peace around here."

"You sound like they're the Justice League or some shit," you reply.

"Might as well be," he says. "Those little Arsonists fuckers have been a pain in the ass for the nightlife. They burn down shit just for fun. Class 6s with daddy issues is what I say."

"You know 6s," you reply. "They never give a fuck."

"So you back, man, or what?" he asks, taking a pull from his vape, holding his words so that the cloud inside can hit the air slowly.

"Nah, man," you say. "I'm just here to make a drop and check on my place. I'll be out again in a day or two."

He looks disappointed, like he wanted to have you over for dinner for or something.

"Damn, man, I wish you were here longer. I know some folks that could use a Class 7."

"Well, I'm trying to stay out of the spotlight these days," you say humbly. "You wanna grab a drink now?"

He grins. "I already had a few over at the Hitching Post," he says. "But fuck it. Let's roll. Where you wanna hit?"

"I don't even understand this place no more. You lead the way."

And he does just that.

The walk up Dekalb in the autumn cool is energizing. Brooklyn Hospital has doubled in size and has become yet another stack of transparent bricks complete with a double helipad and a parking deck almost as tall as the hospital building itself. South Portland and South Oxford seem untouched by the metamorphosis that has you walking the streets like the star of a *Hookers at the Point* special. Chee says something about slowing it down, that he feels like you're going for a gold medal or something.

Madiba, the South African joint that had become Fort Greene's Cheers for the young, hip, and dangerous, now has a 24-hour spa on top of it. It seems counterintuitive that one would have a heavy meal and then want to get in a hot tub or sauna, but doing it the other way around actually sounds kinda nice.

"You wanna hit Madiba?" Chee asks. You shake your head. You've been there and done that, and you don't miss it. Fort Greene still looks the same, even with the bike paths and all the Lego stacking, until you arrive at Heaven's Prisoners, just west of Washington Ave. You are shocked that it's still standing. It was the only place on that block that stayed open until four on weeknights. And it doesn't look too crowded.

"This is it," you tell Chee. You and he switch chairs and you step into the pilot's seat.

The bartender looks around 50, with a salt-and-pepper beard and Welsh features. He pours you a Jameson and Chee a vodka tonic. And then, in the name of drinking and a good playlist, the good times begin. The first song you remember coming on is the Family Stand's "Ghetto Heaven," then it switches to Mike's "P.Y.T.," James Brown's "Hot Pants." Then it goes hip-hop. Chubb Rock's "Yabadabadoo," M.O.P.'s "Hardcore," and back-to-back Jigga with "Imaginary Player" and "U Don't Know." Bobby Womack's "Across 110th Street" wanders out of the speakers and then Tribe's "Sucka Nigga," and after that you lose count. The shots hit you in waves with the water backs receding the tide.

"I missed this fuckin' place," you say, directing the words at Chee, but instead they catch the attention of a little biracial who barely looks old enough to be in the place.

"Where have you been?" she asks.

"DC," you say.

"Doing what?" she asks.

"I have a restaurant," you say.

"What kind of food do you serve?" she asks. You feel the rhythm, and you know the beat, but the last thing you need is another interlude. What you need, right now, in the middle of all of this avoidance and on-the-lam behavior, is a really dope album, a man/woman experience with a variety of moods and movements, a treatise about two people trying to find their way in the world together and not just into one's bed. The youth and inexperience, and the scent of classic thirst reading off an aura that might be a 2 on its best day, encourage you to keep this conversation brief and polite. You understand here what women your age mean when they see guys in their 40s with women in their 20s. She truly is still a child. And you hate talking about your restaurant.

"African American fusion," you say.

"What's it called?" she asks.

"The Queen and Country," you say.

"Are you British?" she asks, as if your Southern American Negro accent is a made-up invention and you actually talk like Idris Elba.

"No," you reply. "I named it after one of Denzel's first movies when he was playing a British soldier who comes home to live in the projects where he grew up."

"I've never heard of that one," she says. "And my mom and grandma have seen all of his movies." That line would be the erection killer, if you had one.

"It came out in '88," you say. "But excuse me. I need to use the restroom."

You can only fully gauge the state of your sobriety when your feet are planted firmly on the ground. And when you land, said sobriety is a few hours, a half gallon of water, and a meal away. Each step to the men's room reminds you of this, and there's enough in your bladder to produce a healthy stream.

You get the door to the one-person john open and closed and feel the waters sprint forth like Moses pointing his staff at that rock in Exodus. And then, at the most inconvenient of times, your phone rings, your phone and not the work one in your bag that's either back in Brownie's truck at the yoga-infused hall of justice of a library light-years away from the here and now. You answer midstream, almost dropping the device into the commode, but you save it with a flat and open palm. Then a hologram of Rena jumps out of it. Luckily you're holding it above the waistline.

"I wasn't sure if you really even wanted me to call you," she says with that universal look of female dissatisfaction on her face, the one that says that it's beneath her to call a man who left her in a strange apartment without a word after they'd just had sex. Even drunk you can't argue that your actions were anything close to Prince Valiant.

"I had a lot on my mind," you say. "Things moved kind of fast."

"Are you going to pretend that you didn't want it? Because you pressed pretty fucking hard to get it."

"I wouldn't say I pressed," you reply.

"I would," she says. "Now zip up and talk to me."

There is something incredibly surprising about this turn of events. It's not so much that you thought about her in the face of Lolita outside, but it's that you're actually happy to see her. You lose your footing and stumble back a step. And this has nothing to do with the liquor. You do as you're told and zip.

"I'll expect a hand wash when convenient," she says. She is in her concierge clothes, possibly at work, possibly just off.

You switch modes on the phone so that it's audio only and take it back out into the bar that now seems like it's packed to the brim. So you shoulder your way out the front door and continue your conversation on the street.

"Where are you?" she asks.

"Brooklyn," you say. "Fort Greene."

"Is Madiba still there?" she asks.

"How come everybody knows Madiba?" you reply.

"Because that's where all the cool people go."

You lean against the brick outside the bar and then slide down to a sitting position.

"I didn't know that you'd ever been to Brooklyn," you say.

"You barely know anything about me." She laughs. "Do you really want to know more?"

"I left my number, didn't I?"

"That was passive-aggressive at best," she says. "It was a great night, love. But it was just one night. It's okay if your head was somewhere else."

You allow yourself to embrace the memories of what is barely a day old but now seems so much further away.

"I would have stayed, but I had a job to finish," you say. There is more truth in this statement, though you intended for it to be comfortably ambiguous.

"Is that what motivates you the most? Your job?"

"Is that sarcasm or a real question," you say back to her. Her aura is so dense that you can't penetrate it. You don't really know her intentions. You have to feel your way through.

"I don't know you," she says. "But I want to. So I'm asking."

"The job is always easy," you say. "Everything is hard. You follow the instructions and you take the hits when shit goes bad. In the job there are no feelings involved."

"Did someone hurt you? Or was it someone you hurt?"

"Are you working the night shift? I saw you had your uniform on."

"Don't dodge the question, mister. It's unbecoming of a real Black man."

"I take it that you've dealt with a lot of fake Black dudes?"

"It's trial and error with you people, no matter which country you're in."

"That makes you sound like a world traveler for love."

"I get where I need to go," she says.

"I wish you were here right now," you say. Is this the liquor? It has to be the liquor.

"Don't tempt my ability to problem solve," she says. "Look, I know you're out and about and very under the influence, but I want you to call me back. Don't be afraid of me. I'm not afraid of you."

"I don't know what to say." You exhale.

"You don't have to say anything," she says. "I'll let you talk more the next time." Then she does both the most fucked-up and the sexiest thing she could ever do. She hangs up on you.

You lock her number into the phone and place her on your priority call list. Then you upload the data file directly to the cloud, just to make sure you don't lose it.

There is a tingling in your hands and feet as you are engulfed in a warm red. Everything in your world is a single color. You think of heat. You think of blood. You think of passion. But it still takes you a few minutes to get back to your feet.

Back inside, you order up a trio of club sodas as a discussion unfolds about whether or not they're going to put tolls on all of the bridges.

"They'll get away with it this time," Lolita argues. "This city has more debt than a hundred times its population."

"I don't know," the bartender argues, "Cardi B swears to God that if she wins this election she'll put a stop to it."

"You got a lot of faith in a woman who used to be on the pole," the guy with the beard next to Chee argues.

"Jesus was on the pole for a while too," says a man wearing a priest's collar and raising a snifter of Hennessy. "And look what he did when he got off."

"I never expected to hear that analogy," you say. Then the entire bar erupts with laughter.

It's well after midnight when the discussion ends and the music gets turned back up. Chee looks at the time and accepts his fate that it's finally time to go home to his wife.

"I said I wouldn't be home for dinner, but this is the doghouse hour." There is no better statement for a buzzkill. The bar fleet breaks up. Chee heads back down Dekalb toward parts unknown and you hang a left on Washington, heading straight for Kum Kau.

Once the most respected Chinese carry-out in Brooklyn, Kum Kau is now a dining experience. In addition to the take-out business, they bought what used to be the Five Spot across the street and have a dine-in service with 100 tables and live music. It's only 400 capacity, but from the line outside you would think it was Madison Square Garden. A female voice can be heard through the small speaker outside the doorway. She is singing an acoustic version of Maxwell's "This Woman's Work," a cover of a cover. Her voice is a softest soprano with only the guitar and brush snare underneath. She makes you think of Rena, and of the night before, and maybe your momentary freedom from the sense of doom you've felt hanging over your head for years while you wait for something to happen. Now everything's happening. It makes you smile as you wander into the carry-out to place your order.

A small chicken with broccoli and a quart of lemonade iced tea mix will take fifteen minutes of your life to be ready. You plan to sit and listen to the conversations of others waiting: the minutiae of their cell phone chats or maybe the way the white guy holds the cute Vietnamese girl who fits perfectly in his lanky arms. But there is no more time for poetic observation. Your phone rings again. It's Avery.

"Avery is geeked!" he begins. "The mayor was in here tonight."

"Like the mayor of the city? Bowser? When does she ever cross the river?"

"Well, she was in here tonight with her whole crew. They bought out the bar, cleaned out the fridge. We might have to shut down for a day just to restock."

Instantly you are a legit businessman again filled with managerial expertise.

"No, don't do that. Spend the money and get fresh everything as quick as you can. We'll have a mob for the lunch rush."

"Why do you say that?" he asks, sounding high on something beyond life. There are female voices in the background. And then there is Buster. And then a champagne cork pops. The party has once again gone on without you.

"Kevin Durant and now the mayor? When it rains it pours."

"You gotta get back here, man. We're George and Weezie about to hit the East Side."

"And I thought we were already there," you say. "But look, I'm about to eat and take my ass to bed, though I'm not sure where."

"What happened to Jelly and her crew? Your money came in, by the way. All 61K."

"It's supposed to be 60," you say.

"Avery thinks that's a good thing."

"Avery and Buster need to make sure nobody nuts where food is either prepared or eaten."

Avery chuckles. "Roger that. Later."

"Later."

First a homegrown basketball star and now the mayor. The Queen and Country is moving up in the world and you're moving backward, gearing up for Chinese takeout in a neighborhood that is no longer yours. Irony is reigning supreme tonight.

You get your food and dump the white rice because you don't need the extra carbs. And you don't need the sugar either, but fuck it. You cross the intersection, barely avoid a rogue cab running a red light, and say hello to old friends.

There is an ache at the center of your skull, a combination of fatigue and jet lag. The soles of your feet feel raw, and you don't know where to go. So much is unclear, and all you know is the terrain. Then you look across the intersection of Myrtle and you see three men standing there on the corner, sharing a pint of something brown with fresh plastic cups to boot. It's Wes, Raheem, and Michele. And they are wearing camouflage ponchos. Then the once-clear sky above darkens, and it begins to rain.

"Well, look who it is," Raheem says. "Gilda said you wouldn't be around for a while."

"Since when does Gilda come down to talk to you?" you ask.

"Boy, everybody talks to us. We always look out for our friends," Raheem says.

"See what they done to all of this here," Wes adds. "We told you it was comin'."

"How come y'all are way over here and not back down the way," you ask, giving each of them a pound of dap delayed by the new rain. But the falling water doesn't bother you.

"We are always where it's about to be," Michele finishes, as cryptic as ever. The years show on their faces and in their stances. Time has passed and they have continued to keep it moving.

"Water and fire. That's why they call this firewater," Raheem says, downing his shot before pouring himself a little more, but leaving plenty for the others. "It's *Clash of the Titans* out here. You ready?"

"I don't know what I'm ready for," you say.

"Sure you do," Wes says. "Ain't nobody told you no lies. You just ain't seen the whole picture yet. It's not the same people and same shit. It's new people and old shit."

"Other players in the game," Michele continues. "Other camps. Other factions. Trying to pull out the weeds before they choke down the plants. All under one God."

"What does this have to do with me?" you ask.

"You think people forget about you, but nobody forgets," Wes continues. "They prioritize. You roll out for a while and that's one less thing they got to worry about. But now you back, and you think it's a different crew but it's the same crew. You lay them out seven in the street and they just multiply.

"They don't know truth. They don't know peace. They just get more guys and they keep coming at you. You see them in town, and you see them out of town. They get word that you're about to be somebody and they want their taste of the cake. You gotta pay the price and you gotta pay the toll."

"Who are the Arsonists?" you ask.

"They're the kids, the young bucks who think they just figured out the world was round," Wes adds. "And they swear to God that they can do it better than you even when all they got is a license to thrill and not kill."

"You spent all this time thinkin' about Gilda and her moving in on what you got planned," Raheem snorts, at the bottom of his cup again. "But Gilda's got the cake and connections. She's got a bullseye on her back way bigger than the one on yours."

"Are you saying that she's not the reason why I had to leave?"

"What we're saying is that Gilda's the only reason that you're still alive," Michele erupts. "There's a difference between clipping your wings and pulling you off the nipples before it's too late. You were running around like Tom Cruise in *The Color of Money*, beating people at their own game. You were a lightning strike liable to get someone else cooked."

"Sixes get to the point, but Sevens end the war," Wes says, folding his arms. The rain intensifies. Now you're starting to feel soaked.

Then there's a rumbling under your feet, accented by sirens hitting the air. Multiple police cruisers shoot down Washington and Clinton and all the streets in between. They zip by one after the other, cutting through the rain like blades.

"And the cops are a gang unto themselves," Raheem says, shaking his head.

"They're headed for the Navy Yard, aren't they?" you ask.

"And you wonder why they needed you to come back."

Kum Kau's chicken with broccoli is nourishment for the soul. You walk and then begin to run, chasing after New York's finest like a Dalmatian after a fire engine. There is no cramping from digestion. There is no fear of what to do next. It's almost like you've been here before. The only thing you don't know is what or who started the whole thing.

CHAPTER THIRTEEN

Everyone becomes a leader once somebody follows them. And once you follow someone, by default you start to figure out how to be either a good or a bad leader. There are rules to this shit, there's a hierarchy, and when you're young and bright and angry you think that you can take parts out of the machine and no one will notice. One wheel keeps another turning. One circuit connects to the next to the next, all on the same motherboard. If one thing goes out of whack, the whole thing does.

Gilda had a lot of respect for you. You were young and from out of town, and that made you naïve about the ties that bind, not just by blood or lineage or circumstance, but the fact that we all eat, breathe, and shit in the same air. What one person does ends up in the other person's backyard, and sometimes to keep the peace in a house, things have to go. It's not always official either, and it damn sure ain't personal. But if a cop gets a badge and a gun, he's not only bound by the rules that come with it, but he's protected by all the other cops who took the same oath. So when a call comes in with the right code or designation, every blue and white makes a beeline to the destination, trying to lend a hand. And whether you're friend or foe to their mission, if you have no cruiser and you have no badge, you're always going to end up a step behind the whole game.

You ask yourself why you are running toward the cop cars. Why don't you just head back toward what you know? The answer is simple and doesn't require any rambling in poetic prose. You are sick and tired of being on the outside, tired of making up excuses for why you shouldn't be a part of the game. You picked up bad habits that wouldn't let go of you. And now it's finally time that you pried them loose.

You can see all the brake lights from the cop cars once you turn onto Flushing. And you can see that the island, Gilda's tiny little piece in the work, where you took the "sink or swim" test and passed with flying colors, is on fire. And it's not just a small fire. The whole damn thing is burning to ash, lighting up the night for at least two different boroughs. You feel the blisters forming between big toe and insole. But you keep moving toward it, somehow knowing that the answers you've sought all of this time are down there somewhere.

You can see the barricade going up and the

signal flares, but as a pedestrian it's easy to stick to the shadows and be unnoticed. You walk under the elevated freeway until the island is in view. There are other people down there, more than you might have expected. They're surrounding what appears to be a red SUV with someone standing on top of it all.

You turn corners and walk between spaces, closing the gap between you and them. The NYPD has their guns drawn, and the megaphones are out calling for surrender. But what can the cops do against a bunch of teens and twentysomethings with their auras covered in flame? And their king is standing above them wearing a gleaming crown on his head not unlike those air fresheners the players put at the backs of their cars in the Deep South and the West. Their king is a man you know, a man you fought once. You beamed with pride when you broke his leg at the ankle, and when you stole him in the face until his eye swole shut over some damn white girl so long ago that you have to think about it to remember her name. The girl that lied and brought all of this into being. The Pillsbury Doughboy is now the head of his own little army. And he has that right, because he's a made guy. You were just the Class 7 fucking up the game for him.

The dots connect like pixels on a screen. The whole thing at the Drummer's Circle wasn't as much a threat as a means to keep the peace, because they knew what you were and they knew what they owed you from the minute they opened up the books and gave you a key to all the secrets of that thing of theirs, that "Head Wrap" thing, as you and Khujo describe it jokingly.

This can't be all of these "fire kids." The Warriors on the corner described them almost like a legion. And if this is the stand they're taking, burning down a closed-off island that Gilda has risen above, then they are truly a day late and a dollar short.

They begin to chant, taunting the cops.

"Burn baby burn, burn baby burn," singing it like the Trammps' disco anthem but with this sinister air. Without warning a police cruiser explodes, and then another, flipping over like rigged cars as their gas tanks are ignited and aural pulses lift them a story into the air before they come crashing down again. They are foolishly convinced that they are powerful enough to take down the police, just this handful of people.

What you know is that aural energy burns quickly. You don't have enough at any given time to block bullets forever. You can't move through solid matter that's a football field thick. Anyone above a Class 5 starts to fall into Patriot Act territory. This is why you don't have men and women with aura ratings running around in costumes trying to save the day. But you were flying real high back then, pulling off the impossible and thinking that no one was taking notice. This is what Gilda wanted to avoid happening with you, and you were a lot closer to it than you ever thought.

You don't pay attention to the words coming out of the mouths of both sides. Instead you watch the violence ensue. The cops open fire after repeated warnings. The Arsonists retaliate. Burning bodies in uniform fly through the air. The kids go down one by one. None of them escape, and because he's the big boss with the smallest aura, the Doughboy, having lived out his *Long Live the Kane* album cover moment, is cuffed and shuffled into a police cruiser only after he is stomped by a hundred boots and left a bloody mess sentenced to hard time at the closest medical center and then on Rikers Island.

The rain does not quell the burning island, nor does it lessen the wreckage there at the edge of the water where you were once upon a time invited to witness the whole deal from a distance. This is the sum of that last day in town. This almost makes sense of that dream long ago that you still can't forget. You turn away, disgusted by a smell that you don't want to admit is cooking flesh in the air. You limp as far as you can, and then with the last of your phone battery you flag a car, carelessly selecting the luxury option. It doesn't matter what Khujo or any of them said. You list your destination as the house that you own on Hancock Street.

You can hear the cars streaking across the Brooklyn-Queens Expressway overhead. When the Lexus SUV arrives with a chrome crucifix and a gleaming silver cross hanging from the rearview mirror, you cannot be shocked to learn that the driver is none other than Shaheed.

"I should've lost my leg," he explains. "But after a bunch of pins, a bunch of surgeries, and the Lord Almighty, I don't even walk with a limp. So I just keep doin' what I've always been doing."

His hair is salt and pepper now and he's leaner, wearing a V-neck sweater with a shirt underneath. Fred Hammond is playing on the stereo. The song is called "No Weapon."

"They wouldn't let me come see you when you were in intensive care," you explain. "I felt like shit about what happened."

"I knew you had been there, my brother. And I never doubted that I'd see you again. You were always a good customer. We don't know why the Lord asks us to take the hit when he does. But we plant our feet and we take it. Then he makes sure that we get back up again."

It's a short ride down Myrtle to Nostrand, but time seems to stand still.

"Wherever you've been, you've been fighting the Lord's fight too," he explains, braking before another rogue cab runs a red light.

"I don't know about that," you say. "All I do is run a kitchen. I work with some guys that have been inside, come home, and need jobs. And some cool ladies who believe in them too."

"And you don't think offering the condemned a second chance is God's work? You don't think that's what the Holy Spirit is in the world for?"

"But there's nothing holy about what I do on the side," you explain. "People like you have gotten hurt because of me."

"I'ma say it again. People get hurt because they need to get hurt. Folks die because it's their time. Things end. Love turns to hate. You forget to get oil changes and your engine goes. None of it is personal. It's all a machine, all one big system. The things we play out in our lives are nothing more than reflection of what goes on in heaven."

"I'm tired," you say. "I've been walking all night."

"But you're almost home." He smiles. You see the whiteness of polished implants in his rearview mirror. You don't always get to keep everything you enter the game with. "And when you couldn't walk anymore, I was here to carry you. You're a good man, Kango. Sometimes you're just too hard on yourself. I don't know what's going on in that head of yours, but I don't think this is some in-and-out trip. I think you might be back for good."

"I don't know about that," you say. "My restaurant's blowing up. My dude told me the mayor ate there today."

"But there's a new mayor every few years. There's new hustles. New people. It only becomes a loop if you let yourself get trapped in one."

"Yeah, but I feel like I've been in a box for a long-ass time," you explain. Your eyes close. Your body is crashing just as the car pulls to a stop.

Shaheed hands you a business card. "It's the same number, but I didn't think you had it anymore. Lock it in. Call me when you need me."

"I will," you say as you force yourself out of the car and up the flight of steps. You punch in the code on the keypad and the door comes open. You know everything that's happened to this place since you left. You've directed every upgrade and repair. You even have your apartment cleaned for dust once a month. You were always ready to go back to the way things had been before.

You climb the stairs. There's a slight creaking pain in your left knees, your primary reminder of aging other than the few grays in your goatee. You scale one flight of stairs and then the next. And the next thing you know you're back at your own door, and there is a note on the door written in Khujo's handwriting:

> *Opening the window*
> *You feel fire under the chair*
> *The door opens and then it closes*
> *Who goes there?*

You snatch the paper off the green pin holding it in place. A chill runs down your spine. You know those words from long ago. They are not from Brooklyn. They are not from Caramel City. It's first poem you ever wrote in the seventh grade, daydreaming while you stared at fine-ass Miss Glenn's bottom as she wrote vocabulary words on the board. You didn't know what it meant. They were just words, words you kept for yourself in an orange folder that no one has ever seen, a folder in the attic of the house where you live now.

You still have boxers in the drawers and jeans and shirts in the closet. There is still that .380 in the holster right under the couch. The fridge is empty save for bottles of water that are kept there just in case. There are gluten-free frozen dinners, both meat and vegetarian, in the freezer, for the same purpose.

The hot water jets out brown, clearing out unused pipes. You let the sediment go down the drain and then you hop in, lathering yourself with a single bar of black soap still in its package. As you lather down you count five blisters, two on your left foot and three on your right. You remember Jenna's feet, but those ancient memories are replaced by Rena: the gold rings on her middle toes, the wear on the heel repaired daily with some kind of lubricated therapy.

Rena doesn't want you to be afraid of her. And she's not afraid of you, and aura never came up the whole night. And there was no crazy shit you had to do for her or with her to make the night great. It just happened. It didn't feel forced, and she showed the strength of a real woman in everything she did, just by being there.

You kill the water and dry off. Those tenants you knew are long gone. Now you've got a married white couple and a traveling classical musician who is Eastern European, based on her renter's application. They pay the rent and you don't have to know anything about them. You own the space and they rent it. No business deal is simpler than that one.

You turn off the water and towel off. You go into the living room and turn on the lamp in the corner. Then you look at Khujo's note again.

Opening the window
You feel fire under the chair
The door opens and then it closes
Who goes there?

You cross the living room floor, enter the bedroom, and crank open the insulated casement window above the radiator. You come back and sit in the papasan chair, knowing that the jar of weed and incense holder are no longer there. Those are relics of the past from years of the dragon. But the .380 is locked and loaded, heat ready to be hammered.

But what you don't expect is the warbling that begins to happen at the center of the room in front of you. It starts as a hum and then becomes an increasing black mass, a hole in space. Jelly and Shango and Khujo are back in your head now. Then the woman steps out of it, a woman you don't recognize. One eye is slightly larger than the other, the possible product of thyroid disease. Her long locks are salt and pepper, her small breasts sag, hanging loosely underneath a thin black garment. Her head is covered like a niqab muslimah. But you do see what comes out of the portal behind her.

It stretches up to the ceiling with white slits for eyes, its claws extended. Its tail wraps around her like a snake, almost as if it's a part of her. This is what you saw in London. This is what tried to keep you from taking the Bible, the contents of which are still not fully known to you.

"Hey, Denzel, baby," she says. "I've been waiting for you."

Your eyes bulge in horror, remembering the story and the night and how you left her place quietly, a shtick that became all too familiar in those post-Jenna years where you figured it was smarter to be ghost before they ghosted you.

"What are you doing here?" you demand, trying to play off the fact that the woman just materialized in your living room. Your finger brushes the butt of the gun. You think about it. It's not a question of whether or not you will shoot this woman and this thing. It's only a question of whether or not you have to.

"You don't know why they told you to stay away, do you? They didn't want me to get to you."

She is grotesque, and not in physical appearance. It's not that she's aged or gained weight. Such is life. But there's this clicking underneath her voice that almost seems serpentine. And she laughs like Pat from *Saturday Night Live* in the '90s.

The shadow part of her draws closer, almost sniffing at you. You think of saying the Lord's Prayer, assuming that you're being visited by some demon in human form. But the truth is much simpler. Whiskey changes faces and takes away the good sense God gives you to get out before it's too late.

You don't know what she is, but you do the math. If no one is lying to you, and she speaks the truth, then she is the fuel underneath the fire children they call the Arsonists. Deductive reasoning is your best friend on the right while faith holds you down on the left.

"Bingo!" She laughs in a shrill alto that reduces dick and balls to nothing.

But your mind stays calm.

> *Opening the window*
> *(You've opened the window)*
>
> *You feel fire under the chair*
> *(The gun is within your grasp)*
>
> *The door opens and then it closes*
> *(She came here through a portal)*
>
> *Who goes there?*
> *(the girl with the whip around her neck)*

Deductive reasoning is your best friend on the right while faith holds you down on the left. You pull the gun, pretty certain that bullets won't do shit to whatever this thing is. But that isn't the point. Your mind remains calm. There's a wire attached to the gun. When you pull it from the holster, it will pull the pin that starts the timer on the nice chunk of C-4 under the papasan pillow.

You know all of this because you set all of this up. You're the only person who can do the job because it's always been your job. But before you go on explaining this to yourself, there is more warbling, and more portals begin to open throughout this house of yours.

Arsonists step in, igniting their auras, ready and willing to do you in. That Walther holds seven rounds. At your last count there are now

14 people in your apartment. You pull the gun and blindly fire, heading for the window, knowing that it's better to break a leg or two if you land the right way than to burn to death once the kids and their master get going.

As predicted, those little bullets of yours don't do a damn thing, and you barely dodge the wall of fire that comes out of the floor. You count to three, taking long and broad steps through your own bedroom, heading toward the window you just opened. If you're right this is absolute suicide, the ending to the sad story of a middle-aged man who just didn't try hard enough, a man with no babies, a man with no wife and a restaurant that might be on the verge of crossover success.

You leap, taking a Greg Louganis as the charge goes off in the living room, destroying the only home you have and hopefully reducing Pat and her homies to nothing but ash. Then you feel the gravity and the night air, and the drop, and you start wondering if you're even going to clear the wrought iron fence surrounding your brownstone's courtyard. Flames send shattered glass into the air above you.

You think of all the times you thought it was good enough for you to die for the sake of others, and all the times that you woke up the next morning regardless of how certain you were that you wouldn't be there. So when that warbling starts underneath you, and you start to feel the way you might on some Starfleet transporter pad, you start to believe in what the code in that Bible is all about.

You do not land as a splatter of bone, blood, and brains on Hancock Street. Instead you smack against the concrete floor of the basement of the library where you told Shango and Jelly and Brownie and all the rest of the Teen Titans to go fuck themselves because no one was going to make you do anything you didn't want to do, the attitude of an overgrown child or at least of a man who hadn't been part of something for a long time.

There are writing and symbols in white chalk all around you. There are white candles lit in the corners of the room. They stand all around you in a circle, looking down not with pity but with relief.

"Did the shit sink in yet?" Khujo asks.

"Do you believe now?" Shango asks.

"Yeah," you say, catching your breath. "I do."

"Then stand up," a voice both foreign and familiar says. It is beyond your field of vision, but when you get to your feet, Gilda and Josh and the Twins are there. The old gang and the new one have merged, and you're the bridge between them.

"We need to talk," Gilda says.

You have not seen her in a long time, but she still stuns.

"Yeah," you say. "We do."

From *King Reece*

PROLOGUE

April 9, 2009

The man's naked, chiseled torso dripped with sweat as he pounded out a set of pushups. Headphones covered his ears, blasting raunchy rap music at ignorant levels. The song hadn't been released yet, but the man had an exclusive copy. He jammed the song so much that he knew the lyrics by heart.

He rapped, "When it come to my bars, niggas fear 'em like prison, they start squealing like pigeons, praying to God that I miss 'em! Oooooh!!!"

The last line hyped him up so much he hopped from the floor and threw a few imaginary punches at the air. He was in his zone now, doing his normal routine to break the monot-

ony of his predicament. He lived vicariously
through the music. When he bumped his tunes,
he drowned out the sounds of prison. With the
right song playing, he wasn't confined to a USP;
he was a teenager again, roaming the halls of
71st Senior High looking for a classmate to battle. Or he was in the trenches again, putting in
the work that would make him a legend in the
streets. The right song dictated his mood. With
the now-popular trap rap booming in his ears,
he reveled in his status as a Trap Lord, and for a
brief moment, he wondered what would have
become of his life if he had decided to pursue a
music career on his terms.

However, when the music stopped, he was
forced to deal with the reality of who he was.

King Reece pushed the headphones from
his head and allowed them to rest on his neck.
He inhaled the stale air inside his cell and focused his attention on the wall in front of him.
Taped to his wall were newspaper clippings and
photos of the last four years of his life. It was his
shrine of sorts, the thing that kept him going.
Each portion of the collage served a purpose
for him.

On the top left of the wall was the article
that started it all. The headline read, "Heavy Is
the Head That Wears the Crown." The article
spoke of his trial and the mysterious five-year
plea agreement. The article made him seem
larger than life, mythic even. It detailed some
uncorroborated stories of his drug empire—
tales of kidnappings, murders, and lynchings.
They estimated he and his gang, the Crescent

Crew, had amassed more than $50 million in just two short years, and that his personal wealth was somewhere around $30 million. In the article, the writer stressed that the Crescent Crew lived their ethos—Death Before Dishonor—to the letter, in that no one from his organization turned rat in his absence. They were rumored to still be operating in his absence and stronger than ever.

King Reece had placed this article strategically first in his collage. He read the article daily to remind himself who he was and of his purpose. Being in prison was a constant battle of the mind, and even the strongest man fell weak at times. This article reminded King Reece of his stature, of his family who believed in him. This article reminded King Reece of the empire he had built from the ground up and why he couldn't fall victim to the instability of his incarcerated thoughts.

Beside the first article was another clipping. The headline read, "Music Mogul Dodges Prison." This article spoke of Qwess, King Reece's right-hand man, brother, and co-founder of the Crescent Crew. King Reece had taken his plea agreement to save Qwess from any further investigation by the feds. Qwess was on the cusp of superstardom as a rapper, producer, and label head when King Reece was apprehended and set to stand trial. Before his trial began, Reece had one of the Crew abduct one of the juror's children in exchange for a not-guilty verdict. He acted ultra-cocky at trial, and the federal prosecutor knew the fix was in. To insure a conviction, the government arrested Qwess and threatened to pin a charge on him unless Reece took a plea agreement. In the end, Reece sacrificed his life for that of his comrade.

Beside this article were numerous photos of Qwess attending industry events, photos of him on *60 Minutes*, *Forbes* listing photos, and other media clippings.

This section was important to Reece because it bore witness to the strength of their brotherhood and the results of his sacrifice. King Reece would travel out of the galaxy and fight the sun for his brother Qwess to live in peace, and he knew Qwess felt the same way. They lived, breathed, and were willing to die for each other. This was Crew Business.

A Young Jeezy song screamed from the speakers around King Reece's neck, a song about how amazing he was. Reece could relate, so he threw the headphones on, hit the floor, and got some money. After he completed his set of fifty pushups, he stood and studied his mural again.

The next section of his mural was a testament to false love, his only mistake and Achilles heel in an otherwise beautiful tapestry of the right decisions in life. The headlines read, "Disgraced FBI Agent Resigns Amidst Conspiracy Suspicions," "FBI Agent Has Lovechild from Imprisoned Kingpin." There were no fewer than ten articles surrounding a picture of the woman they spoke about: Katrina Destiny Hill.

This section of King Reece's mural was the most important for him. Although it ripped his heart like old stitches every time he looked at his wall, he forced himself to endure the pain just to remind himself to never make that mistake again. She had caught him slipping, warmed up to him, then served him on a cold platter to the federal government. King Reece—the Five Percent God-Body—adjusted his mantra to that of the Jews: never again.

The orthodox Muslims turned toward Mecca and offered their prayers every morning, the Buddhists meditated. For King Reece, this wall was his shrine, the place where he cleansed and replenished his soul every morning. His time inside was nearing its end. He had to prepare himself to reclaim his place in society and right all the wrongs inflicted upon him, beginning with Destiny.

The country had just elected a black man to the Oval Office. Surely, the world was ready for the return of King Reece.

From *The Safe House*

1

MY AFTERLIFE

I felt my consciousness slipping into a quiet place. It almost seemed weird because there was no noise around me. It felt soothing to finally be in a peaceful place. There was no one in this dark place but me. Why hadn't I done this before? Why was I afraid to leave that other world? Here I have no worries and I'm pain free. I was told all my life that it was wrong to do what I did. They said that you'd be condemned. But then I realized, it was my way out. In fact, it was a win-win for me. I would get the chance to see my grandmother and my cousin again and they were all that mattered to me, since my life had gone to complete hell. Who would've thought that I would screw my life up? I went from being a college graduate in the field of pharmaceutical science, and working as a pharmaceutical tech, to being a fucking murderer and informant.

I'd been wanting to work in the medical field for as long as I could remember, but I ruined my life by stealing prescription drugs for my drug addict–ass cousin, which led to a robbery gone bad. Not only that, I fucked around and murdered my ex-boyfriend—but in self-defense. But who's gonna believe that? Especially since I paid someone to discard his body. What has happened to me? Why have I allowed these things to corrupt my life? I was doing good for myself. But look at me now. I'm a fucking idiot with a target on my back. What are the odds of me getting out of this? Slim . . .

"Got an A-24! In the bedroom. Need some help!" I heard faintly, and then everything went silent.

Wow! This place is nice. Everything is so white and clean. It kind of has the feel of a hospital, but with no one around.

"Hello," I said, but no one answered. I traveled down what seemed like a hallway, but there was no floor. It felt like I was floating around on thin air. Now, how was this possible? I didn't have superpowers. Nor was I immortal. So, what was going on?

"I can tell you what's going on," said a voice behind me.

I turned around and, to my surprise, my grandmother was standing behind me. Oh my

God! Seeing her standing there before me dressed in all white took my breath away. "Grandma, is that you?"

She smiled. "Yes, it is, sweetheart!"

When she confirmed to me that it was, in fact, her, I leaned in and embraced her. "I thought I lost you," I told her while I held on to her as tight as I could.

"No, baby, you will never lose me," she assured me.

"But I thought you were dead? The agent said that you and Jillian were both murdered."

"Yes, that's true—" she started, but I cut her off.

"What do you mean 'that's true'? And where is Jillian?" I wanted to know. Things she was saying were not adding up.

"I have passed on, darling. And as far as Jillian is concerned, I don't know where she is. But I'm sure she's around here somewhere."

"So I'm dead too?"

"Not quite. You're in a realm that is called the After Life."

"I don't understand."

"Listen, baby, I'm just a messenger that was sent to tell you that your work on earth is not yet done," my grandmother told me, and then she smiled.

"What do you mean that my 'work on earth' isn't done? What am I supposed to do?"

"Misty, God has a calling on your life, so He will not allow you to die. You can't get into heaven by committing suicide. He said that He's going to give you another chance to do it right."

"Do what right, Grandma? You're scaring me."

"There's no need to be scared, darling. You're gonna be okay."

"What am I supposed to do?"

"You're gonna have to help those agents bring those mafia guys to justice. Those guys have killed over a dozen people. They're into human trafficking amongst some other things. They are some very dangerous people. And then you're gonna have to make it right with Terrell's family. You're gonna have to tell his mother that you killed him and show them where his body is."

"I can't do that. I would go to prison for life if they found out what I did."

"I'm sorry, Misty, but you're gonna have to make it right. You won't be able to see me again if you don't."

I covered my ears with both hands and tried to block out every word she uttered. I mean, what kind of demands were these? I couldn't go back, testify against those guys, and then turn my own self in. Who would do that? I refused to snitch on myself. The end result of that would mean that my life would be over.

"Misty, I know that you don't wanna hear what I am saying, but there's no other way around it."

"Please let me stay here with you." I began to sob. Tears started running down my face uncontrollably. I leaned into my grandmother again and embraced her. But this time, I held on to her tighter. In my mind, I wasn't going to let her go.

Somehow she managed to push me away from her. "I'm sorry, baby, it's out of my hands.

I can't help you right now. You gotta do the right thing," she said, and then she started stepping backward.

"Grandmom, where are you going? I'm not done talking to you."

"I have to leave now, darling. Do as I instructed you, and you will be fine. Also tell your mother that despite how she felt, I always loved her," she told me, and before I could utter another word, she disappeared into thin air.

I stood there with a troubled mind and broken heart. Here I was standing in the After Life with my grandmother, hoping to join her, but was told that now wasn't my time. And then to be told that I had to help the agents take down Ahmad and his family, and reveal to the cops that I murdered Terrell. I'd really be committing suicide then. The whole thing was unfathomable.

While I tried to piece together my next course of action, I started hearing voices around me. I heard a woman say: "We just updated her vitals. She's stable and breathing on her own now."

"So, when will I be able to talk to her?" I heard a male's voice ask.

"It's all just a waiting game now," the woman continued.

"Will she remember what happened?"

"Yes, she will."

"Okay. Great. Thank you for your time."

"You're welcome, sir," the woman replied, and then I heard two sets of footsteps. It lasted for a few moments and then I didn't hear it anymore, so I opened my eyes slowly to prevent any light from blinding me. Halfway into full focus, it became apparent that I was in a room, but it wasn't the same room I talked to my grandmother in. This room was different. This room looked like a hospital room. In fact, it was a hospital room and I was hooked to every machine placed around my bed. "Oh no, I'm here. Back here alive," I whispered after I opened my eyes completely. Instantly anxiety consumed my entire body. I didn't want to be here. I wanted to be where my grandmother was. This godforsaken place was nothing short of hell. Bad people lived here and they made sure everyone knew exactly who they were.

"What am I gonna do? I can't be here," I continued to whisper. My heart became very heavy.

"Who are you talking to?" a female's voice asked me.

I looked in the direction in which the voice came from and realized that a nurse had walked into my hospital room. The woman smiled as she walked toward me dressed in her scrubs.

"I was talking to myself," I told her, feeling very saddened that I was lying in my bed alive.

"How are you feeling?" she asked me while she stood alongside my bed. She checked my IV to make sure that it was intact.

"I don't wanna be here," I got up the nerve to say.

"You mean here in the hospital?" she questioned me again. I figured this was a test question, a suicidal test question.

"No, I mean here. On this freaking earth," I boldly replied.

"Why don't you wanna be here?" Her questions kept coming.

"Because there's nothing left on this earth that I want to live for. My grandmother is gone and so is my cousin. I wanna be in heaven with them."

"So you are aware that you tried to commit suicide?"

"I wasn't trying to commit suicide. I was only trying to exchange my life with my mother's."

"Well, I'm sorry to hear that."

"Don't feel sorry for me. Just disconnect me from all of these freaking needles and tubes so I can get out of here," I said quietly, but in an aggressive manner.

"I'm sorry, but I can't do that. You're gonna have to speak with your doctor. He's the one that would be authorized to discharge you."

"Tell him I need to speak to him right now."

"I'm afraid he's in surgery right now, but I will let him know when he's done."

"Yeah, whatever," I said, and turned my focus to the window in my room.

"Is there anything else I can help you with?"

"No, you can't. Just leave me alone."

"There are a couple of federal agents outside the door, and one of them instructed me to let him know when you wake up. So I'm going to go outside and let them know."

"No, don't tell them anything. I just want to be left alone. Tell him I'm still asleep."

The nurse took a deep breath and then she exhaled. "As you wish," she said, and then she opened the door to my room. While she tried to leave, Agent Sims met her at the door because he was trying to come in the room himself. "Excuse me," he said to the nurse.

"No 'excuse me,'" she replied while she scooted by him.

Agent Sims smiled as he approached me. "I'm glad to see you up and alert," he commented.

"I'm not."

"Come on, Misty, it cannot be that bad," Agent Sims responded.

"You wouldn't have the slightest clue," I replied sarcastically, because he didn't. I had a bunch of mess going on in my life. Shit, that would make me look like a heartless bitch. But more important, I would have been in jail for the rest of my life.

"Want to talk about it?"

"No, I don't. But I do want to get out of here."

"I'm sorry, but it's not going to be that simple."

"Explain that to me."

"Do you realize that you tried to commit suicide? If I hadn't come in that bedroom, when I did, you'd be dead right now."

"What'cha want me to say, thank you for saving my life?"

"We can start from there."

"News flash, I wanted to die. And I'm glad I did it too, because I saw my grandmother and we had a nice time talking. She held me in her arms and told me how much she loved me."

"So you're telling me that you went to heaven and came back?"

"Why are you smiling? You think I'm a freaking joke?"

"No, I don't think you're a joke. I just never talked to someone that went to heaven and came back. You know, I see people on TV claiming that they've done it."

"Well, I have, and I'm going back."

"If you went there, and you liked it so much, then why did you come back?"

"Because my grandma said that my work here on the earth wasn't complete."

"She's talking about this case, huh?"

"Oh, shut up! And get out of my face."

"Is your life that screwed up, that you want to die?"

"Give me another chance and I will prove it to you."

"Your doctor has you under suicide watch so you won't try that stunt again."

"Are you done? Because let's keep it real, you only want me to be alive so I can help you put those guys away in prison."

"You're a very smart girl."

"So this is funny to you? You're holding me hostage so I can testify against Ahmad and the rest of his family?"

"This isn't just about putting Ahmad and his family behind bars. Remember, you're getting a get-out-of-jail-free card."

"Are you kidding me right now? You think

you're doing me a favor by testifying against those people? Do you know that I lost my grandmother and cousin behind this bullshit?" I spat, the volume of my voice got louder.

"If you would've kept your hands clean and never took any prescription drugs from the pharmacy, then we wouldn't be having this conversation."

"You know what, fuck you! Fuck you and the boat you got off of."

Agent Sims chuckled. "Don't get upset. It's not healthy. And besides, I don't want to be the reason that you try to commit suicide again. I wouldn't be able to look at myself in the mirror anymore."

"You're so fucking phony."

"What gave you that idea?"

"Will I be free to go on with my life after this case is over?"

"That depends on if you go into witness protection."

"Well, let me be the first to tell you that I won't need you guys' protection. I'm gonna move so far away it would take one of those drones in space to find me."

"Are you sure you wanna do that? Those guys have ties to contract killers all over the world," Agent Sims warned me.

"I'm gonna be fine. Thank you," I assured him. "Has the doctor said when I would be released?" I changed the subject.

"No, he hasn't. I believe he wants you to speak with a psychiatrist before he can make a medical prognosis."

"Fuck a prognosis! I'm fine and I'm ready to get out of here."

"I'm sure you are, Misty. But we have protocol here."

"So you say," I commented, and then I turned my focus back toward the window in my room. Looking outside at all the birds flying back and forth was more entertaining than Agent Sims. All he wanted to do was talk about my testimony for his case. He couldn't care less about anything. But whether he knew it or not, I had a trick up my sleeve, and he and no one else was going to hinder me from doing it.

"Listen, I'm gonna let you get some rest. There are two agents outside of your door, so if you need anything, you let them know."

"Yeah, right," I said nonchalantly as I continued to look in the opposite direction.